TO CHAIN AN ELF KING

ATLEY WYKES

ALDER CIRCLE PRESS

Copyright © 2023 Atley Wykes

All rights reserved. No part of this book may be reproduced or used in any manner without the prior written permission of the copyright owner, except for the use of brief quotations in a book review.

To request permissions, contact the publisher at atley.wykes@gmail.com.

Ebook ASIN: B0BY161VNZ

First paperback edition June 2023.

Edited by Ginger Kane

Cover art by Atley Wykes

Layout by Atley Wykes

Printed by Amazon Printing Services in the USA.

Alder Circle Press

P.O. Box 115

Somers, WI 53171

atleywykes.com

Contents

Dedication	V
Maps of Maeoris	VI
1. Chapter 1	1
2. Chapter 2	11
3. Chapter 3	22
4. Chapter 4	30
5. Chapter 5	40
6. Chapter 6	51
7. Chapter 7	62
8. Chapter 8	73
9. Chapter 9	83
10. Chapter 10	91
11. Chapter 11	101
12. Chapter 12	109
13. Chapter 13	120
14. Chapter 14	132
15. Chapter 15	142
16. Chapter 16	151

17.	Chapter 17	160
18.	Chapter 18	169
19.	Chapter 19	179
20.	Chapter 20	189
21.	Chapter 21	196
22.	Chapter 22	205
23.	Chapter 23	214
24.	Chapter 24	225
25.	Chapter 25	234
26.	Chapter 26	242
27.	Chapter 27	250
28.	Chapter 28	257
29.	Chapter 29	266
30.	Chapter 30	275
31.	Chapter 31	281
Acknowledgements		283
About the Author		285
Newsletter Signup		286

This book is dedicated to all my fellow nerds and lovers of DUNE. When one desert isn't enough, here is another to call home.

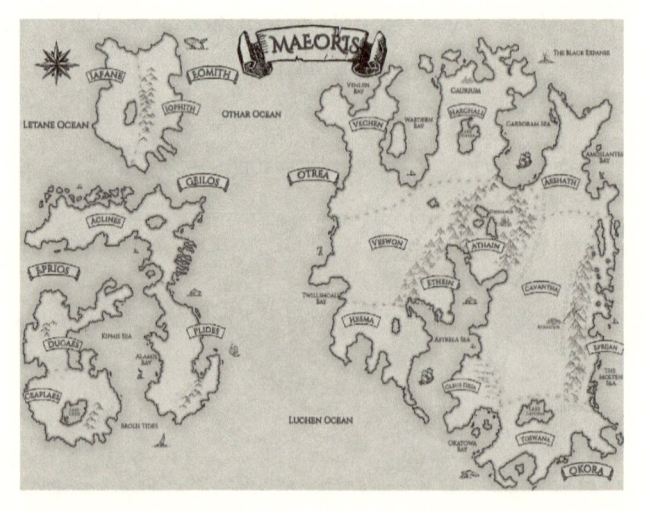

More maps of Maeoris can be found at atleywykes.com

Chapter I
Theron

I blinked, sand scraping my eyes as my vision cleared. They'd chained me to the wall in a desert cave. The stone was red, flaking like shale... Was I in the Red Wilds or somewhere near Sailtown? The latter made more sense given what happened with... A wave of heat and ice flooded my veins, and a growl escaped me before I shoved the emotion away. *No.* I couldn't think about that right now. I needed to keep my head clear if I wanted to survive this.

Light came from a smooth hole in the ceiling above, the hiss of falling sand coming from somewhere nearby as the wind shifted. Earthborn iron rubbed against my wrists, digging into my skin like drukkar claws. I inspected my arms—the wounds were deep, my blood flowing freely onto the sandy floor, forming blackened clumps. My legs were numb, the iron preventing me from calling on any magic to heal myself. I only wore my breeches and boots, the rebels having stripped me of my armor when I was captured. I winced, tasting blood as I sat up, the chain from my manacles clanking.

A scrape drew my attention as a Kyrie Remnant stepped into view. I recognized her... Peregrine, the rebel leader I'd met years ago in that warehouse. The night Calyx had died because the slaves had betrayed me. When Striker had—No. Not Striker. *Her.*

Green eyes that flashed with anger before softening in arousal filled my mind before I forced the image away.

Don't think about her.

Peregrine sneered at me, her yellow hawk-like gaze glinting with malice. "Well, well. Look what the wind blew in. The War Marshal."

Her ebony skin glimmered in the low light, her mangled wings just peeking over her shoulders. A faint limp hinted at a life of toil in the mines, but it didn't diminish her towering presence. She wore her braids like a crown, each one adorned with shimmering beads and feathers.

She didn't try to intimidate or deride me as she stepped closer, instead radiating quiet confidence. A leader who had earned her place through years of hard work and dedication, no doubt earning the respect of her followers.

This wasn't good. A corrupt leader could be negotiated with; it was the noble ones that sent you to your grave in a hurry.

She circled the cave, studying me with her shrewd, yellow gaze. Finally, she stopped in front of me, her voice quiet but laden with unmistakable loathing. "You know why you're here. The question is whether you'll cooperate."

I cleared my throat, my tongue a dry and scaly thing in my mouth. "What do you want from me?"

"Where are the speaking stones in the castle?"

I ground my teeth, refusing to give her the satisfaction of a response.

"Thank you." She laughed then, a harsh sound that echoed off the cave walls. "I was hoping to do this the hard way." Her hawkish eyes pinned me like a mouse in the open desert. "I want you to see what it's like," she intoned, her voice cold as

Sithos' fields. "To suffer at the hands of another. Just like you made so many suffer." She stepped closer and placed one finger on my chin, forcing me to meet her gaze, her nail piercing my skin. "You can't escape this time," she hissed, before turning and walking to a leather bag resting against the wall.

I clenched my jaw, determined not to show any emotion or weakness as she yanked on the chain connected to my manacles, dragging me up until I was almost suspended, standing only on the balls of my feet.

The rebels despised me for what I'd done—bringing escaped slaves back to be punished or executed by Rhazien instead of helping them reach freedom. After the mass revolt five years ago, all I had thought about was revenge. Wanting only to retrieve my sword and bring Striker to justice. It was only recently that I regretted my actions. When she—No. Not right now. Despite my shame and anger, I kept my expression neutral and refused to react to Peregrine's taunts.

I heard the first lash before I felt it. A sharp sting across my back sent a wave of pain radiating through me. I gasped and clenched my fists, willing myself to remain silent as she raised her whip again.

The next blow came fast, this time even harder than the first. I gritted my teeth and bit back a scream, focusing instead on breathing through the agony. She stopped after a few more strikes, waiting until I opened my eyes.

"Where are the speaking stones?" she asked again, her voice cold and emotionless.

I shook my head, and she smirked before continuing with her 'interrogation.' Memories flooded my mind as Peregrine began her work. Of when I was a child and my brother, Rhazien, held me captive. He'd done the same, beating me more for fun and revenge than anything else. I was twelve again, my brother already full grown, his boots echoing down the hall as he approached my cell and I desperately wished I had somewhere, anywhere, to hide as my heart fluttered so fast I thought it would burst.

With each lash, memories of the past came flooding back to the present. Rhazien forcing me into a maze so he could hunt me down. My mother impassively watching me re-break my fingers so I could heal them properly when my cuffs were removed.

"He's dead," I muttered, trying to convince myself, and Peregrine paused.

"Are you ready to talk?" She walked around to face me, my blood dotting her skin like crimson freckles. I averted my gaze, and she glared, striding away to resume her onslaught on my body.

I closed my eyes, willing the memories to fade away until all that remained was the pain. Agony was easier to endure. But thoughts of *her* crept in. Kael. My *Sihaya*. I didn't want to think about her, but I couldn't help it. I remembered the first time I saw her, standing at the edge of the platform in the colosseum, dressed in sheer white. The setting sun illuminated her silver hair, outlining her curves as she glared at everyone below her. But then her eyes had met mine and my heart clenched as if she had speared it from across the arena. The need to claim her had been overwhelming. I'd found her hate refreshing; I'd thought her *honest*. Too open in her loathing for us to deceive me. Even when I'd realized she was a rebel, I hadn't cared, thinking what we'd shared was bigger than that. I'd thought that she'd felt the same, even if she'd been too afraid to admit it.

But it had all been a lie.

A trick to get close enough to kill Rhazien. I'd delivered myself to the rebels, trusting that we'd be together, and pleaded with her to tell them the truth. Her eyes had hardened into an expression I knew all too well, her brother by her side rejected me. I could still taste the bitter bile that had risen from my stomach as I realized she'd been lying to me from the start.

I'd been a fool. Falling for the daughter of a rebel leader. The assassin that had stolen my sword. So desperate for love that I lied to myself. None of it had been real. Red clouded my vision to near blindness as rage coursed through me, blocking out the pain.

All that remained was my need for vengeance—revenge against Kael for breaking my heart, revenge against Peregrine for making me suffer like this, revenge against the rebels for sending Kael to me. With each lash, a new determination formed within me—no matter what happened, I would find a way out of this prison and exact revenge on her for all she had done. I didn't care how many times Peregrine's whip ripped the flesh from my bones. Nothing would stand in the way of my retribution.

Her lashes picked up in intensity until I couldn't hold back my screams or stay conscious for long periods. She continued to break and batter my body for what seemed like an eternity of agony before she stepped away.

"That was just a taste," she panted, exhausted and painted in red. Torture took more endurance than most expected. She tossed the whip into the bag against the wall. "Now tell me where the stones are."

I opened my mouth to respond, but all that came out was an empty croak. Peregrine laughed—a cruel sound that echoed in the surrounding caves—before turning away and releasing the crank on the chain. I collapsed to the ground in a heap, my face half-buried in the sand.

"I'll be back with more questions, War Marshal. And you better have answers for me."

I lay there for what seemed like hours afterward, trying to ignore the pain as best I could, imagining what I'd do to Kael once I'd claimed her once again. First, I'd take her over my knee, reddening her ass until she squirmed. Then I'd… I tried to ignore how the air reeked of hot sand and blood, with visions of Kael begging me for mercy. I'd gotten through floggings before I'd reached my immortality, and I could do it again.

Quiet footsteps came closer, and I forced my eyes open. I wouldn't give the rebel leader the satisfaction of breaking me. If Rhazien and my mother hadn't, no one would.

But it wasn't Peregrine.

It was *her*.

She wore loose pale breeches tucked into her boots with a matching jacket underneath a red hooded cloak. Her hood was pulled up, obscuring her face in shadows, with my swords strapped to her back. It was how Striker always dressed on raids. How could I have been so foolish to believe she was a man? Her sinewy grace and slight curves were even more erotic than the enhancements Carita had forced upon her. She looked powerful—a warrior. She paused just inside the threshold and glanced around at the gore-painted walls with wide eyes, sucking in a breath as she pushed her hood back, revealing her silvery hair.

I pushed myself to sit up—although it took all my self-control—so I could look her in the eyes. Hissing in pain as sand shifted in my wounds, I gingerly leaned back against the stone wall so she couldn't see the extent of my injuries. She was still battered from her ordeal; one of her eyelids was swollen, a shadow of a bruise darkening her pale skin. I longed to reach for her, to comfort her, an instinct that I quashed under a mountain of pain and hate.

"Theron," she breathed, her voice barely above a whisper.

I narrowed my eyes at her, wrath sweeping through me like a raging sandstorm. I wanted to shout and rage at her, to demand she explain why she had tricked me, why she seduced me in the first place, to *punish* her—but I held it in. All I could do was glare at her as an oppressive silence filled the air between us.

Kael stepped closer, reaching out for me with trembling hands; but I batted them away and rose, staggering back against the wall as I swayed.

"Was any of it real for you... or was it all an act?" I growled.

She paled and retreated from me, her arm raised before her body like a shield. The fear that crossed her features shook me—and all I desired was to pull her close and forget everything. My *Sihaya* never cowered. Rhazien had taken something from her, broken something, and all I wanted to do was help her mend it.

But the agony was too much, the betrayal too raw.

"I never said it wasn't," she whispered. "I did what I had to do. Just like you."

"You had to do what? Betray me? Turn me over to your rebel friends?" I sneered at her, my voice sharp as pain coursed through me.

She flinched as if I had struck her, her eyes shining with unshed tears as she clenched her jaw. "No, Theron, I never wanted that. But I had to kill Rhazien—"

I shook my head, my hands spasming at my sides. "You should have told me, Kael. You could have been honest with me after I'd told you what he'd put me through." My chest heaved, a gaping maw opening where something vital had once been. "Do you think I would have stopped you? I would have helped you kill him. But you lied to me, used me…"

"I never meant to use you," she protested. Rage boiled inside of me and I lunged forward, my hand wrapping around her throat as I pushed her back against the wall. Someone had removed the collar I'd put on her to claim her as mine, and it only enraged me further.

"You used me!" I shouted, my voice breaking in a rough crackle. "Just like everyone else in my life."

Kael gasped for air as I tightened my grip around her neck, her hand clutching at my arm as she struggled to breathe. The urge to hurt her—to inflict the same pain I felt—was so overpowering that I didn't know if I could stop myself. But as I looked into her eyes, I hesitated. Something shifted inside of me, a flicker of emotion that I couldn't place.

I released my hold on her and took a step back, my body trembling with pain and the effort to control myself. Kael stumbled forward, gasping for air, her hand rubbing her throat.

"I never meant for this to happen," she gasped.

I laughed bitterly; the sound echoing off the stone walls. "You think that makes everything alright?"

"No, I don't—" She cut herself off as Peregrine returned, a large male Inferi Remnant with shorn dark hair graying on the sides beside her. Haemir.

Kael straightened her shoulders, schooling her expression until it was one of annoyance. No trace of the hurt that had been there a second before. No wonder I'd been deceived. She was a masterful liar.

"What is the meaning of this? The Marshal is *my* prisoner," she said, ignoring me when I snorted. "I told you I wanted to be present for his questioning."

Peregrine tilted her head, staring at Kael for a long moment. "Your presence wasn't required."

Kael opened her mouth to argue and Haemir held up a hand, glancing at me. "Let's have this conversation in private."

"Fine by me." Peregrine turned, leaving the cave without a second look. Expecting Kael and Haemir to follow, something that goaded my *Sihaya* based on the look she shot at the older woman's back.

"Come on," Haemir said, guiding her toward the tunnel as if trying to usher her away from me as quickly as possible.

She glanced over her shoulder, those cool green eyes meeting mine once more before she turned and followed him out of the cave. It felt like a part of me had been stolen—all the trust I'd put in her, in anyone—and I didn't know how to come back from it.

I tried to stay standing but eventually gave up, collapsing onto the ground with a heavy thud. I was alone, surrounded by memories of what had happened between us. What could have been… if only things were different. If only we'd been honest with one another from the very beginning. But that time had passed.

All that remained was vengeance.

Chapter 2
Kael

I followed Teodosija and Haemir out of the cave toward the larger caverns. My stomach churned like a stormy sea, each wave crashing against the walls of my throat, threatening to spill over. The scent of the blood, sweat, and bile—everything reminded me of Rhazien's assault. I felt like a ghost, my feet leading me down the path as I gazed ahead with unseeing eyes as I fought the tide welling up inside of me. Memories of Rhazien's attack kept pressing up against the surface of my mind; the feel of his breath on my neck, Zija's cruel laughter, and my helpless despair as I waited for Theron to come before I fell blessedly unconscious. I shuddered, trying to push the thoughts away, praying to any of the gods for blissful ignorance to return like it had when I was a child. But it was as if a dam inside me had burst, and all that had been festering in the darkness of my mind was out for everyone to see. As if I was translucent, my hidden hurts on display as the desert wind rasped against my skin like sandpaper. It was skinning me alive.

No. He's dead, I reminded myself. I killed the Beast. And Zija and all those other concubines whose mockery had formed the vile chorus of my assault. They were dead, and so we're all the bastards that had hurt me as a child. Haemir had slaughtered them. I was safe now. *Safe.* I repeated, trying to convince my racing heart to slow as I mentally wrapped myself in a blanket as if I could shield my fears from prying eyes. I wasn't the one being hurt. Not this time.

It was Theron.

I tried to focus on the present, to see the roughened stone walls and sand-covered floors, but everything was blurred by the rage burning within my blood. I welcomed it; anger was easier than dealing with what had happened.

"What's the meaning of this?" I said, my voice tight with fury. "He's *my* prisoner, and I didn't give you permission to question him."

Teodosija whirled around to face me, her eyes blazing. "You are not in charge here, Kael," she snapped. "I am the leader of this camp and as such, I can do whatever I deem necessary."

My jaw clenched and determination filled me as I squared my shoulders. She may be the head of the rebellion, but I was Striker. The person our fighters would follow into battle. The one who risked her life to kill the Beast, and our people knew it. Part of me wanted to throw that in her face. To challenge her and take the position for myself, but I knew I shouldn't. Not unless I had to.

"He's mine," I growled through gritted teeth. "If anyone has earned the right to torture him, it's me."

"Do you think you're the only person here that he's hurt?" Teodosija asked, crossing her arms as she lifted a brow. "His army sent half the slaves here to Adraedor. Almost all of us have lost a relative to his Harvestmen dragging them back to the mines."

I understood that, but it didn't make me any less angry.

"He ruined my life. I was there when he razed Caurium," I spat, and Haemir's eyes widened. I never talked about it, not to him or anyone. "His horde ripped apart the city, killing my father as he tried to escape with me. We lost Orya to his soldiers. He took Haemir's hand. I was—' I stopped, panting as the memories threatened to overwhelm me, Rhazien's rasping laugh echoing in my mind. I sucked in a breath, collecting myself as Haemir and Teodosija shared a glance. "This isn't just about revenge," I said, keeping my voice low and steady. "He's the heir to the Thain Empire. Holding him as a prisoner gives us an edge. But not if he's dead. Which he will be if I don't help him soon."

Teodosija paused for a moment, her expression unreadable. Finally, she nodded, her posture loosening. "You're right. We should use him as a bargaining chip if need be."

Relief flooded through me and I let out a breath I hadn't realized I was holding. They wouldn't kill him. "He can't heal himself with the earthborn iron on and no electrum. I'll have to dress his wounds."

Teodosija raised a brow. "You seem to have learned a lot during your time undercover."

I swallowed, a wave of nerves washing over me. The thought of telling them any of the things I did... Of what happened to me when I was in the palace... I didn't want to think about it, let alone talk about it. If they knew, then we might have a better chance of winning this war... But I was scared—scared of how they'd react if they found out that I was a Sálfar Remnant. Or what they'd do if they learned what I'd done with Theron. Or that I'd almost considered one of his Harvestmen a friend. Did I want to take that risk?

"Not much," I replied, feigning nonchalance as I shifted my stance. "Just what some of their metals do. A little about their alliances. It was mostly dinner parties."

I could feel Haemir's gaze on me, but I refused to meet his eyes. I had a feeling that he knew exactly what I wasn't saying. He could always tell when I was lying. But thankfully, he said nothing as Teodosija narrowed her eyes on me.

"Any bit of intel is helpful. Roza said you were pretty beat up when you arrived in Sailtown..."

She let the sentence hang and the same icy anger as before rose in me and I had to fight off the urge to snarl at her. "I finished my mission. That's all that matters."

"Kael—" Haemir's voice was soft, and I cut him off, unable to have this conversation.

"Not now. We have a bigger problem." Haemir gave me a hard look but didn't push. He could tell I wasn't being honest, but he also knew me well enough to know that if I didn't want to talk about it, then he couldn't make me. "We have a leak."

"What?" Teodosija's mouth snapped close, her teeth clicking. "How do you know?"

"I overheard the Beast telling the Marshal about our base in the Red Wilds. Someone gave them our location. That's how they captured Gavril and the others."

Haemir swore. "We need to find out who it is and deal with them," he growled, his voice low and dangerous as his fiery eyes flashed. No one threatened his family and lived. "We can't afford to have a traitor in our midst."

Teodosija nodded, her expression grim. "We'll start an investigation immediately."

"What about the plan?" I asked, crossing my arms and leaning against the rough cave wall, kicking loose rocks away from my feet. I was exhausted, but I was determined not to show it. Teodosija's grand plan to retake Adraedor, the whole reason I'd risked going undercover in the palace in the first place, was supposed to begin tomorrow. "If there's a leak, then the attack is compromised."

"Kearis' wings," Teodosija muttered as she paced, her own stunted wings flicking out in frustration. "This is a mess."

"We'll have to divide the offensive squads and change the times." Haemir rubbed one of his horns with his hook absentmindedly. "If we have smaller groups and one of them is breached, we'll have the others in reserve and an idea of who the traitor is."

"How're we supposed to split our attack force when half the royal guard is out here scouring the desert for us? And that's before they realize we've captured their prince."

"I'll lead one," I offered, and Haemir shot me an exasperated look, his eyes blazing orange.

"Absolutely not. You're only half-healed and limping."

"I can handle myself."

Teodosija interjected, her voice cold. "You think you can go against my commands and come back here making demands?? No. You're staying here for the time being. You've done enough."

"But I killed—"

"You defied orders and burned my best contacts in the palace. I don't have any eyes there anymore."

I winced, remembering how Kadir had fled. Apparently, the others had as well.

"Is Kadir alright?"

"He's fine." She waved a dismissive hand. "The issue is that you believe you're not subject to the same rules as everyone else here."

"But—"

"She's right, Kael." Haemir cut me off. "You need to heal."

My stomach squirmed. I couldn't stay in one place. I needed movement. To keep myself busy so I wouldn't have time to think.

I sighed, defeat slumping my shoulders as I tried to come up with a new plan. There was no way I was going to sit back and let others do all the work while I wasted away in some cave. I'd prove that I could still be an asset to this rebellion, even if my body refused to cooperate. "Then I'll talk to our raiders, and see if they have noticed anything suspicious."

Teodosija exchanged a look with Haemir before nodding. "Fine. We need to find this traitor before they can cost us everything. Don't tell anyone what you suspect. Everyone is under suspicion until I've cleared them."

"Alright." Haemir agreed. "What about the Marshal?"

"I'll go get supplies to dress his wounds," I blurted, and Teodosija held up a hand.

"No. You rest. I'm sure your father and brother want some time with you. I'll send a healer to see to the Marshal."

The idea of someone else touching him made my heart sink. Teodosija saw the look on my face, and her expression softened as she misinterpreted it. "I know you're desperate to help, Kael. But you need to let someone else do this for now. Rest."

I nodded, knowing she was right. I'd been pushing myself too hard these past few weeks and my body was paying the price for it. My bones still ached where Theron had pieced them back together, the damage so bad even his magic couldn't fix it all.

"Why don't you go relax and I'll have Gavril bring you some food?" Haemir asked, and I nodded. I needed to regain my strength and I wouldn't do it if I kept running myself ragged.

"Fine. But no one questions or tortures the Marshal without me present."

Teodosija eyed me for a long moment before dipping her chin. "Deal. I'll put a guard on him."

"Your brother is waiting for you, kiddo." Haemir's cheek creased. "Why don't you go see him and I'll join you two soon?"

I nodded, and he smiled, turning to let her lead him down the twisting paths.

Sighing, I watched as Haemir and Teodosija went off to discuss battle plans, leaving me in the cavern by myself. I stared up the trail that led to Theron's cell, remembering the streaks of dried blood painting the wall. He'd hidden his back from me, but it had to be horrific. Guilt twisted my stomach, and I took a shaky breath. How different were we from the Elves? We'd tortured him the moment we had a chance. Just like the Beast...

Theron hated me now. There'd be no more soft smiles and teasing jokes, no more confessions in the dark as he wrung pleasure from me. He hadn't realized the depth of my hatred when he'd selected me, and now our positions were reversed. He loathed me as thoroughly as I had him.

He'd grabbed me by the throat when I'd gotten too close to him, though he hadn't squeezed hard enough to truly cut off my air. What stopped him from killing me? I ran my fingers over my neck, my thoughts drifting back to the feel of his skin against mine, the softness of his lips... Shaking my head, I tried to clear it. I couldn't think about him like that. He was the enemy, the one who had hurt me and so many others. If anyone knew what happened between us, I'd face banishment at best, and death at worst.

We all had our secrets, our demons that we kept locked away from prying eyes. Mine were more literal than most; wounds carved into my skin by a Beast who thought he'd broken me until I escaped his claws and he fell into my trap. It wasn't easy living with those scars. Maybe Haemir was right that I needed time to heal.

I took a deep breath, trying to push away the memories of my torture. And that was what my rape had been. Just one more means of torment. I refused to think of it as sex or anything resembling it.

Even wounded, I was still one of the most skilled warriors in the rebellion. If they went forward with the plan, they'd need me and I'd have to be in fighting shape. I needed to be ready. With one last glance at Theron's cave, I turned and headed in the opposite direction.

As I returned to the base, I tapped on the walls, restless energy burning within me as I tried to distract myself. My mind kept wandering back to Theron, to the way his powerful arms had felt around me, how he'd gazed at me with such intensity when he professed his love for me. It was wrong. I knew it was wrong, but I couldn't stop thinking about him.

I pushed aside the thought as I stepped into the rebel base. It was a massive underground cavern, roughly carved out of sandstone. Light filtered in through a series of openings in the ceiling, giving the chamber an almost ethereal glow. Everywhere I looked, I saw warriors preparing for battle, sharpening their weapons, and patching up their armor. It was a hive of activity and there was an air of determination that hung over the place like a thick fog.

The cavern was vast, extending far beyond what I could see with my own eyes. But it wasn't just about size—everything had been carefully crafted and designed to maximize efficiency and create a safe fortress. We had reinforced the walls with metal beams and steel rods to ward off any potential invaders; the entrance had multiple layers of security, from sentries posted at various points along its perimeter to barriers that would be triggered if anyone unauthorized attempted to enter. It wasn't as impressive as our encampment in the south; the hidden city felt like a home—this was a military base. But it was closer to Adraedor, and an easier launching point for an assault on the city. It was also close enough to the road that we could raid passing caravans for supplies.

I caught sight of my brother, Gavril, sitting outside a familiar tent. He looked up as I approached, a small smile tugging at the corners of his lips.

"Kael." He stood, pulling me into a hug that I returned, awkwardly at first, before leaning into his embrace. He smelled the same, like spice and fire, and embarrassing tears pricked my eyes. I was ten again, in a new place, wondering if I was trading one prison for another, but Gavril had meant safety. He still did. My shoulders shook and his arms tightened around me.

"Shhh. It's alright, sis. You're home now." A sob caught in my throat and I took a shaking breath, trying to force myself to calm down. "I'm sorry I wasn't here when you woke up."

After I'd taken Theron as my prisoner, my exhaustion had been too much for me and I'd passed out once again, waking alone in our family tent. My cheeks reddened when I realized my first thought had been about finding Theron, not my brother or father.

"I'm the older sibling. I should be taking care of you."

He chuckled as I leaned away, breaking our embrace as I wiped my eyes with the back of my hand. I hated crying, and I'd done it twice today.

"Older, but smaller." He propped his elbow on my shoulder, something he knew annoyed me, and I huffed as I pushed his arm off of me.

"Idiot."

His smile fell a bit as he scanned my face, no doubt taking in my residual bruises.

"What happened, Kael?" He took a step forward, trying to get me to look at him.

I shook my head and glanced away, not wanting to discuss my assault. Or anything else.

"Nothing," I said, brushing it off. "I did what I had to do."

"Kael..."

"Just—Not right now. I can't talk about it."

His expression hardened, and he looked older, just like Haemir, with the same bronze skin and fiery eyes. Only his hair was longer, with messy curls. "I'll kill him. You never have to worry about him again. Whatever the Marshal did to you—"

"Gavril, stop." I cut him off. "It wasn't the Marshal, alright?"

He stared at me, his brows drawing together. "Then what happened?"

I tucked my hair behind my ears. "I don't want to think about it right now."

"It had to be bad," Gavril said, his voice low as he brushed a finger over my bruised cheek. "I won't judge you for anything you had to do to survive. You know that, right?"

I swallowed, nodding, even if I didn't truly believe it. He noticed my pointed ears and his expression changed from one of sympathy to confusion in an instant.

"What's with the new ears?" He leaned forward, poking one tip, and I batted his hand away.

"They showed up when my earrings were removed." I stifled my wince as I remembered Rhazien tearing my piercings out.

"Must be a descendent of Thanja," he mused.

"Or a hornless Inferi Remnant," I joked half-heartedly as a worrying thought crossed my mind. Would Gavril hate me if he learned I was a Sálfar Remnant? Would the rebellion even let me stay? There was no telling how they'd react, especially if the things I'd done got out... But what if I accidentally made something explode again? I needed more information, and there was only one person who could give it to me.

Too bad he hated me now.

Chapter 3
Theron

My hands balled into fists, my nails cutting crescent moons into my palms. I shook so hard I didn't know if I would have enough control to stop myself from lashing out at the wall. Memories of Peregrine's whip cracking like thunder as it split my skin, my screams echoing off the walls, bouncing off the stone; all of their torture was nothing compared to my anger at *her*. Anytime I thought of Kael, fury flooded my chest, making my heart pound against my ribs and my temples pulse until it felt like my veins would burst. How could I have been so naïve to believe her lies, so blind not to see her deception? Rhazien was right. I was so desperate for love that I'd tricked myself into believing she cared for me. Even as she shouted at me about how she hated me. I wanted to rail at her, to demand answers, to shout and scream until I was hoarse. But she'd left me, leaving only a ghost in the shadows of my mind, and the only sound that echoed in the thickening air was that of my own broken breath. It was my fault. I'd convinced myself of her affection when there was nothing there.

The crunch of gravel came from the path with a slight tremor in the ground under my skin. I tensed as the distinct clank of metal armor and the stomp of boots grew louder. A single guard appeared in front of the opening of my cave, but he wasn't alone.

A woman accompanied him, an Inferi Remnant I'd never seen before. She was beautiful—bronze skin, dark curls, and small horns—but there was something about her that made the hair on the back of my neck bristle.

The guard stopped several feet away and regarded me with open hatred. "You have ten minutes, Rabbit. Yell if you need anything."

"Of course," she purred, resting her hand on his armored chest. "I feel so much safer with you here."

He grinned at her, scanning her curves, and I narrowed my eyes. She reminded me of Tannethe. Using her body as a weapon to cudgel men into obedience.

My gaze shifted from the guard to the woman, who sauntered forward with an almost flippant grace. She set a bag down on the ground, then turned her attention to me, her lips quirking in an inviting smile.

"I'm Andreja," she said, extending a delicate hand that I ignored. "I'm here to dress your wounds."

I stared at her for a moment before turning my gaze away. I didn't trust her—but I needed my injuries attended to or I wouldn't survive. Despite the direness of my situation, something inside me rebelled against accepting this woman's help, as if by doing so I would be betraying myself yet again.

"Give me the supplies and I'll do it myself," I grunted, shifting away from the wall. Searing pain blazed down my back—I hadn't realized my bloodied skin had dried to the rock—and I swore as my blood flowed freely once more.

"Can you reach your spine?" she asked, a flicker of mischief dancing in her eyes as she stepped closer to me. "It's hard to clean wounds if you can't even get to them."

"I'll manage."

"Oh, come now," Andreja crooned. "Let me help you. I promise I won't hurt you."

She smiled at me and moved nearer, her fingertips brushing against my skin as she inspected the damage and I shuddered. She kneeled by my side and began to work on cleaning my wounds with an astringent liquid that spread like fiery tendrils across my back.

"Where's Kael?" I demanded. I hated not knowing where she was. Did she have a husband here? A male that she was reuniting with right now as I languished in a dusty cave?

"You mean Striker?" Andreja stopped her ministrations, but the pain of hearing that name was worse than anything she'd done. "I think she's with her brother. He was pretty worried about her. Even though it was her fault." She muttered the last sentence under her breath, but I caught it.

"What do you mean?" I looked back over my shoulder, locking eyes with the Remnant. She schooled her features to blandness, but not before I saw an ugly expression cross her face.

"Striker wasn't supposed to be on that mission. Our leader told her not to go, and she did anyway." She began dabbing liquid onto my wounds. "And of course, she comes back acting like a hero again and everyone loves her for it."

I gritted my teeth, acid rising in my throat. Kael had gone against orders and had put herself in danger to kill Rhazien. She hated us more than she cared about her own life. I couldn't help but feel a pang of worry for her, even as fury burned hot in my chest. What was she thinking? Did she not understand the risks she subjected herself to?? And what was she going to get up to now that Rhazien was out of the way?

"If she's with her brother, where is he?" I asked, trying to keep my tone level. I needed to know what was going on, even if I didn't want to hear it.

Andreja shrugged, her movements gentle as she continued to clean my wounds. Her fingertips brushed my spine, and a shiver ran through me, followed immediately by my stomach churning. It wasn't her that I wanted to touch me. "I'm not sure. I overheard some guards talking about them leaving for Adraedor, but not much else."

I sucked in a breath. Had Kael abandoned me here amongst her allies? Part of me had foolishly thought she'd stay close when she'd claimed me as hers to Peregrine. Red pulsed at the edges of my vision, but something in Andreja's voice made me hesitate. She was lying. But why? To make me focus on her instead of Kael? As if that would ever happen. My *Sihaya* dominated all of my thoughts, whether I wanted her to or not. This woman could never compare to her.

I turned my head to look at Andreja, studying her. She was still working on my wounds, her movements slow and methodical. But there was a tension in her shoulders, fear in her eyes that she was trying to hide. She knew more than she was letting on.

"What are you not telling me?" I asked, my voice low and dangerous.

"I don't know what you're talking about," she said, a hint of amusement in her tone. "I'm just here to help you."

I set my teeth, resisting the urge to lash out at her. I couldn't let my anger get the best of me. Not now. Not when I was so vulnerable. I took a deep breath and tried to calm myself, but it was difficult when every nerve in my body was on edge. "It must be hard trying to live in Striker's shadow."

Her movements stopped. "I don't live in anyone's shadow."

I shrugged, then winced when the pain was too much. "Everyone has heard of Striker, not—What was your codename again... Rabbit?"

She scowled. "Some of us have jobs that require more stealth and intelligence than others."

I made a noncommittal noise, resting my forehead against the rock. She wasn't giving up much, and the pain was building until the muscles in my legs and arms quivered uncontrollably. To distract myself, I went over everything that had happened during the last day. One thing kept nagging at me in particular: Kael's ears. Why did someone try to hide their shape? Most of the Remnants from Thanja's and Vetia's lines had pointed ears like the elves, though you'd have an odd one out here and there. What was she hiding from? Why would she be ashamed of her heritage?

Unless...

She wasn't a Remnant at all.

My heart leapt as I followed the thought, only for Andreja to interrupt me. Unless she'd been talking the entire time and I hadn't paid attention.

"I was the one who was supposed to go on the mission." She pitched her voice low in a seductive purr. "Would you have picked me?"

I glanced over my shoulder at her, taking in her lovely features and lush hair. Still, the sight of her left me cold.

"No," I said, turning away from her so she could no longer reach my back. "I'll finish dressing my wounds. If your leader wants to talk to me, send in Kael. She's the only person I'll speak to."

"Why not me?" She asked, her voice dripping with honey. "You don't even know me. I can be *very* friendly."

I remained silent as she sent me a lascivious smile, but Andreja was determined to get an answer out of me. She brushed a stray lock of hair behind my ear and I jerked away from her.

"Because," I drawled, "I'm not interested in you."

Andreja's face fell, but she quickly recovered and smiled sweetly at me.

"Oh come now," she said as she reached to spread ointment onto my back and I caught her hand before she could touch me. "Surely you can make an exception for a beautiful woman like me?"

"Touch me again and I'll snap your neck," I growled and her eyes widened as she scrambled back. I hated women like her; ones that always assumed their touch was welcome, as if I was a lust-driven fiend that would take anything I was offered.

"You're a monster," she spat, her face twisted in outrage and fear. I stood up, looming over her as I glared down into her frightened eyes.

"I am," I growled, stepping forward. "Think of that next time you come in here twitching your hips."

Andreja scrambled to her feet, her gaze still fearful as she kicked the medical bag at me and ran. Atar's hammer, what I wouldn't give for a healing plate.

I watched her go, my attention lingering on where she had stood moments ago before I leaned down to grab the bag of supplies, groaning as my wounds moved. She hadn't stitched anything yet, and strips of my skin slipped over each other.

"Dinner." The guard stepped into the room carrying a bowl of porridge, which he tossed at my feet. The bowl clattered onto the floor, spilling its contents everywhere. He snickered as I sighed. "Eat up."

My stomach grumbled despite my best intentions as the warm scent of porridge filled the air. When I was in Rhazien's cage, he had often left me to starve, with only a small portion of food allotted each day. This was a much larger meal than what I had been given then, but it felt like a cruel joke. One more attempt by Peregrine to manipulate me into submission.

Still, I knew that if I didn't eat something soon, I would be in no condition to fight if my Harvestmen showed up or if I managed to escape from this place. With a heavy sigh, I grabbed the bowl and knelt on the cold ground, and began scooping up the porridge from the floor.

They were trying to break me by making me choke down their disgusting food. As if I hadn't lived on slop for years. I took a bite of the mixture; bland little balls of some sort of grain with a hint of spice amongst the sand. I'd seen the slaves eating something similar. I think they called it seffa.

The porridge was tasteless and gritty, but it did its job; within minutes, my hunger pangs disappeared. I'd need all the nutrients I could get to heal.

I turned my attention to my wounds, pulling out some bandages from the bag and beginning to dress them. I winced as I applied pressure to clean the bloody cuts I could reach. The Niothe had trained me in self-sufficiency and I wouldn't allow myself to be broken by something so trivial as food deprivation or a flogging. I couldn't sew them, so I'd need to wrap them tight and hope for the best.

As I worked on my wounds, my mind raced with thoughts of Kael. Was she really with her brother? Or was there some other reason she wasn't here with me? My jaw clenched so hard that the metallic taste of blood filled my mouth. That she could be with another male enraged me. It didn't matter that she'd betrayed me. She was still *mine*. My plans with her may have changed, but she belonged to me.

Always.

But first, I needed to break free from this place. I stood up, testing my weight on my weakened leg. It held, but just barely. My back was another story. I had to move carefully if I was going to get out of here alive.

I scanned the room, looking for any escape, gripping the chain tight and yanking. Dust escaped from the anchor point, fluttering to the ground, and I grinned. It would be tedious, but I could work it free.

I had nothing but time.

Chapter 4
Kael

I blew out a breath as I escaped our tent, hurrying off before Gavril followed me. I'd had to tell him I needed to relieve myself for him to stop hovering over me. He was treating me like an invalid—a victim—and I couldn't stand it. After he'd been tortured, I had treated him normally, even if it had only been for a few minutes. I'd trusted him. Having him act as if I could barely walk was annoying. But how could I say that without being a bitch? *Sorry you worried about me for days and I know I came back looking like hell, but can you leave off with all the love and affection?* Doesn't work too well.

I pulled up my hood, not wanting to draw attention in the camp. I didn't want to talk to my brother, let alone anyone else, right now.

The sound of soldiers working, their clanking armor, and muffled conversations filled the base. Smoke from the campfires tickled my nose as a warm wind brushed against my skin, carrying with it a hint of creosote. My heart tapped out a staccato beat, mirroring the sense of urgency that permeated the air.

The strike teams were preparing to leave, their loved ones holding them tight. And the spy might be any of them. How many of our people would die tomorrow because we were rushing ahead? I understood why Teodosija wanted to push forward with the plan. There was only a brief window of time while the city was unstable, but the risk of the elves being warned... I watched them pack, wishing I could be beside them fighting, rather than here. The sand shifted under my feet, light filtering through the cavern's openings coming at a slant. It was almost sunset. Had Theron eaten today?

I ducked into the seffa line behind a group of soldiers, grabbing a last meal before they left and grabbed a large bowl before hurrying back toward the cave. I just wanted to ask about the Sálfar. That's the only reason my pace quickened as I turned his way. I was solving a mystery about myself, that's all.

I stopped in my tracks when Andreja emerged from Theron's cave, straightening her clothes and brushing sand from her breeches. The guard returned, and she smiled at him, flirting before she noticed me.

"Striker." She inclined her head regally as if acknowledging me was some grand gesture.

I narrowed my eyes, stepping in front of her so she couldn't pass. "What are you doing here, Andreja? The Marshal isn't to be questioned without me present."

She raised a delicate brow. "Someone sure is possessive."

A growl rumbled in my chest that I couldn't suppress. "I'm not possessive. I'm cautious. Now answer the question."

Andreja stepped back, her hand going to her hip as she eyed me coolly. "I was tending to his wounds."

I scoffed. "You're no healer, unless you count healing blue balls."

Her lips curved into a half-smirk. "Maybe I should heal his, then? It wouldn't be a hardship. He's handsome. For an elf."

My temper thrashed at the thought of Andreja touching him. Or anyone else putting their hands on him, for that matter. Fire burned in my veins and I clenched my teeth together so hard they creaked. She was insufferable. We'd never gotten along; she and Roza had bonded immediately, especially with their shared dislike of me. Though Andreja was more subtle in her jabs than the fiery Sirin Remnant.

"It's my job to question him," I ground out. "Don't go into his cell again."

Andreja smiled slyly. "Why? Are you jealous?"

Yes.

"Of course not," I sneered, crossing my arms. "He's my prisoner. I know more about him and the right questions to ask. That's all."

"Sure." She smirked at me and for a moment, I didn't see her. I only saw a haughty Inferi Remnant gazing at me with dislike. *Zija.* White-hot fury raced through me, my heartbeat thundering in my ears. I advanced on her, intent on flaying the skin from her bones when she stumbled backward, the fear on her face bringing me back to myself. Andreja, not Zija. The concubine was dead.

"Go," I snarled, and she scampered away, muttering under her breath that I was crazy.

I watched her leave before turning to the guard, who eyed me warily. "Take a break, I'm going in."

He nodded and stepped aside obediently, recognizing me. The responsibility of my position weighed heavily on my shoulders, but I pushed it away. I didn't want to be Striker right now; I just wanted to be Kael.

The guard's eyes followed me as I made my way into the cave, the bowl of food for Theron in my hands. He was on his knees in the sand, struggling to reach his wounds, his arm muscles rippling as he stretched to mop up the blood trickling down his spine. The scent of an astringent ointment that I knew well filled the air. I stopped, sucking in a breath.

His back.

Peregrine had whipped him until his skin only hung in strips in some places, a multitude of cuts large and small, ranging from his shoulders to his hips.

A pit formed in my stomach and it grew larger when he didn't acknowledge me, his ragged breathing the only sound in the cave.

I cleared my throat, and he finally looked up at me, bronze eyes smoldering. My heart constricted in my chest, but I held firm against it, even though every instinct screamed for me to speak. I didn't know what I'd say. I wanted to say something to make him stop looking at me like that, but I didn't have the words.

Pulling back my hood, I set the bowl of food next to him on the floor.

"You need to eat," I murmured, folding my arms across my chest as I backed away out of his reach.

He scowled at me. "You don't need to fear me, *Sihaya*. I plan on doing many things to you," he drawled, his eyes lingering on my scant curves. "But I won't choke you again."

Something loosened inside me. This banter was familiar. He wasn't treating me like some broken thing, but like an equal.

"Is that right?" I sank to the floor opposite him, so we were at the same height. I'd once dreamed of standing over him, but now that I had...it wasn't what I thought it would be. "Will I be whipped or flayed first?"

He narrowed his eyes at my sarcasm. "Why are you here, Kael? I've already eaten your prisoner slop."

He gestured to his empty bowl, and I could see the blood still dripping down his sides. My chest hurt and I looked away, studying the wall as if it wasn't the same boring red stone as the rest of the caverns.

"That isn't prisoner food," I mumbled. "It's seffa–everyone eats it here, not only prisoners."

I picked up the bowl and held it out to him again. He hesitated before taking it from me, bringing it up to his mouth. He stopped just as his lips brushed against it, eyes flickering up towards mine. "You first," he murmured, holding it out to me.

Heat rose in my cheeks as I took the bowl from him, a pinch of hurt going through me as he avoided brushing his fingers against mine.

"It's not poisoned." I took a bite of the spiced couscous before passing it back. It reminded me of when he'd fed me that first night by the firelight; how he'd coaxed me to drink from his cup as he gentled me with his touch.

He ate methodically, as though he was trying to conserve every morsel, and I watched him, wishing I could do more before chastising myself. He was my enemy. I shouldn't feel this fucking guilty.

"I can dress your wounds while you eat." The words were out of my mouth before I could stop myself, and I winced.

He stared at me for a moment before nodding, a flicker of surprise in his eyes. "Alright," he said gruffly, trying to hide the relief that flashed across his face.

I pressed my lips together, irritated with myself, and looked in the bag for a needle and thread.

"I'll have to stitch these," I warned, holding up the needle. He eyed me for a long moment before nodding and I began suturing his wounds while he ate in silence. He winced whenever I accidentally touched a deep spot, but otherwise didn't speak as I stitched his split skin together. Even so, it was like a conversation between us. An apology as I gently bound his injuries.

I'd seen worse hundreds of times in the slave quarter, but I'd never had to dress them before. A confusion of emotions roiled within me; shame, guilt, and a vicious glee that he was experiencing the pain he'd subjected so many to by sending them to Adraedor. But it was short-lived. Mostly I felt... hollow. The satisfaction I'd expected to feel after killing the Beast and capturing Theron was absent, leaving only a yawning void in its place. I'd been changed by my time in the palace, and I didn't know how much was because of my assault and how much was because of the man before me.

"Where are we?" Theron asked, his voice nonchalant. As if I'd fall into that trap.

"A cave."

I finished applying his bandages, carefully wrapping gauze around him and ignoring the heat of his skin as I pressed against him to pass it around his front.

"There. You're already healing."

Theron looked down at his bandages, eyebrows raised in surprise. He made a noise of acknowledgment, but contempt filled his eyes as he glanced up at me.

"Did that soothe your guilt?"

My spine stiffened, and I shot him a hard look before snapping back, "I have nothing to feel guilty about. You tortured my brother, and I didn't even get the chance to dress his wounds."

His brow furrowed as realization dawned on him. "You're the one who released the prisoners." He laughed bitterly. "Atar's hammer, I've been a fool." He shook his head. "The daughter of a rebel leader. Of course, you freed them."

"You would have killed them."

"Most assuredly," He agreed, his demeanor angrier. "And now those slaves' deaths aren't just on my hands. They're on yours too."

I glanced at the ground, unable to meet his eye. "They always have been."

He pulled back, and I stepped away, the sudden distance feeling like an abyss between us.

"Come here," he ordered.

I lifted my chin and stared him down. "No."

He smirked, and my breath caught. "You know you want to." He breathed, his voice full of promises. Ones I knew he could fulfill.

I shook my head, my stomach fluttering. I didn't trust myself around him.

"You don't make the rules anymore," I held his gaze. "You're *my* prisoner now."

"Better hope I don't decide to talk to Peregrine then. I'm sure she'll enjoy hearing how much you loved fucking me. How you screamed my name when you rode my cock."

"Fuck you." My hands shook as I glared at him.

"Later, *Sihaya*." He grinned before his expression softened. "Come here."

Reluctantly, I stepped forward, and he gently cupped my face, checking over my bruised eye. His calloused hands were gentle, and I had to fight to keep my eyes from closing.

"Why are you really here, Kael?" He whispered as if hiding a secret from the guard I'd sent away. His fingertips ran over the tip of my newly pointed ear and I gasped. His breath ghosted over my skin as his gaze searched mine for an answer.

"Did the Svartál kill all the Sálfar?" I asked, holding my breath as I gazed up at him.

He looked pleased that I asked, and his mouth twisted into a satisfied smirk.

"No," He whispered. "Not all of them were killed. Many went into hiding and were hunted down over the years by the Carxidor emperors. But some survived and remain hidden in caves and forests."

I shivered at his words, my heart racing. I was so close to knowing the truth about my heritage. "What about Sálfar Remnants?"

"Not possible." Theron smiled, tapping his finger against my chin lightly before dropping his hand away from me. "Use your head, Kael," he said with an amused glint in his eye. "Atar is still alive."

"Atar?" A chill ran through me as I realized what he meant. Magical blood won out over humans, and if someone was born of two races, one was always dominant. There weren't any Sálfar Remnants because they all still had their power from Atar. Which meant I wasn't a Remnant at all...

I was an Elf.

I staggered back, my breath coming in quick gasps as I tried to make sense of the implications of his words.

"What? I'm–"

The truth crashed into me like a violent tidal wave, shattering the fragile illusions I had clung to. My head spun, my vision darkening around the edges. Fuck, I was going to pass out. I leaned forward, breathing hard as I fought off the wave trying to pull me under. The bastards who'd persecuted us all these years were actually...my kind. It was almost too much to comprehend.

Shame coursed through me, so deep and raw that it threatened to consume me whole. Growing up, I'd looked up to the Fae Remnants in Haechall, hoping I was one of them. When I came to Adraedor and met Sirin Remnants, I thought they might be my people. I'd never known which gods were mine and had prayed to them all, even though they were gone. But Atar wasn't dead. He was hiding away in shame. Just like me.

What would happen now? Would Haemir and Gavril accept me? Would they view me differently?

Theron's expression had gone from smug to alarmed. "Most people would be delighted to know they have magic."

I shook my head vehemently, tears streaming down my face as I glowered at him. "Why would I be happy to find out I'm related to the people that enslaved me? That killed my father? Everything I've thought I'd known is a lie."

He ran a hand through his hair as if struggling to find the right words. He opened his mouth to speak, but I cut him off before he could say anything.

"Oh gods, when do I stop aging? I'm going to have to watch Haemir and Gavril grow old." A sob caught in my throat and he moved to embrace me. "They're going to die and leave me here. Alone."

His expression was tortured. "*Sihaya.* Come here"

But I stepped away, overwhelmed. I couldn't handle being touched. I didn't want comfort right now—everything had changed too much. Hurt flashed across Theron's face as I fled from him, hurriedly pulling up my hood to hide my tears as I ran up the path to the desert.

The evening air was cold against my skin as I stumbled away from Theron's cave. The wind came from the mountains as night descended, bringing with it the scent of ice and pine. My mind spun, trying to process what he'd said. I staggered towards a rocky outcropping and collapsed in the sand, burying my face in my hands. My entire life had been a lie. Why had my father never told me? He'd said my mother didn't know what type of Remnant she was. Yeah, because she wasn't. Memories from decades ago flitted through my mind; the isolated cabin, always living on the outskirts of the city, the sword training… Things clicked into place that I'd never understood.

My thoughts swirled as I cried into the sand, my sobs drifting away from me in the chill wind. What about Gavril and Haemir? All I could think about was how much time would pass before everyone else aged and died—leaving me behind. I'd be alone again. Always alone.

But that wasn't true anymore.

Theron would still be there. Determined to keep me.

For eternity.

Chapter 5
Kael

I woke up in an empty tent. Haemir and Gavril had left earlier, probably to deal with something regarding the invasion of the city. Rubbing my eyes, I tried to clear the fog from my mind. I had been out late last night, crying in the dunes, and they'd already been asleep when I'd finally collapsed on my sleep mat.

I forced myself to get up, to push past the pain and the hurt. Maybe if I just went through the motions, acting like everything was normal, I'd feel like myself again.

Stumbling towards the seffa line, I grabbed a plate of food and tried to ignore the way my stomach twisted. Just a regular day. Groups of rebels sat in loose circles in the sand, nodding at me with respect and admiration in their eyes. I'd earned it over the years, always willing to take the hardest missions after they killed Orya. She'd begged me to do more for the rebellion for months, but I'd hidden instead. If I'd done more, she might still be alive.

"Kael." Gavril hailed me, standing and hurrying over to me, a canteen at his side.

"Here. I couldn't find yours, so I bartered for a new one for you."

"Thanks." I took it gratefully, gulping down the liquid as if my life depended on it. I'd gotten used to the palace with its endless supply of water and luxuries. But that life was gone now, and I needed to relearn my water discipline. "Where's Haemir?"

He lifted a shoulder. "He had a meeting with Teodosija early. They're keeping it quiet, though."

I made a non-committal noise in the back of my throat. Probably something regarding the leak. Part of me wanted to talk to Gavril about it; there was no way he was the mole, but I also didn't want him to tip off anyone with his behavior. If Haemir hadn't told him, then I wouldn't either.

Gavril motioned towards a group of people sitting in a circle, laughing and chatting. "Come on, let's hang out with the others."

I followed him, feeling awkward and out of place. Roza, Cithara, and Evadne sat around a small fire, heating cups of tea in the hot sand. But no Andreja, thank Vetia. Roza shot me a dirty look as I approached, but I ignored her. She had always been rude to me, and I was more than happy to reply in kind.

"Kael!" Evadne said, jumping up and welcoming me with a hug. She was a lithe Fae Remnant with black hair like her sister, but both her eyes were a vivid violet, unlike Cithara, with her mismatched purple and green eyes. "Thank you so much for saving Cithara. I was going crazy after they captured her."

I swallowed. Remembering that night only made me think of Theron—him kneeling in the sand with his back torn to shreds. *No. Remember Gavril instead*—his swollen face, the bruises where they'd beaten him. Herrath's casual cruelty in discussing how to break him. The elves were the enemy. But I was an elf too...

The circle quieted, and I realized that I'd been silently staring at Evadne, and too much time had passed.

I cleared my throat. "It was nothing."

"It was very brave," Cithara put in airily as she looked up from her sewing project and frowned. "Where did your new breasts go?"

Gavril coughed as Roza cackled.

"She doesn't need them now that she's not fucking an elf." Roza lifted a brow. "Unless you still are? Andreja said you visited the prisoner by yourself."

I advanced on Roza, but Gavril beat me to it.

"Fuck off, Roza. No one hates the Marshal more than Kael. You're just jealous that she killed the Beast."

She stared at him in shock. Gavril had always been kind to Roza, treating her as a surrogate sister after Orya passed. It made sense; he'd thought Orya was his mate, so he considered her his sister-in-law. But he was *my* brother. She shot him a rude hand gesture but stayed quiet, and he sat back down, ignoring her in favor of talking to me.

"Have you talked to Dad about leading a group to Adraedor?"

"Yeah. But Teodosija nixed it. She wants me to stay and heal more."

"Not a bad idea. I'll stay with you..." He kept speaking, detailing ideas of things we could do around the hideout, and I did my best to pay attention, but all his words ran together in the soup of my mind.

The other rebels followed suit, trying to make conversation. They were all friendly, but the whole thing was awkward. I had been through an ordeal that none of them could understand, and it seemed like they didn't know what to say or how to relate to me anymore. Still, I forced a smile on my face and tried to keep up the facade of normalcy. But underneath, a constant, low-level panic filled me. It was as if someone had wound me too tightly and I was just waiting for something to break.

Gavril's cheerfulness only made it worse. He seemed almost too happy, like he was desperately trying to make everything alright again. But it wasn't.

Cithara and Evadne weren't helping matters, either. As Fae Remnants, they couldn't lie, and their discomfort with my situation was clear in everything they did. Every time they glanced at me, their eyes were filled with worry and concern. The gentleness of everyone around me made me feel like they didn't see *me* anymore. I'd been regarded as a pillar of strength before—one of the best warriors in the rebellion—now they were treating me as if I was weak. Helpless. Anger simmered deep within me, and my jaw locked shut.

I stood up abruptly, my plate clattering to the ground. All eyes were on me, their collective confusion and pity suffocating.

"What's wrong, Kael?" Gavril asked, his voice laced with concern. "Do you need something different to eat? I can go get—"

"I don't need your pity," I snapped, the words tumbling out of my mouth before I could swallow them. "Stop coddling me and treating me like I'm some kind of fragile thing that needs to be protected. I'm a warrior, godsdamnit. I've faced worse than this before and I will again."

The silence was palpable. Gavril stood up, his eyes narrowing. "No one is treating you like that, Kael. We all understand what you went through—"

"Understand? You can't!" I shouted, my voice echoing across the camp. "You weren't there when the Beast tortured me, when he—" I cut myself off, noticing everyone staring at me. Not just in our group, but in the entire cavern.

Cithara shook her head, her eyes wide. "No, we weren't, but we are now."

Tears threatened to fall and I blinked them back furiously. I didn't want their pity, their sympathy. I wanted to be strong, to be in control of my own emotions. Not this wreck that cried at everything.

Roza rolled her eyes. "Why do you always have to be so dramatic? It's not about you all the time."

I turned to face her, clenching my fists. "What is your problem?"

Roza didn't back down; instead, she glared at me with fire in her azure eyes. "You heard me. You act like the world is ending whenever things go wrong and it gets old fast."

My heart pounded in my chest as I stared down Roza. She smirked and something in me snapped. I lunged forward, shoving her. She stumbled back, and before I could blink, she was coming at me with a flurry of punches. I dodged, landing a blow on her chin that sent her reeling.

"You bitch!"

I dove at her, knocking her to the ground as I struggled to pin her. We grappled for a few moments before Gavril rushed over and pulled me off of her.

"Enough!" He shouted, yanking me back even as I threw an elbow into his ribs. "Kael, Roza—that's enough."

I panted, adrenaline still coursing through my veins as I shook off his hold. My fists ached, but it was an odd relief to have let out some of my anger on someone else. It wasn't her fault that I was a mess after everything that had happened, but I couldn't help liking it. And she should have shut her fucking mouth.

Everyone around us stared in shock, their faces almost comical in their surprise and confusion.

Roza straightened her shirt and brushed off her hair calmly. "I'm fine," she said coolly. "Kael's just having a moment, as usual."

"Fuck you," I kicked sand in her face, and she swore, scrambling to her feet to fight me again, only for the fae sisters to hold her back.

Gavril turned to me, his eyes narrowed in warning. "Kael, go cool off and take a walk around the camp." He let go of my arms and took a step back. "You want to be alone? Go and be alone."

I stood there, my chest rising and falling with each breath as I glared at Roza. Alone. Did I want to be? All my tears last night had been because one day I would be. That I'd lose everything and have to continue by myself.

I opened my mouth to speak, but nothing came out. I didn't want to be alone, but I didn't want to be here either. Turning on my heel, I walked away without another word. Their eyes followed me, but I didn't care. I needed to get out of there.

I hurried through the camp, my shoulders hunching under the weight of all those eyes as I fled the underground caverns into the desert.

The air was stifling, and the sun blazed down on me, but I didn't feel it. Not really. How could they treat me like this? I was still me. The same person I had always been. Wasn't I? But now it felt like everyone was walking on eggshells around me, afraid to say the wrong thing or trigger some kind of emotional breakdown. But hadn't I proved them right? Maybe I wasn't who I thought I was anymore...

I looked up at the sky, tears streaming down my face as I growled in frustration and dashed them away. The sun rose behind me, heating the wind that whipped past. In the distance, a figure emerged from the shadows and started walking towards me.

"Kael?" A familiar voice called out.

My heart hurt as I spun around to face him. Haemir approached me, his brows drawn down into a line. He had always sensed when something was wrong with me and this time was no different. "Am I trouble?"

"No. Roza needs that thick skull rung now and then." He chuckled as he sat down beside me. "Are you alright?" He asked as he wrapped his arm around me in a loose hug that he ended quickly. "I've been looking for you. We haven't had a chance to talk much since you got back."

I shifted uncomfortably, digging my hand into the warm sand. Soon it would be hot enough to burn. "I've just been busy."

Haemir raised an eyebrow. "Too busy to talk to your dad?"

I sighed, feeling guilty. Again. "I'm sorry. I've had a lot on my mind."

Haemir nodded. "I understand. That's why I came looking for you. I thought we could take a walk together, and clear our heads."

I hesitated for a moment before nodding. It would be good to spend time with Haemir. He always seemed to know the right thing to say, even if it was hard to hear. I stood, and we walked in silence for a few minutes, lost in our own thoughts.

Finally, Haemir spoke. "Did I ever tell you about my mate and triad?"

I shook my head. I had never heard this story before, too worried about dredging up painful memories to ask.

Haemir took a deep breath. "My mate, Amalia, had been enslaved in our homeland. The governor had a liking for her as a girl, so he kept her as a slave in his own home. She endured terrible treatment and conditions, things that no one should ever have to go through." He paused, glancing at me. "I'd already found the rest of my triad, Adar and Niam, men who were like brothers to me. We'd become well known for our trade—"

I broke in. "What did you do?" He never spoke of his life before coming to Adraedor, and I was dying to know.

He smiled, his expression wistful. "We built homes. Together, we built beautiful things. Adar had an artistic eye, and we'd created a good life. Built a home for the mate we hadn't found yet. Not until the governor requested for us to come to his home and build an addition onto his mansion. That's when I first saw Amalia." His eyes were distant, staring at the shifting dunes. "For some, it takes years to recognize their mate upon meeting them, but I knew it the moment I saw her. She'd been hurt, and afraid, but together we charmed her as we worked on his home, trying to give her enough courage to run away with us."

He took a shuddering breath. "We'd made plans to help her and steal her away, but in the end, she'd come to us. The governor had tried to take what she didn't want to give again, and she'd attacked him, almost killing him. She'd escaped and ran to our home, still covered in his blood. We fled south to the Molten Sea that night, abandoning everything. Anything to keep her safe." He met my eye. "It took her years of hard work and love from our triad to heal from the trauma she had experienced. Eventually, though, she started smiling again and when she was ready, we were married."

Haemir's voice softened, his eyes misting over with emotion. I listened intently, my heart aching for Haemir's loss. I knew something terrible was coming, and I desperately wished he could have lived in those moments with her and his triad forever.

"Things were good for a while," Haemir continued. "We had Gavril, and we were happy. But then the governor found us. I was out with Gavril, getting a snack for Amalia and wearing out Gavril for bedtime. She was pregnant again and had a craving for honeyed pears." He heaved a breath, his fiery eyes dark. "He and his men killed my mate and the rest of my triad that night. I was the only one who made it out alive, with Gavril in tow."

My eyes widened in shock. "I didn't know."

Haemir shrugged. "It's not something I like to talk about. But I wanted you to know, Kael. To know that you can recover. With time and love and understanding, you'll heal from whatever happened to you in the palace."

I swallowed hard, tears pricking at the corners of my eyes. "How did you end up in Adraedor?"

He shook his head. "That's a story for another time." Haemir's eyes were distant as he spoke, his gaze fixed on the horizon. "I've had a long and difficult journey, but it was worth it in the end. I learned much from my triad, especially about love and resilience. We had to be strong for each other during our darkest times. Because that's what family does." He patted my back, knowing that I didn't hug much. "And you're my family, kiddo. You're the daughter we'd always wished for. No matter what happens in life or how hard things may seem, never forget that you are strong enough to survive anything. And I'll always be here to remind you of that."

"Thank you," I said softly before burying my face in his chest, my shoulders shaking as I fought the tears threatening to fall as he embraced me. He held me as I wept, comforting me as I had never let him before, murmuring soothing words.

He pulled away and wiped my tear-stained cheeks. "I'm here, Kael. Whenever you're ready to talk about it, I'll be here to listen." He smiled at me warmly, his eyes full of understanding and compassion. "It's alright if it takes time. Just know that I'm always here for you."

I returned his smile, grateful for his support. I wanted to tell him about everything, but I couldn't yet. It was still too raw. The thought of reliving those memories filled me with dread. I remembered what he said earlier; he was worried about something but I didn't know what.

"What's wrong?" I asked. "You said you needed to clear your head."

He hesitated before sighing and looking away from me. "It's Teodosija," he finally replied. "I'm concerned about her and the rebellion." He looked back at me, his expression grave. "I know she wants to get revenge on the elves, but we need more than that to gain our freedom. She refuses to see it."

"What do you mean?"

"She's too focused on retaking the city, with no other plans," he continued. "Adraedor is only the first step towards freedom, but she doesn't seem to understand that." He paused, letting out another long sigh before turning back to me. "We have the highest number of Kyrie Remnants in the rebellion since we're in Cavantha. They are always surrounded by what they lost. But if we seize Adraedor and they decide all they want is their country, then it's only a matter of time until we're enslaved again."

"As long as the empire exists..."

"Then we're not safe," he finished my thought. "It needs to fall, and the only way we can win is by keeping our forces together and maintaining momentum." He shook his head. "It's alright, kiddo. We'll figure it out."

His words sent a chill down my spine. Taking down the empire seemed like such an impossible task. I couldn't help but think of what that would mean for Theron... I forced the thought away, not wanting to dwell on it now.

"Come on," Haemir said softly, sensing my unease. He offered his arm, and I took it, letting him pull me to my feet."Are you ready to head back?"

I nodded.

"Good. Because it's time for you to interrogate the Marshal."

Chapter 6
Theron

I yanked on my manacles, straining against the thick metal chain that was bolted into the wall. I had spent hours working to loosen the anchor, and the sound of grinding stone echoed as I tugged against the links.

Footsteps approached, and I stilled, kicking the pile of rubble aside so as not to alert the guard of my plan. My progress was impressive—it wouldn't be long before I could escape. But stealth was more important than speed, especially with how slowly I was healing.

"Has anyone come to speak to the prisoner?"

I recognized Peregrine's voice from outside the cave's entrance, though I couldn't see her past the bend in the tunnel.

"Not since Striker yesterday, ma'am." The guard answered.

"Did you get information from him then?" I could practically see how Peregrine's bird-like eyes would narrow.

"No," a woman replied shortly and my chest thumped painfully when I recognized her voice. Kael. "He'd passed out, and I finished dressing his wounds."

Lying to her leader. Interesting.

"Find out everything you can about Adraedor's defenses. I don't care how you do it, just get results."

I stayed still as they stopped outside my cell. Teodosija studied Kael's guarded expression, and I held my breath in anticipation.

"I always do." She cleared her throat. "I don't want an audience. All of you leave, and I'll report back when I'm finished.

A twinge of hope stirred within me. This might be my chance to escape with Kael. If I yanked my chain free and used it as a weapon, I could reclaim my swords and be unstoppable...

Teodosija spoke again. "You can't be alone with him. He's an enemy soldier—a murderer—losing you to the Marshal would be a blow to the rebellion."

"I was secluded with him for days. I can do this."

Haemir joined the argument. "Kael is right," he agreed. "I trust her, and you should trust her judgment in this, too."

I didn't hear Peregrine's response; it was lost in the sound of shifting stones as sand fell from above.

Kael stepped into my cave, her eyes locking with mine. I studied her for a moment, my expression stoic as I tried to keep my thoughts hidden. My heart was in turmoil—the desire to dominate her, to *punish* her, warred with my need to protect her. I was still filled with the certainty that she belonged to me, regardless of what she'd done.

She broke the silence, her voice demanding and cold. "Tell me about Adraedor's defenses."

My lips quirked as I crossed my arms over my chest. "What makes you think I'll tell you anything? You betrayed me." Her mouth pressed into a thin line, but I could see the hurt in her eyes. There was so much more going on beneath her surface. Had something happened?

I dismissed the thought and asked my question. "Have you come to terms with what you are yet? Or are you still disgusted about being a daughter of Atar?"

Kael sidestepped the conversation and lifted her chin. "That's none of your concern," she replied, keeping her tone even. "I only want to talk about Adraedor's defenses right now."

I scoffed, unable to hide my disappointment at her determination.

"You can help me save lives." She pressed.

"Why would I care about rebel lives?" I challenged her, though part of me knew why she was doing this. I stretched my arms over my head, trying to relieve the insufferable itching of the wounds on my back as they healed. Kael's eyes drifted down my muscular frame and I saw a spark of something else there—attraction.

"We'll figure it out regardless," she said, tearing her eyes away from me. "But if you help us, you can save Elven lives."

I snorted. "You have a lot to learn about being an elf. We don't give up. Ever. Elves don't surrender, so no matter what you have planned, I won't change the outcome."

"They've killed a lot of royal guards in the desert," she murmured. "I don't know if it was Raenisa and Zerek or those Rhazien sent to search for me. But this could keep them safe."

I laughed, not believing a word she said. "You expect me to think that you care about their fate?"

"I like them," she replied, her voice barely above a whisper, almost as if speaking to herself. "More than I should."

I raised an eyebrow, intrigued despite myself. "Tell me more."

She stared at me for a long moment, her green eyes hiding whatever thoughts passed through her cunning mind.

"Same deal as before," she said finally. "A secret for a secret."

My mind raced as I considered her offer. On the one hand, I couldn't trust her. She'd betrayed me before, and there was no guarantee she wouldn't do it again. But I also needed to learn what was going on in the city. And if there's any chance I can use this to my advantage and escape, I had to take it. Not only that, but I wanted to know about *her*. To learn what secrets she kept hidden behind that mask of anger.

I nodded, my eyes never leaving hers. "Alright," I said, my voice low and hesitant. "I'll do it. But you go first."

Kael sighed and looked away for a moment before turning back to me. "I hated all of you at first," she said, her voice matter of fact. "The way you used water like it was nothing. How you never seemed to care about the fact that we were in the desert and needed to conserve every drop… All you cared about was power and posturing. I couldn't understand it." She shook her head and laughed sadly. "But then I realized you all were doing what you had to do to survive, just like me. And I learned how easy it is to take water for granted when it's all around instead of something you have to work hard for. Raenisa and Zerek weren't bad people, just different. I don't hate them anymore." She glanced over at me, almost as if she was expecting some kind of response. But before I said anything else, she continued. "I still hate you, though."

I laughed. "Of course, *Sihaya*."

"Your turn. What defenses does Adraedor have?"

I rolled my eyes. "Three impenetrable walls. You need to be more specific, Kaella."

She glowered at me when I used her full name. She'd told me it the last time we'd played this game.

"Fine." She leaned back against the wall. "What do you want to know?"

I considered for a moment, then asked the question that had been on my mind since I'd seen her. "How old are you?"

A slight smirk played on her lips as she replied. "Twenty-four," she said with a mischievous glint in her eye. "Much younger than you, old man."

I laughed and shook my head. "Elves age slowly once they reach their immortality," I explained. "So while I'm over two hundred, in terms of maturity, I'm probably closer to your age. You'll be settling into your immortality soon."

A new thought occurred to me. What if she went through her change when I wasn't near her? When the magical races set into their immortality, everything became more heightened; including their need for sex. It was insatiable for the duration of their transition. Some only took hours, others days. I'd fucked my way through half the lesser court during mine. I'd have to have her out of here by then, otherwise, I was liable to chew through my wrist to kill whatever men she had servicing her.

A growl escaped me, and she stared, opening her mouth to say something before thinking better of it. "How can I breach the fortress?"

"Scale the walls."

She shook her head. "That won't work. I need more."

"Make them let you in," I said, a plan already forming in my mind.

Kael nodded and waited for me to ask my question.

"When did you come to Adraedor?" I asked, knowing the answer but needing to hear it from her lips.

Her expression shifted as she realized what I was asking. "I was sent here when I was ten," she mumbled, her gaze dropping away from mine. My heart sank. Ten years old meant that she had been in Haechall when I razed Caurium. Had she seen the horrors that I'd inflicted on her people? "Tell me about the speaking stones."

"We have two sets. One is hidden in the throne room." I swallowed hard, my mouth parched. "You were there...during the Fall of Caurium, weren't you?" I asked, dreading the answer.

Kael held my gaze and nodded. "Yes," she said simply as if that one word was enough for me to understand her pain and sorrow.

My heart ached for what must have been an unbearable experience for such a young girl, and I wanted to reach out and comfort her despite my anger. We stood there in silence for what felt like an eternity as shame threatened to suffocate me. I let out a shaky breath and closed my eyes as regret washed over me in waves. Light filtered through my eyelids and it was like I was back there, the firelight so bright I could see it whether I wanted to or not.

When I opened my eyes again, Kael was still watching me, her muscles quaking as if preparing to run. "Did you see me?" I asked, not sure I wanted to know the answer.

Kael nodded and her voice trembled as she began. "I watched you on the rooftop. You looked like a cruel god, impassively staring down at the destruction that your army wrought. Everywhere you went, death followed. Children separated from their parents and women crying out for their lost loved ones or screaming as they were raped." Her eyes were distant, but I knew what she saw. The same memories haunted me. "I can still hear the anguished cries of mothers searching for their children, being swallowed by the endless abyss that the city had become." Her tears fell like the river coursing through Caurium before it, too, was poisoned on my orders.

I bowed my head in shame, unable to look her in the eye anymore.

"My father died trying to protect me," Kael continued, her voice wavering. "Your soldiers killed him after they dragged me from his arms. He fought to get to me until one of your soldiers stabbed him in the heart." A sob tried to escape her, and she took a shaky breath. "He bled out in front of me, trying to tell me that he loved me as his blood choked him. Then a soldier packed me in a wagon full of prisoners destined for Adraedor as I screamed for him."

My breath hitched as images of that fateful night flashed before my eyes like some sort of sickening slideshow. It melded with my memory of my father's death; how he'd told me to run, his blood thick and cloying in the air as Rhazien laughed. No child should ever be subjected to that kind of cruelty.

"I'm sorry, *Sihaya*," I breathed. "I'm so sorry." No apology could ever make up for what happened that night, but it was all I could give her. "I was following orders—"

Her eyes flashed. "You burned down an entire city because your uncle told you to? That's your excuse?"

The bitterness in her voice made me flinch. "I had no choice," I said defensively. "I was a soldier, complying with orders."

"A soldier?" Kael spat out the word as if it were poison. "Try murderer. You killed innocent people, women, and children. You destroyed homes, families, lives. The city was a burned-out shell. Nothing survived inside it."

Her words struck me like a physical blow, causing my stomach to churn. The bitter taste of truth mingled with the sourness of regret in my mouth, threatening to overwhelm me.

"You're right," I admitted. "It was wrong. I've spent years trying to make up for it. That's why Varzorn sent me to Adraedor in the first place because I refused to sack another city."

Kael looked at me, a swirl of emotions in her gaze. She didn't speak, but I felt the weight of her unspoken words settle on my shoulders. I knew that no matter what happened, there was nothing I could do to undo the past. But I had to try.

Kael took a deep breath as if trying to regain some semblance of composure before speaking again.

"How does the palace control the water?"

"We use a series of pipes and channels to divert water from the mountain snowmelt into underground cisterns in the range," I explained, my voice barely audible over the pounding of my heart. "The same system allows us to draw water out of certain areas as well."

"Like flooding the tunnels?"

I nodded, wondering if she had escaped from those very tunnels five years before.

"Yes."

Kael was silent for a moment as she processed this information. She was smart and her mind worked quickly to piece together the puzzle before her.

This might be the first time we had ever truly opened up to one another, with no subterfuge or hidden agenda between us. It was what I thought we'd had before, but that had been nothing compared to the intimacy of this conversation. She hadn't shown me her hurts then, hadn't told me about the pain

I'd caused her. I admired how strong and unflinching she was after all that she had faced, both before and during her captivity. She refused to back down or give up, no matter how difficult the situation became. The way she held herself was a testament to her resilience and bravery in the face of unimaginable horrors.

"What happened after you arrived at Adraedor?" I needed to know it all.

Her expression shuttered. "That doesn't matter."

The weight of her words hit me like a ton of stone. Something terrible had happened to her... and it was my fault.

"What happened?" I growled.

"I was a ten-year-old girl without a father who was dropped into a slave pit with no protection. What do you think?" She snapped.

My stomach rolled, vomit rising in my throat. I'd only thought about the horrors I'd inflicted on the city, not about what happened after I'd sent her to Adraedor.

"How did you escape?"

Her eyes were hard. "Haemir killed them all and saved me."

Them. Gods.

I swallowed the acid in my mouth, gratitude to a man I hated filling me.

"No wonder you hate me," I whispered, my voice thick. "I ruined your life." In her eyes, I was no different from Rhazien. I was her tormentor, as he had been mine. My eyes met hers, and my chest ached as I saw the pain and hate reflected there.

I was a fool to ever believe she could forgive me.

"The controls for the water pipes are in the mountain and only reachable through the palace," I began woodenly. "The tunnel is hidden behind the grotto."

My mind went back to that day that we'd swam together. She'd challenged me then, asking me how I didn't care about the plight of the slaves. I'd been so entranced by her I hadn't thought it through.

But I was now.

"Kael, if you care about your people and the Rebellion, then you have to run. Varzorn will send an army to Adraedor once he finds out that Rhazien is dead. Take the slaves and run south, beyond the reach of the empire. You can make a new life for yourself and your people there."

My breath stilled in my chest as I awaited her response. Would she heed my advice? Or would she ignore it and march on to her destruction?

"For how long?"

"What do you mean?"

She narrowed her eyes on me. "How long do you think it would take for Varzorn to send the Niothe south after us? Would you lead them? Drag us back to Adraedor and the mines like before?" She glared. "Fuck you, Theron. You're a coward. I won't abandon these people to their fate."

My heart twisted painfully as she sneered at me.

"Kael, you might be brave, but it won't save your life or the lives of your people." I narrowed my eyes on her. "The Rebellion isn't strong enough to stand against Varzorn's forces. If you try to fight him here, you'll all die."

She laughed bitterly. "It doesn't matter. We have nothing else left, anyway. We can either fight for our freedom or die trying—I would much rather do the former than the latter."

She crossed her arms and looked at me, determination in her eyes, daring me to argue with her.

I ran my hand through my shorn hair, frustrated. "A secret for a favor, then?"

"I'm not freeing you."

"That's not what I'm asking."

She pressed her lips in a line. "Then what?"

"When Varzorn comes, run. Live to fight another day. Otherwise, you'll have to live through the fall of another city."

Chapter 7
Kael

As I left the cave, I couldn't shake the image of Theron hanging his head from my mind. The sight of his bowed figure haunted me, his defeated posture etched into my memory. I had the inane thought that if I kissed him, I'd be able to taste his regret, bitter and caustic. The mere idea of it left a tang of remorse on my tongue. A part of me hated him, but another couldn't help but understand. Hadn't I done horrible things too? I tried to push my conflicting emotions away and focus on the task at hand—reporting my findings to Teodosija and Haemir.

"Hey. Wake up." I kicked the young guard lounging against the wall on the opposite side of the cavern, his arms and ankles crossed as he slept. I took it as a compliment rather than a dereliction of duty.

He stirred, red staining his cheeks as he realized who was standing over him.

"Striker—Shit. I'm sorry. I don't know what came over me."

I frowned as he stood with a groan, brushing off the sand. "Have you switched guards at all?"

He shook his head, and I growled in my throat. "I'll take care of it. Stay on your feet until relief arrives. Alright?"

He nodded, relief flooding his face. "Yes, ma'am. Thank you."

The caverns buzzed with hushed conversations and the clatter of weapons being readied. The low rumble of strategic discussions mixed with the occasional clash of swords being tested for battle. Warriors hurried past me, their faces smudged with dirt and determination, their armor reflecting flickering firelight. Raiding parties leaving to attack Adraedor. I should be with them, damn it. Especially if we have a spy in our midst. Maybe if I could convince Teodosija and Haemir that I'm more useful on the front than anywhere else? An idea came to mind, but it was risky...

I stepped into the makeshift war room, my mind still reeling from my conversation with Theron. The room was a natural cavern the size of a small house with rough walls covered in intricate carvings, its interior illuminated by several fire bowls. A large sandstone table stood at the center, around which several members of Teodosija's rebels sat, their faces stern as they discussed battle strategies. Various maps of Adraedor were pinned to the wall, marked with arrows and red dots showing enemy movements. On another wall hung weapons of all kinds—swords, spears, bows and arrows, knives. The scent of smoke blended with that of oil used to sharpen the blades, giving it an almost festive atmosphere.

In one corner, Haemir stood studying a map on his own while the others discussed tactics around him. Peregrine's piercing eyes followed my every step as I advanced toward them. Next to Haemir sat a pile of scrolls and parchments that looked like they had been hastily strewn together and forgotten.

Haemir looked up from his maps as I came closer, a relieved smile on his face. But it was another rebel that caught my eye.

"Kadir!" The exclamation slipped out of my mouth before I could call it back.

He turned from where he'd been arguing with Teodosija and faced me.

"Kael." Kadir stepped forward, raising a hand for me to shake before lowering it. "It's good to see you again." He greeted me awkwardly, neither of us sure if we were friends or not. "I never thought you could kill Rhazien by yourself—but here you are."

"Here I am," I agreed, hiding the shudder that the Beast's name caused. "Thank you for helping me. I know I made things difficult for you."

"You did." He agreed, and Haemir narrowed his eyes at him.

I waved off his concern and turned back to Kadir. "What are you doing here?"

Teodosija answered. "He's giving us information on the palace since he spent so much time there. I'd like to hear your report as well."

"Being grilled is more like it." Kadir shot me a look that Teodosija couldn't see and I had the impression that he didn't like her much.

"The prisoner told me how to access the water controls," I said, quickly explaining the grotto, "and that the speaking stones are in the throne room."

Teodosija nodded thoughtfully, her eyes going distant as she considered the information. "Anything on breaching the walls?"

I shook my head. "The outer wall is weaker sandstone, but the inner two are solid. We won't be able to breach them without being welcomed in."

Haemir chuckled. "No chance of that happening."

Teodosija's expression remained serious. "The stones and water are useless to us until we breach the palace."

"Unless we arrange a siege," Haemir suggested.

"We'd die of dehydration before them." I pointed out. "And we can't demolish the walls since we'll need them to defend ourselves when the Niothe arrives."

My declaration was met with quiet, and Kadir cleared his throat. "If you need nothing else, then I'll work on something more useful. Like making Kael a new outfit."

I scoffed. "There's nothing wrong with my clothes."

He gestured at me with a flourish. "You look like a sheepherder."

Someone snickered behind me, and I turned to see Gavril, Roza, and a few other rebels I recognized. Roza smirked at me and I stepped forward, ready to brawl again when Haemir cleared his throat.

"This is our last group to brief."

Teodosija nodded. "Roza. Gavril. Your teams will not be involved in the initial breach. We're holding you in reserve until we see the outcome of our smaller sorties."

A muscle pulsed in Gavril's jaw, but he didn't speak. Roza had no such restraint.

"What the fuck? You told us we were going in a large group and now it's all these little raiding parties. What's going on?"

Teodosija ignored her outburst, continuing in a calm voice. "We plan to breach the outer wall of Adraedor. Our forces will slip in amongst the miners, who are mostly unaware of our plans. Then we'll sabotage the outer door so it can't be closed. Once that's done, more forces can go in. Your teams."

Gavril and Roza nodded, their postures loosening, and I cut in. "What about the city? Is it running as usual?"

Teodosija shook her head.

"No. One of the Harvestmen, Herrath Tavador, is now running things, which means there will be extra guards watching for any sign of rebellion or infiltration."

I narrowed my eyes. "He's a cunning one. We'll need to be careful."

Gavril growled in agreement. "That's the bastard that tortured me while the Marshal questioned me."

Herrath was the person in Theron's entourage that I trusted the least. "Have none of the other Harvestmen returned then?"

"No. We believe they've received word of the Marshal's abduction and are currently searching for him."

A thought teased the back of my mind. "This is the first time we're sending out people since we brought the Marshal back, right?"

Haemir frowned. "Yes. Why?"

I glanced at the gathered group. I knew Gavril wasn't the spy and, for all her faults, Roza would rather die than work for the enemy. Could they be trusted?

"Can I speak freely?"

Teodosija raised an eyebrow and nodded. "I've cleared them."

I blew out a breath. "If the leak is with one of the raiding parties, then we can expect them to converge on our position in the next day or two. We'll need to move camp."

"Leak?"

I shushed Gavril and motioned for her to respond. Teodosija pursed her lips. "I made sure everyone in the raiding parties had at least one relative that stayed behind as insurance against them selling us out. We should be safe."

"Not with the bounty Theron will warrant. He's the emperor's heir now. The ransom will be outrageous."

Teodosija eyed me and I couldn't help but feel like she was scrutinizing me too closely. I shifted uncomfortably.

"What are you suggesting then, Kael?"

"We send word to anyone we have left in the city and see if we can get them to let us into the inner wall and wait on our attack. Otherwise, we'll end up trapped in the outer ring of the city with no supplies. Pinned and waiting for the Niothe. This will give us time to root out the leak without compromising our position."

"It's too late, Kael." Haemir itched one of his horns. "The first groups have already left."

I swore. "Then let me go. Maybe I can—"

Teodosija shook her head. "Absolutely not. You're not cleared to go back into battle yet."

"What if I could turn the tide?" I asked, licking my chapped lips. I needed to get used to less water.

"And how would you do that?" Roza sneered.

I paused for a moment, feeling the weight of their collective gazes on me. How could I explain my magic without admitting my heritage?

"I think I have magic," I blurted out. All four of them exchanged glances and stared at me in shock. Roza's face twisted into a smirk of disbelief and she laughed, while Gavril looked as though he wanted to come to my aid, but didn't know how.

"Why do you think that?" Teodosija asked, her expression carefully neutral as she glanced at Haemir. They thought I'd cracked, that my mind broke because of what happened in the palace.

I took a deep breath. "When I was in the palace, I touched some celestial metal, and things seemed to explode around me without warning," I explained the situation with the tiara, and Teodosija's face morphed from skepticism to understanding as she made the connection between metal and magic.

"Are you saying you're... an elf?"

I tucked my hair behind my newly pointed ears. "These showed up when my earrings were removed." I pushed away the memories of my assault as Rhazien tore my piercings from my body. *All but one.* "And the Sálfar elves were known to have white and silver hair."

"Kael..." Haemir breathed.

"She's an elf?" Roza sneered. "We can't trust her. You should throw her in the cell with the Marshal."

Gavril stepped forward, his face contorted with rage. "Fuck off, Roza. Kael's done more for the rebellion than you have."

Haemir held up a hand and Gavril fell silent. "We can trust Kael," he said. "If she's a Sálfar, then we should make training her a priority."

Roza shook her head. "That's stupid. She could turn on us."

"I'm right here, bitch." I growled and Roza shot me a rude hand gesture.

"Enough. We don't even know if what she says is right." Teodosija eyed me before stepping to the wall and yanking a short dagger off the wall. "This is made of silver. Try to use the metal."

"I've never done it on purpose—"

"Just try."

I took the blade from her, hefting its cool weight in my hand. The smooth hilt fit snugly against my palm, providing a sense of familiarity and reassurance. I looked around at their faces, full of confusion and fear. Taking a deep breath, I squared my shoulders and placed my hand on the blade.

I closed my eyes and thought about what I wanted to do. Theron told me before that to use the magic, he had to push his intention into the metal. But what was silver supposed to do? Was it speed? I tried to remember all the things that Theron had said about his magic, but all of his words were jumbled in my head.

I opened my mind and tried to push my thoughts into the metal, warmth spreading through my hand as I did so. *Speed.* I felt lighter as if some sort of weight had been lifted from me. I took a step and gasps rang out. When I opened my eyes, I found myself on the other side of the room. A soft glowing light emanated from the blade, and its surface shimmered with energy.

The others were wide-eyed with shock as they looked from me to the blade and back again. Roza's face still held disbelief, but there was also wariness in her gaze now.

"It—it worked," Gavril whispered in awe. "Vetia's horns."

Teodosija met my gaze, a satisfied expression on her face when a scream in the distance broke the moment.

"What's—"

A chorus of screams grew louder, and I took off at a sprint through the carved tunnels. As I rounded a corner, I let out a string of curses as I pulled my swords. A giant scorpion-like monster attacked the main encampment, its enormous claws whipping through the air as it slashed at anything that came near it.

"Fuck. That's the biggest scopscion I've ever seen," Gavril panted beside me. People ran in panic, some trying to flee while others fought against the beast, poking at it with spears as they avoided strikes from its wicked tail.

"Let's go."

Gavril followed behind me, his sword drawn and ready for battle. I made my way through the chaos, dodging claws and poison tail strikes as I got closer to the beast. It reared up on its hind legs and I had to duck out of the way to avoid being hit. Gavril shouted and lunged forward, lashing out at one of its legs with his sword.

"I'll keep it busy! Cut off its tail!"

Gavril attacked the creature's front while I charged in from behind. My blade bounced off its carapace, and I grimaced. Shit, how should I do this? I jumped forward, sliding onto the beast's back. I slipped, almost falling on its slippery shell. Aiming my sword where the plates separated, I dove forward as it moved again, my blade slicing deep into its thick flesh. The beast shrieked in agony as my blade dug deep and I yanked, slicing its tail off.

"Kill it!"

I jumped off of its back and rolled on the sandy floor, rocks scraping my exposed skin. The beast caught a man in its claw and he screamed as it crushed him. Gavril used the opportunity to strike at its exposed stomach, diving underneath the monster. The scopscion reared in pain as Gavril stabbed its soft underbelly.

"Gavril!" Haemir shouted, jumping into the battle with me. He swung his great hammer, smashing the creature in the face.

The giant beast collapsed in a heap of black exoskeleton and yellow ichor—with Gavril underneath.

"Vetia's fiery tits, get me out of here." Gavril's shout was muffled underneath the massive carcass.

Haemir and I rushed forward, lifting the beast off of Gavril. He groaned as he emerged, covered in yellow ichor. He had a long gash across his forehead and cuts along his arms and legs, but he was still alive.

"Are you alright?" Haemir asked, concern in his voice.

Gavril nodded, his gaze flitting around the carnage that lay before us. The creature had been so large that even with its death, it seemed to still loom over us in a way that made my stomach churn.

Haemir pulled Gavril into a hug, the two of them embracing for a long moment. I watched in silence, feeling out of place.

Haemir released Gavril and looked over at me, gesturing for me to come closer. He opened his arms wide, and I stepped forward cautiously until he enveloped me in a warm embrace, Gavril joining us. A sob escaped me and I swallowed, trying to hold back the tide of tears that wanted to escape.

"What's wrong?" Haemir drew back, looking at me. "Are you hurt?"

"No, it's just that Gavril smells so bad—"

"Oh, shut up," Gavril laughed, rubbing some of the ichor onto my cheek, and I jerked away with a choked laugh.

I ducked my head. "I just thought that when you found out I was—" I couldn't finish.

"You think that your heritage changes things?" Haemir asked, his voice soft.

I nodded, tears pricking at the corners of my eyes. "I thought you'd hate me," I said, my voice breaking. "That I wasn't what you wanted me to be."

Haemir's hand came up to cup my cheek, his touch gentle. "Kael, you could be a wyrm and it wouldn't change how we feel about you," he said firmly. "You're my daughter, Gavril's sister, and that's all that matters."

My heart ached, and I held them tighter.

Haemir's expression turned serious. "Kael, I won't let anyone hurt you. I'll do whatever it takes to keep you safe."

Warmth spread through my body as I hugged him back tightly in an awkward three-way hug that was more comforting than any I remembered.

Chapter 8
Kael

I sat next to Gavril, watching him use sand to scrub the ichor off his armor.

"Here." I handed him my canteen. "You can have the rest of my water to clean it off." Vivid memories of Theron's opulent bathing tubs tantalized my mind, but I pushed them aside, focusing on the rhythmic motion of polishing my swords. They didn't need sharpening. Nothing could dull the edge but other god-forged blades, which were thankfully in short supply, but I found the process calming.

"Thanks. Gods, I'd kill to go for a swim right now. Though Roza would be liable to drown me." I forced a small smile, appreciating his attempt at levity. But I still couldn't find the right words to broach the conversation we needed to have.

The weight of his unsuspecting gaze added to the ball of guilt in my stomach as he looked up at me. "I'm glad you finally told us what was bothering you." He set his armor aside and focused on me. "I knew you were hiding something, but I didn't know what. I'd worried it was something horrible." He chuckled to himself. "As if Dad or I would care that you're an elf. Dumbass."

I forced a laugh. "Yeah."

He didn't notice my hesitation. I had only told them a small part of the truth, and I was still hiding so much more. How could I explain it? How could I tell him I was afraid of what they would think of me once they knew everything? That I was terrified of being cast out if they learned what I'd done with Theron? That my secrets weren't just secrets, but my shield, my protection?

A lump formed in my throat as I looked into Gavril's eyes, not wanting to speak the words and reveal my fears.

Gavril softened, sensing my warring emotions. He smiled, his expression warm and understanding. "It's alright," he said, squeezing my shoulder. "You don't have to say anything. You're home now and I'll kick anyone's ass who tries to mess with you."

"Like I need help with that."

He rubbed his chin. "I don't know. You barely touched Roza."

I shot him a rude hand gesture, and he laughed, tending his armor in silence. I tried to shake off my frustration, but the tension in the air around the rebel encampment made it impossible. Everyone was on edge. With half the force on a mission and the scopscion attack, it made sense. But that didn't explain the whispers as the other rebels watched me from the corners of their eyes. The respect I'd earned over the years was gone—in its place was wariness, if not open hatred. To them, I'd become the enemy. It was bullshit. I'd done so much for the rebellion, risked my life countless times, and yet they still saw me as an outsider because of something I couldn't control.

Gavril noticed my unease. "Everyone is just weird because of the scopscion. It's unusual for them to attack such a large group. Some predator must have flushed it out of its den and it was trying to claim fresh territory."

I knew better. I could sense their distrust, their suspicions pressing on me like a storm on the horizon.

"They're looking at me, not watching for more scopscions," I grumbled, letting a handful of sand trail from my fingers.

"It's going to take time." Gavril pitched his voice higher, trying to reassure me. "They'll come around, eventually."

"Sure." I nodded, but I wasn't convinced. Hate for the elves had been bred into us for generations. That's not something that just goes away.

I needed to get away from this camp for a while. Nervous energy burned within me, and I stood up abruptly. "I need some fresh air."

"I'll come with you." He made to stand, and I shook my head.

"NO—I mean, no thanks. I want to be alone for a while."

He eyed me for a long moment before nodding. "Alright, take all the time you need." He turned back to his armor and continued working as I walked away from the fire, ignoring all the eyes trailing me as I escaped into the darkness.

The night air was cool on my skin, the twin moons chasing one another across the sky. Ydonja's stars were bright above me and in the distance, the low call of an owl hunting its prey drifted over the dunes. Moths fluttered around me in the soft breeze, as if they were guiding me somewhere undiscovered.

I'd never thought that I'd love the desert. It was inhospitable, killing with the same dispassionate ease of the sea. But it was beautiful too, serene in a way that I'd only once associated with the forest. It was *more* than that. It tempered you, honing you into something deadly.

But it wasn't comforting tonight. The sound of shifting sand scraped against my nerves, causing the hair on the back of my neck to stand up.

I turned around and wandered through the winding corridors of the caverns, lost in thought. The weight of my secrets and the tension within the camp had settled onto my shoulders, and nothing seemed to ease it.

Until my legs took me in a familiar direction—to Theron's cell.

The same guard as before swayed on his feet, about to drop from exhaustion. Fuck. I'd forgotten to mention it to Teodosija.

"Hey. I'm here to relieve your shift."

He shuddered in relief, an enormous yawn escaping him. "Thank Thanja. He hasn't been any trouble. I'll be back in the morning."

I nodded, wondering if the expression of respect on his face would be replaced with fear when he returned. "Get some rest."

"Kael."

The sound of my name startled me, and I turned to see Haemir approaching. I composed myself and tried to act as if I was just following an order.

"What are you doing here?" he asked, his eyes narrowing.

"Just... checking on the prisoner." I kept my voice light, but I felt foolish. Haemir could always tell when I lied.

Haemir stepped closer and I could smell the familiar scent of sandalwood and sweat on him. It was an odd mixture, but it had become as comforting to me as my father's voice had been. Haemir had always meant protection and now was no different.

"Is everything alright?"

My shoulders slumped under his gaze and I mumbled, "Everyone was staring at me and whispering."

Haemir's expression darkened, and he stepped forward, patting my shoulder. "I'll talk to Teodosija. If Roza is spreading rumors, then—"

"But it's not a rumor, Dad. It's the truth. And I just have to deal with it."

His eyes crinkled. "If you think calling me 'Dad' will help you win this argument, you're absolutely right." I laughed, and he continued. "But you can't let other people's opinions influence how you think about yourself. So you're an elf. Does that change your favorite color or the fact that you hate sleeping on your back? No. You're still *you* and you always will be."

I nodded, my eyes burning with unshed tears. "I know," I said, my voice barely above a whisper. "It's just hard sometimes."

Haemir's expression softened. "We're in this together, kiddo. We'll figure it out."

With that, he turned and walked away, leaving me alone with my thoughts once again. I glanced back at Theron's cave, wondering if he was still awake. I edged inside, my steps silent on the shifting sand. He sat on the ground, his back against the wall, staring off into space. A streak of moonlight illuminated the weariness etched into his features, and a pang of guilt hit my stomach.

I wondered if he felt as alone as I did.

He turned and stared at me. I'm not sure what emotion flitted across his face. It wasn't hatred or anger, but something else—something familiar. I couldn't put my finger on it, but it drew me in closer.

He broke the silence first. "Not in the mood for company," he growled, but there was an edge of vulnerability in his voice that belied his words.

I raised my eyebrow and replied lightly, "I didn't think the day would come when you didn't want to see me."

His lips twitched into a half-smile. He enjoyed our banter as much as I did. "I didn't think you'd ever voluntarily come to visit me."

My heart thumped against my chest as our eyes met. "Who says it's voluntary?"

He rolled his eyes and my attention locked on how one side of his smile tipped higher. "I doubt Peregrine would send you in to question me in the dark of night. Unless this is a sexual rendezvous." He raised a brow. "I've never been the one chained before, but I'm willing to try it for you."

Heat rose in my face and I hoped he couldn't see my cheeks redden in the low light. I took a step forward and stopped, my heart beating wildly with anticipation. He was trying to seduce me—but I wouldn't let it work.

"Tempting... but no."

He chuckled and shook his head. "So much self-control." His voice was soft and inviting, but his eyes were full of challenge. "But do you want to bet that you can resist me? You weren't able to before and I like a challenge."

"I won't ever fuck you again," I said, my voice firm even though my knees went weak at his words.

His lips tipped into a smirk and he leaned forward, closing the gap between us until only inches separated us. "I didn't think we were lying to each other anymore?" His gaze locked on mine and the surrounding air thickened with desire as neither of us spoke or moved apart.

"So tense. If you didn't come to me for relief, then why are you here? What's got you on edge, *Sihaya*?"

"I'm not in the mood for your games, Theron," I lied. "I just needed to get away from all the staring."

He clucked his tongue. "Ah, they found out about your little secret, did they?"

I nodded, my stomach churning with unease. "Yeah. They know."

Theron stepped closer, his expression softening. "Kael, you're still the same person you were before. Don't let anyone make you think otherwise. Even yourself."

His words echoed Haemir's, but I still didn't believe them. I met his gaze. "Do you mean the person I was before I found out I was an elf or the person I was before Rhazien raped me?"

His jaw clenched, an inner rage boiling under the surface that I watched him slowly quell. He placed a gentle hand on my shoulder, his touch warm and comforting.

"I'm sorry," he whispered, his voice thick with emotion. "I should have been there for you."

I shook my head. "It's not your fault. I should've been more careful, and scouted more. If I had just planned better, it never would have happened."

"Kael, it's not on you. Soldiers don't expect to be raped on the battlefield—no one expects it."

Theron brushed a strand of hair from my face and cupped my chin in his hands, tilting it up so that our eyes met. "I'm sorry I wasn't there for you," he murmured.

Tears filled my eyes as I tried to accept his apology, a wave of sorrow washing over me as memories of everything that had happened that night flooded me. "I know," I managed to choke out around the lump in my throat.

"I won't lie to you and tell you that you can just get over it." His gaze was distant, and I knew Raura was filling his thoughts. "But it gets easier with time and the help of friends." He turned his gaze back to mine. "You'll make it through this, Kael. You're like a diamond forged through fire and pressure. Harder and stronger, but still made of the same stuff. You're precious, and anyone who can't see that is a fool."

I shook my head, guilt pressing down on me like a mountain on my chest. I wanted to show him a sliver of the truth, to give him that. "Have you ever heard a man cry out for his mother when he's about to die?"

His brows furrowed as if he couldn't see where I was going with the conversation. "Of course."

"I'd never understood it." Averting my gaze, I stared at the wall, memorizing every crack and crevice. "I've been near death more times than I can count, and I'd never called out for anyone. Not my father, or Haemir or Gavril. I don't think I've ever had someone that I trusted fully to take care of me. The way those men think of their mothers. Someone who will always protect me." I lifted my eyes to his golden gaze, molten in the moonlight. "But that night, when Rhazien was ra—hurting me. I called for *you*. Prayed to all the gods that you'd come save me."

The column of his throat bobbed as he swallowed, his eyes tortured. "*Sihaya...*"

I stared at him, trying to see past his skin, and into his soul to find the man that hid there. He'd never tried to lie to me or manipulate me. He'd been honest from the beginning. I was the one who'd lied from the start. I was the poison.

I cleared my throat, stepping back. "Have you eaten? I can get you more food or water."

"Don't do that." He reached for me. "Don't retreat from me. Stay."

I hesitated, not sure of what to do. He was my enemy, my prisoner. I shouldn't want to stay here. Shouldn't feel relieved that he asked me to. But the thought of going back out to the cavern to be judged and stared at...

"Please," he whispered, his voice barely audible. "Just for tonight, let's have a truce." He raised his shackled hands in surrender. "I swear I won't hurt you or do anything else." He paused before adding softly, "Please, Kael. I just want to hold you."

Conflicting thoughts raced through my mind, too fast to fully form, my heart pounding in my chest. I wanted to trust him, but was it worth the risk?

I let out a shuddering breath and nodded. "Alright." I took off my swords, throwing them on the opposite side of the room and out of his reach, making him roll his eyes.

He lifted his shackled arms, and I hesitated before I stepped into them, allowing myself to be enveloped in the safety of his embrace. His warmth cosseted me, melting away the pain of the past few days and making me feel safe for once.

"Come here." He pulled me with him to the ground, grunting as his back scraped against the stone.

"Is your back—"

"I'm fine, *Sihaya*." He situated me in between his legs, so I rested on his bare chest, my cheek pressed against his firm skin. "This makes up for any discomfort I have."

He kissed the top of my head and sighed contentedly as we both settled into each other's embrace.

"This might be the dumbest thing I've ever done. If anyone sees me, I'll be killed for treason." I couldn't muster up the energy to move, though. I was relaxed for the first time in days.

He snorted. "No. The dumbest thing you've ever done was steal my sword."

"You mean *my* sword."

His laugh rumbled under my ear as he ran his hand through my hair.

He held me like that for hours until sleep claimed us both.

Chapter 9
Theron

I woke up in my cave happier than I'd been in days, even though I was shackled to the wall and covered in sand. Because I had Kael sleeping in my arms. Brushing my nose over her hair, I breathed in her scent, my shoulders loosening. Gods, I'd missed this. I was still angry with her for betraying me, but learning the things she'd endured had mollified my anger. Of course, she wanted revenge—I would have done the same. Punishment would still need to be dispensed, but instead of her pleading for mercy, images of her in bed, begging me to fill her, ran through my mind. I could see her, sprawled on the red blankets, her skin practically glowing as she guided me into her tight cunt... I shifted, painfully aware of my hard cock, when movement in the air alerted me we weren't alone.

Haemir stood at the entrance of the cave, watching us, his expression unreadable. He lifted a finger to his lips.

"Whisper. I don't want to wake her." His voice was barely audible.

I narrowed my eyes, settling the way a forest cat does when the winter has come and prey is scarce, conserving energy and waiting for an opportunity to strike. He had the upper hand and knew it. I'd have to be canny.

He was older than the last time I'd seen him, more gray peppering his hair. But he was still the powerful male of before, muscular and proud. He shifted his weight, crossing his arms over his chest, thick biceps bunching. A thick iron hook replaced the hand I'd taken from him. Commanding the trust of his people with his steady presence. I'd once thought that he was helping me, that he'd wanted to improve the lives of the slaves with me, but it had been a ruse to trap me that night. To kill me and my Harvestmen.

"What do you want, Haemir?" My lip curled even as I did as he wished and stayed quiet.

"I came looking for my daughter," he replied, his tone light as he sank to his haunches beside us. "Why does she keep returning to you when she's upset?"

I kept my expression neutral as a conflicted sense of pride filled me. She trusted me, even when she should hate me more than anyone else.

"Perhaps she sees something in me she recognizes in herself."

Haemir hummed, his gaze searching mine. The air seemed to thicken around us until he spoke again. "I think it's more than just your shared heritage."

My brows went up. I'd expected him to berate me, not this.

"Despite all you've done, I see a better man than the others do." He paused before adding, "I still remember the man who wanted to help the slaves when no one else would."

"And look where it got me now." My lips quirked in dark amusement. "Chained and beaten in the desert. Though I can say it's an upgrade from when your people tried to blow me up and killed my friend."

Haemir's eyes hardened. "I didn't know about that plot. I wouldn't have allowed it."

At that moment, he reminded me of my father. Stern; a man of morals, but also kind and honorable. I shifted, uncomfortable with the comparison.

"Calyx is still dead," I growled and his eyes darted to Kael, where she stirred on my chest, nuzzling my skin in her sleep before she stilled again.

He chuckled sadly, his eyes crinkling. "I don't know if I've ever seen her like this. She never sleeps well." He met my stare, his fiery gaze soft with affection for his adopted daughter. "What happened in the palace?"

I shook my head. "If she didn't tell you, then I won't."

Surprisingly, he smiled. "It's good that you keep her secrets. It may save her life."

"What do you mean? I brought her here to be safe. If they want to hurt her because she's an elf, then let me—"

He held up a hand, stopping me. "That's not what I'm worried about. It's this—" He gestured to where Kael held onto me in her sleep. "They can ignore her heritage. She isn't the only elf on our side." My brows went up as I caught his meaning, but he continued before I could question him. "What they can't forgive is *this*. Her feelings for you."

My jaw locked, and I looked away. The idea of us *not* being together had never crossed my mind. In all of my imaginings, she was there. Regardless if I had dreams of retribution or adoration, she was by my side. The thought of her not being in my life... I shook my head. It was unfathomable.

Haemir continued. "The rebellion won't accept a relationship between the two of you, Theron." His fingers brushed Kael's hair off my shoulder in a gentle gesture that made me want to stab him. "It's too dangerous for both of you."

I scowled and ran a hand over my face, the reality of his words sinking in. He was right; they wouldn't accept it if they knew about our feelings for each other and it would be too risky for us to be together in the empire. They'd kill her for murdering Rhazien. She'd already made it clear that she wouldn't run away with me. My gaze drifted to Kael as she lay on top of me, and my heart clenched at the thought of not being able to express how much she meant to me without risking her life and mine.

She wouldn't stop until the empire had fallen, or she died trying. The idea of her in danger made my stomach churn, but I knew it was true; no matter how much we might care for each other, it would never be enough for them to accept us together.

"What do you want from me?"

Haemir looked away and let out a heavy sigh. When his gaze trailed back to me, it was determined and unwavering. "You need to escape. I'm not stupid; I can see the anchor is almost loose enough for you to pull it free. Go south and you'll reach Adraedor." He paused and seemed to struggle with something before continuing, "Leave my daughter out of it. If you care for her, then leave her behind."

My heart tightened in my chest as I stared at Haemir in disbelief. Abandon Kael? How could he ask me to do that? I'd sooner stop breathing.

"Never," I growled.

His fiery eyes darkened, like coals burning low at night. "I'll kill you myself if you harm my daughter."

"And you'll never see her again if she finds out you tried to take her choices from her."

"Well played." He stood, towering over me. His kind and understanding expression had been replaced with the hard stare of a man willing to do anything to protect his family. "Think on my words well, Marshal. And remember that both my problems would be solved with your death."

He turned, walking out of the cave, and anger pounded in my temples. I'd never been on the receiving end of a parent thinking I wasn't good enough for his daughter—usually they were parading them under my nose—but I found I didn't like it. Even if I knew he was right. I didn't deserve her, but that wouldn't stop me from keeping her.

Kael stirred, making a soft mewling sound as she stretched. My breath caught as she pressed her legs together against me and I groaned, unable to stop my cock from twitching to life again in my breeches. She ground against it, a quiet moan escaping her as she cupped one of her breasts. I ran a hand down her back, gripping her full backside and squeezing.

"Gods, *Sihaya*." Her eyes fluttered open, her gaze clouded with sleep as she looked up at me.

Our eyes locked and my heartbeat stuttered at the look she gave me. She rubbed her cheek against my shoulder and I shivered, unable to tear my eyes away from her tender expression. My heart lurched as she smiled at me before rolling off of me. Her smiles were always few and far between, making each one even more precious.

Her shoulders stiffened as she took in the room, only now seeming to remember we were in the cave and not back in our suite at the palace. I sat up as she ducked out of the circle of my arms, wanting to reach out and touch her, but knowing that if I did, she would only push me away. She had already constructed her walls, and she wasn't letting anyone in.

"Kael," I breathed, my voice soft in the early dawn light.

She flinched and my heart sank at the sight of her retreating from me once more.

"This was a mistake." Her green eyes glittered with emotion as she stared up at me defiantly, daring me to say something that would make it easier for her to retreat further into herself.

My jaw clenched as I fought against my frustration. I wouldn't give her the fight that she wanted.

"Is this what you want? To ignore what we could have together, so the rebellion accepts you?" I asked her, my voice steady despite the turmoil within me.

She took a deep breath as if steeling herself for whatever she had to say, even though she couldn't meet my gaze. "There's nothing between us."

I scowled at her, knowing that there was more going on behind those eyes than she would let me see.

"Liar."

"Fuck you," she growled, reaching down and scooping up her swords and slinging on her bandoliers. "You were my mission. That's all."

"That's not what you said last night, *Sihaya*," I drawled, my control of my temper slipping.

Her eyes flashed, angry that I'd brought up what she'd admitted to me in confidence and I wished I could take the words back. "I hate you."

"I've heard that before."

"Sharp-eared asshole." She threw at me and I snickered.

"Your pretty little ears are sharper than mine, *Sihaya*."

She glared, her posture still rigid. I sighed, wishing she would let me in so we could work through this together.

"Kael," I said, reaching out a hand to touch her arm, but she flinched away from me. "Do you want us to end like this? To sabotage what we have because you're scared?"

Her lips trembled as she pressed them into a line. She squared her shoulders and faced me again. "I'm not afraid of anything."

"Then why do you keep trying so hard to push me away? Why are you so adamant about keeping me at arm's length and convincing yourself there's nothing between us?"

Her chin lifted, her Sálfar heritage shining through. She looked like the queens of old before the Lightcurse damned us all. "Because it's the truth."

I chuckled, leaning into her space. "Lie to yourself all you want, *Sihaya*. But I know it's not true."

She glared at me before turning and stalking towards the tunnel. I watched her go, feeling like a fool. Kael's booted steps faded away until all that remained was the sound of my harsh breathing in the silent cave.

Well, fuck. That could've gone better.

I stood up, my movements sluggish as exhaustion settled over me once more. I tested my wounds and was pleased when they barely pulled. Most of my energy had gone to healing my back, but now that I was mended, I'd be able to regain my strength. Even with their bland seffa.

Sometime later, the guard entered and wordlessly offered me a bucket so I could relieve myself. With nothing else left to do, I grudgingly accepted before drinking my allotted water. I turned my attention back to the anchor in the wall, pulling on it again, slowly grinding away the softening stone. I was going to escape.

And Kael was coming with me, whether she liked it or not.

Chapter 10
Kael

The heavy air was filled with the pungent smell of sweat and grime, mingling with the indistinct murmurs of conversation and the shuffling of feet as they repaired the damage the scopscion had caused. I spent the entire day feeling useless, like a burden to the community I had sworn to protect. No matter how much I tried to help, no one wanted me around. They recoiled whenever I approached, their eyes darting away as if I was contagious. Their stares were suffocating, and I'd retreated to our family tent.

It was like they knew a truth I didn't, a truth that made them afraid of me. Clenching my fists, I tried to control the onslaught of emotions building inside me. I had always been an outsider, but this was different. They revile me now. Still, I wouldn't leave. I couldn't abandon the people who had entrusted me with their safety, even if they didn't want me here.

And I couldn't leave him...

Theron.

I closed my eyes, letting the memory of his touch wash over me. It was a foolish thing to do, to let my guard down and stay with him last night, but I couldn't help it. His voice echoed inside my mind, haunting me with his accusations. It was as if he etched his words into my soul, and I couldn't escape them, no matter how hard I tried. Because he was right. There was something between us, but I couldn't afford to have feelings for him, not when any association with him would lead to my banishment. Still, he dominated my every thought.

Oppressive heat radiated from the stone walls as Gavril and I sat in the corner by our tent. I couldn't shake the unease that gnawed at my insides. Waiting for news from the raiding teams, every passing moment, only intensified my anxiety. My guilt was palpable, a weight that nothing eased.

Gavril's attempts to distract me were valiant but futile. He knew me too well, and the small smiles I mustered were not enough to fool him. I was grateful for his company, but the pit in my stomach grew for burdening him with my problems. He was uncomfortable around me, just like everyone else.

"Kael? What do you think?" I looked up to see Gavril waiting expectantly. Shit, I hadn't heard his question. I tried to focus on the conversation, but my mind kept drifting back to Theron. It was like he had taken up permanent residence in my thoughts, and I couldn't shake him loose.

"About what?"

He shook his head. "It's nothing. Why don't we talk about what's bothering you?"

"The raid—"

"Nope." Gavril saw through my feeble attempts at distraction, cutting me off before I finished my sentence. "I was talking about the raid, and you weren't listening. What's on your mind?"

He was right. Guilt was a constant ache in my stomach, a reminder of everything that I'd done wrong. But I couldn't tell him the truth, not about Theron. It was a secret I had to keep, even if it meant carrying the burden alone.

I cast about for something to say that would ring true without having to discuss Theron. Gavril wouldn't understand. He hated him and blamed him for Orya's death. He'd think that I'd betrayed her memory. The thought of her made my chest ache, just adding more to the ball in my stomach. He'd accepted my heritage without blinking, but telling him that my thoughts were consumed with the Marshal would be a bridge too far.

"Everyone hates me," I muttered. "I tried to help today, and no one wants me around. Not even digging a new latrine."

He whistled. "That's low."

"Yeah." I huffed a laugh. "Can't even get shit duty."

"It's alright, sis. They've known for what, a day? They'll get used to it. Just be yourself and they'll remember that you're the same person."

I blew out a breath. "Everyone keeps saying that I'm the same person. But I don't think I am." I lifted my eyes to his. Losing Orya had done something to Gavril that the mines never had, hardening him. He wasn't the same gentle boy as he'd been then. And I had changed from the person I was before the mission.

"Is that such a bad thing?" He asked, his expression earnest. "I know you don't like change, but isn't that what we're trying to do? Change the world? It makes sense that we'll change along the way, too."

I smiled weakly. "What if I become someone I don't recognize? Or so much that I don't fit into our family anymore?" The last sentence came out as a whisper.

"Kael," he said, grabbing my hand. "Dad and I will always be your family. It doesn't matter that you have magic and won't age or anything else. All that matters is that we love and take care of each other. That's what it means to be family. Nothing you do will change that."

"You don't know everything I've done." I couldn't meet his eyes.

"Then tell me. I can see that something is tearing you up inside."

My heart pounded as I looked up at him. He was right. We were family. Maybe it would help to talk about it. I took a deep breath. "When I was in the palace—"

"Kael. Gavril."

Haemir approached, walking fast. I hadn't seen him yet today. He'd been gone when I'd returned to the tent early this morning and I hoped he'd thought I'd spent the night on the dunes again.

"You have news about the raid?" Gavril asked hopefully.

He nodded. "We're putting up a good fight, but they're outnumbered by the Elven forces." His expression was grim. "They're stopped in the slave quarter and unable to breach the inner rings of Adraedor."

I swore. "This is what I wanted to avoid. The elves can turn off the water to the outer forums."

"They already have. They were able to set aside enough to last them a while, but nowhere near as much as they'd need for a siege."

Gavril crossed his arms over his chest, frowning as he thought. "We can't just march right in and expect them to let us pass. We'd be slaughtered before we got within fifty feet of the palace gates."

Haemir nodded. "The plan is to go into the tunnels and try to sneak through unnoticed." He glanced at me uncertainly before continuing, expecting me to object.

"You already know what I'm going to say. They'll flood the tunnels."

"That's what I believe as well. Teodosija thinks differently."

I growled. "This is stupid. We need to redirect our attack. Find the pipes in the mountains and cut off all the water supply. Or try to climb Atar's anvil and sneak in that way. Fucking something."

Haemir rubbed his scalp where it connected to his horns with his hook, something he always did when frustrated. "I know, Kael. But Teodosija is in charge here and we still haven't found the leak."

"Then I'll go by myself again and see what I can—"

He held up a hand. "If you go off without orders again, Teodosija will exile you. We can't risk it. We'll wait a day and see if they make any progress."

"It's too risky." I shook my head. "I'm going to talk to Teodosija."

He sighed. "Kael."

"What? I said I just want to talk to her."

He rolled his eyes. "Try not to shout too much if you want her to listen to you."

I snorted. "No promises."

Hurrying through the cavern, I dodged stares before I made it to the tunnel that led deeper into the caves.

Andreja stepped out of the shadows, her horns freshly polished and her skin glowing. How did she look this fresh if she'd just gotten back running messages?

"What are you doing?" she asked, blocking my path.

"I'm going to talk to Teodosija," I replied, trying to sidestep her.

"She's busy," Andreja bit out, not moving. "You'll have to wait."

I crossed my arms and glared at her. "I don't have time for this. Our teams need all the help they can get."

She raised an eyebrow. "You're not on the mission, Kael. You should mind your own business."

I ground my teeth together, trying to keep my temper in check. "Is there a reason you're standing in my way?"

Andreja narrowed her eyes. "Roza told me you said there's a mole, but I know better. You were in the palace and you're the only one saying there was a leak. Pretty convenient."

"My brother almost died. I would never betray us like that," I snapped. "Now get out of my way."

I tried to move past her again, but she stepped in front of me once more and I growled, ready to shove her out of the way. I knew it wouldn't help my reputation, especially after brawling with Roza, but I couldn't help it.

"I don't trust you," she said, lowering her voice. "I've always known there was something off about you. It makes sense now that everyone knows you're one of *them*."

"Fuck you, Andreja."

I advanced, ready to smack that smug look off her face when a noise up ahead distracted me. Someone shouting and the sound of metal clashing. I tried to pass Andreja again, but she blocked me once more. She wasn't trying to stop me from talking to Teodosija; she was trying to distract me from something else.

Realization raced through my veins like fire.

Theron.

I shoved her aside with more force than necessary and she fell into the wall, hitting her head. Taking off down the tunnel, I sprinted, drawing my sword over my shoulder as the sound of battle grew louder.

I rounded the corner, my heart pounding, when I found Theron fighting against Roza and her accomplices. He was still shackled, chains rattling as he whipped them around in a deadly arc, keeping his attackers at bay. He was glorious—his shirtless torso rippling with muscle as he fought, his sharp features focused as he drove back his opponents. The sight of him took my breath away.

I charged forward, wounding one man trying to get behind Theron. I guarded his back, my eyes locked onto Roza's, the two of us circling each other like predators in the sand.

"What the hell are you doing?"

"Get out of my way, Kael," Roza snarled, her eyes narrowed in anger.

"Not a chance." My voice was low, hard. "Theron is *mine*."

Roza bared her teeth, lunging forward with her sword. I sidestepped her attack and slashed with my dagger, drawing blood. She hissed in pain but didn't back down.

"Just walk away, Kael. This doesn't have to concern you."

"I won't let you do this." I spun, kicking her in the stomach. "He belongs to me."

Theron fought his attackers, his movements fluid and graceful despite his restraints as he bashed one rebel in the head with his chain. He spotted me out of the corner of his eye, and his expression changed from one of fierce determination to surprise.

"Kael, what are you doing here?" he called out, ducking under a sword strike.

"Saving your sorry ass," I replied, gritting my teeth as I parried Roza's next attack.

Theron grinned, a glint of amusement in his eyes. "I thought you hated me."

"I do," I said, lunging forward with my sword again. "But I hate Roza more."

He placed his back against mine and something clicked into place as we moved together in a sensual dance of blades. We fought as one, seamlessly, like we'd been meant to fight side by side for eternity. I felt invincible—adrenaline coursing through my veins, my heart pounding in my chest. There was something intimate about fighting together that sent a thrill through me. I kept stealing glances at him, unable to look away from his rugged beauty or the strength he displayed with his rippling muscles. Strong. Powerful male. The need to dominate him and be dominated in return filled me. It almost made me miss Roza's attack, and I blocked it at the last second.

I managed to knock the blade out of Roza's hands and disarm her. She staggered back, her eyes wide with shock and fear. *No one takes Theron from me.* I advanced, putting my sword to her throat, ready to deliver the killing blow, when Theron's voice cut through the air like a dagger.

"Don't kill her," he commanded in a low growl.

Surprised, I looked over at him and saw that he had knocked out another one of Roza's accomplices and the others had run off. He gave me an intense look, daring me to disobey him. I lowered my sword, unable to. "What are you doing?"

He tied Roza's hands behind her back as she swore at him before gagging her. "Saving your life, *Sihaya*."

Theron grabbed me by the arm and pulled me towards him. "Let's go."

I stood my ground, refusing to move. "No."

Theron's gaze softened as he gazed down at me—the anger in his eyes replaced by something else entirely. He moved closer, resting his free hand on my cheek. I trembled beneath his touch, my heart swelling at the way he looked at me—like I was the only person in the world that mattered.

"Come with me," he whispered, stroking my face with his thumb. "I won't let anyone hurt you again."

My breath caught in my throat. "I can't—"

"You can."

I shook my head, raising my sword. "No. I can't let you leave."

Theron's face hardened, disappointment and fury emanating from him in waves. He let go of me and stepped back, his voice cold. "They came here to kill me, Kael. If I stay, they'll keep trying."

"I can't let you go," I said. My voice shook, and I swallowed, trying to get my emotions under control.

We stood there, both of us breathing heavily as we stared at each other—neither one of us willing to budge. Theron attacked first, and I dodged out of the way, bringing up my sword and blocking the chain as he whipped it toward me. Our moves were desperate and wild as we clashed against each other—our weapons striking sparks that lit up the cave like a million stars. It was a battle of wills more than skill—a struggle between two people unwilling to give up on each other despite all the odds stacked against us.

Determination lit up his eyes as he pressed me, not holding back. He was a warrior like no other, and it took everything in me to keep him at bay. For anyone else, I would have retreated and waited for reinforcements, but I couldn't. The thought of never seeing him again...

Something in me shifted.

I had to fight for what I wanted, even if that meant making him hate me. I moved forward with renewed strength, my sword clashing against his metal, until his chain wrapped around my blade and he pulled me close. Heat from his body soaked into mine as we pressed against each other and I struggled to free my weapon.

"Kael, stop," Theron said, his voice low and urgent. "I don't want to hurt you."

But I wouldn't listen. I couldn't. I had to fight for him. Letting go, I swung my fist as if to hit him and feinted at the last moment, sweeping his legs from underneath him. Theron fell, and I scrambled on top of him, pressing my chain-wrapped sword to his throat.

"You're not leaving me," I growled. "I won't let you."

Theron glared up at me, his eyes hard as a group of rebels ran into the cave to find me perched on his chest, my sword at his throat.

"Then I'm as good as dead."

Chapter II
Kael

Theron's eyes promised retribution as the guards dragged him away. A thrill of fear and excitement went through me, crackling over my skin like lightning. Fighting him had awakened something in me, and I couldn't help but remember our frantic first coupling on the floor of his suite. My body responded to his intensity, my nipples hardening as a shiver ran through me, imagining what he would do to me if he were free. I forced my gaze away from him and towards Roza, who was still bound and gagged, thrashing around for someone to untie her.

"What in Vetia's name is going on here?" Haemir demanded as he and Teodosija stormed into the cavern, his voice echoing through the tunnels. They took in the chaos, the unconscious guard, and Roza on the ground rolling like a grub and me standing over them both with my sword drawn.

Haemir looked at me with a mix of confusion and concern. "Kael, what happened here?"

"It's a long story," I said, rubbing my forehead and sheathing my blade. "But the short version is that Roza was trying to kill the Marshal, and when I stopped her, she attacked me."

Teodosija turned her shrewd gaze to Roza. "Is that true?"

She shook her head, her eyes wide. Teodosija considered her for a moment before gesturing to a guard. "Remove her gag and untie her, please."

The guard stepped forward and pulled the cloth away from Roza's mouth. She gasped, taking deep breaths of air as if I'd suffocated her, and I rolled my eyes. And she called me dramatic. Teodosija crossed her arms and looked at Roza expectantly.

"Now explain why you tried to kill our prisoner."

"The Marshal escaped—" She began, and I cut her off.

"That's bullshit. Andreja stopped me in the tunnels and was trying to prevent me from intervening. You were trying to kill Theron."

Teodosija's brows furrowed as she considered us both. "Why were you here, Kael?"

"I was coming to yell—I mean, talk to you."

Teodosija glanced at Haemir, who nodded. "She was with me until about ten minutes ago and left to discuss the situation in Adraedor with you."

"Anyone other than these ones that can verify that, Roza?"

The Sirin Remnant looked down at the floor. "No."

Teodosija sank to her haunches beside Roza, her stunted wings twitching. "You want to try that story again?"

Roza glared at her before glancing at her co-conspirators, no doubt realizing they'd sell her out once Teodosija got to them. "Fine. Yeah. I wanted to kill the Marshal. He yanked his chain free when we walked in and things got hairy."

Teodosija stood and crossed her arms. "So you decided to take matters into your own hands, disobey orders, and execute him?"

"Yes," Roza spoke without hesitation this time, her face as impassive as if she was confirming what she'd eaten for breakfast. "For what he did to Orya."

Teodosija looked at her with a mix of fury and disappointment. "I expected better from you." She stood. "You're stripped of your command. They will take you to headquarters and detain you there until we conduct a full inquiry."

Roza's brows disappeared into her magenta hair. "But that isn't fair! When Kael disobeys orders, she comes back a hero. But when I do it, I'm in trouble?"

"We're not talking about Kael," Teodosija said, her voice sharp. "Get up."

"So you're going to lose one of your best fighters for some fucking elf that deserves to die a thousand times over?"

"You owe your life to him," I snapped, my fists clenching.

"Fuck you," she snarled, lunging towards me.

I threw a punch, savoring the satisfying impact as my knuckles connected with her jaw. She tackled me around the middle and we fell in a tangle of limbs. I scrambled to pin her as we grappled on the ground. Roza managed to hit me and I saw stars before I rained down a series of blows on her. The taste of adrenaline filled my mouth, mixing with the metallic tang of blood as Teodosija rushed to separate us. She tried to pull me away and my fist flew faster than thought, connecting with her nose.

"Shit. Sorry!"

"Kael!" she shouted, clutching her nose. "That's it. Both of you are going to the brig. You can sort out your differences there. Or rot for all I care."

I leapt to my feet. "What? I didn't start the fight, Roza did."

"You punched me in the face," Teodosija said, pinching the bridge of her nose to stem the blood flow. "You're lucky I didn't demote you."

My mouth fell open. "I didn't mean to hit you. It was an accident."

"I don't care. You both need to learn to control yourselves," she scolded before storming off.

I turned to Haemir. "Dad, she can't be serious."

He shrugged. "I know better than to argue with Teodosija when she's in a mood. And it's about time the two of you sort out this feud. Give me your swords so you don't kill each other."

"As if I'd need a sword," Roza muttered under her breath and I shot her a glare.

"Just get it over with, kiddo. You'll be out in an hour."

"Fine." I tore off my harnesses and passed them over to him. "Let's go."

I kept my mouth shut and followed Roza to the cave Theron had just occupied, though there was no longer a chain coming out of the wall, and settled in to wait.

"This is bullshit," Roza muttered for the umpteenth time, pacing around the room. "I can't believe she's forcing me to stay in here with you."

"You got yourself into this mess," I snapped. "If you'd just followed orders, none of this would have happened."

Roza whirled on me, eyes flashing. "That's rich coming from you. What's fucked up is that you get away with everything and I have to go back through the Bone Gap. This isn't even punishment for you. They're using me to teach you a lesson. It's always about Kael." She mocked, pitching her voice to a whine.

"What the fuck is your problem? You've hated me from the beginning. Why?"

"Maybe I just know you better than they do."

"Fuck off."

She sat down and glanced up at me as she dug her fingers into the sand.

"Do you really want to know?"

I nodded, watching as her shoulders slumped, as if all the fight had gone out of her. "I was jealous," she admitted. "Of the friendship you had with Orya. I had to be too much of a mother to her to be just a sister. I hated you got to have that relationship with her, that closeness."

My jaw dropped, and I closed it with a snap. I had never considered how my friendship with Orya could have impacted Roza. "I had no idea."

Roza shrugged. "It's just how things were. I had to work double shifts in the mine to provide for us, and I was always worried that something was going to happen to her. So it was good that she had you and your family to keep an extra eye on her. But she was all the family I had."

My stomach twisted, an uncomfortable mix of guilt and pity rising inside of me. "I never knew."

Roza shrugged, picking up a handful of sand and letting it run through her fingers. "Why would you? You and Orya were always in your own world."

I thought back to all the times Orya and I had stayed up late talking and laughing, sharing secrets and dreams. I realized that to Roza, I'd taken those things from her.

"I'm sorry, Roza. I never meant to hurt you."

Roza grated out a chuckle. "You didn't hurt me, Kael. Life did that all on its own."

I studied Roza's face, trying to see the girl behind the anger and bitterness. She had always seemed so closed off, so unreachable. But now, I saw the vulnerability in her eyes. She protected herself with her snide attitude.

Just like me.

We lapsed into silence, the air thick with tension. I cleared my throat. "Roza, what are you going to do now? What's your plan?"

She shrugged. "I don't know. I guess I'll wait for the inquiry, and see what happens. Maybe they'll go easy on me if I cooperate."

I nodded, unsure of what else to say. There was a part of me that wanted to offer her help, to make things right between us. But all the things she had said and done to me in the past were fresh in my mind, and I hesitated.

As if reading my thoughts, Roza spoke up. "Look, Kael, I know I've been a bitch to you. And I've said shit I shouldn't have. But I'm sorry. For what it's worth."

I glanced up at her, surprised. "Thanks. That means a lot."

Roza nodded, looking down at her hands. "I just wish I could have killed that bastard."

I sighed. "He didn't kill Orya. He wasn't even there yet when she was shot. The moment he entered the canyon, he attacked me and we fought."

She looked at me skeptically. "How do you know?"

"What do you think? That was when I stole his sword. I remember everything about that night." The memory of his mask of rage as I stabbed him, the feeling of his skin parting beneath my blade, and his scream as I twisted it had once been treasured memories. Now they made me sick.

"Me too." I wondered if she was thinking about when we'd trekked back and moved Orya's body together, crossing the Salt Wastes to return her to the sea. It had been one of the hardest things I'd ever done.

"What happened in the palace?" Roza asked, her voice no longer hard.

I swallowed, unsure of what to say. But she'd been honest with me. "A lot. Theron kept parading me around to piss off his family. They're horrible, always trying to stab each other in the back. He treated me like, I don't know, a friend. Then the Beast almost beat me to death before I poisoned him and his harem."

Her eyes widened, and I continued. "Theron healed me. He knew they would kill me for murdering the Beast and he wanted me to run away with him."

"But you captured him instead." She whistled low. "That's a mind-fuck. He's still got it bad for you."

"Not anymore. I think fighting him today finally cured him of that."

She laughed, a rusty sound like an old shaker box. "That's cold as fuck. I should've trusted you."

"What do you mean?"

She gestured with her chin toward the cavern. "You're not like everyone else out there, fighting to take back your home or protect people. You just want revenge. Like me."

I flinched at her words, but I couldn't deny the truth in them. It was my shameful secret, the one that I hid even from Haemir and Gavril. But Roza understood. Of course she did after losing all of her family to the empire.

"That's how it started," I admitted. "It's why I left after Teodosija called off the mission. I wasn't thinking of the rebellion or helping people. I just wanted to kill those bastards."

Roza looked away, her expression unreadable. "Then you know why I did it and why I don't regret it for a second."

"Even knowing it wasn't him that killed her?"

"They all deserve to die."

She didn't meet my eye again, and we settled into an uncomfortable silence. But as I sat there, I couldn't help but wonder if Roza and I really were so different after all.

Chapter 12
Theron

They shackled me to a chair in the cold cavern, much deeper into the mountains than before, my only light coming from a distant torch. They'd bound my wrists and ankles tight, limiting my movements to mere inches. My captors had taken me far from my previous location, and I had no idea where I was now. No sounds reached here anymore, just the constant rasp of falling sand.

My fists clenched as I struggled, trying to free myself, only to dig the chains further into my skin. Kael's name was a hateful litany in my mind, and I consoled myself by imagining all the things I would do to her once I had her in my power once again. I had foolishly believed her soft words in the night, but her actions proved otherwise. She felt nothing for me. I had begged her to flee with me, a chance to rebuild our shattered trust. Her cold refusal was like a vise around my heart, and now I would face the consequences alone.

Quiet footsteps approached, and I set my jaw. It was her; I'd know the sound of her steps, of her breath, out of hundreds. She'd imprinted herself on my soul and I'd know her presence in a black and silent room. I didn't want to see her, not now, never again. But as she slipped inside, I couldn't help but turn my head to face her.

"What do you want?" I growled. She'd already betrayed me—twice—what other humiliations did she want to heap on me?

"I wanted to talk to you," Kael said, soft and hesitant, as she waited at the entry, shifting on her feet as if about to flee.

I snorted. "Talk? What's left to say?"

"I'm sorry—"

"Sorry?" I scoffed, watching as her shoulders straightened. She couldn't help but rise to a challenge, even when apologizing. Atar's hammer, how didn't I see her Elven traits before this? "Are you sorry for betraying me again? For leaving me to rot in this dungeon?"

"I did what I had to do," Kael said, her eyes hardening. "I couldn't just leave with you."

"I trusted you," I spat, my anger rising with every word as I acknowledged the truth to myself. It had *hurt* that she chose them over me. "And you threw it all away for some damn cause."

"It's not just some cause." Kael narrowed her eyes. "It's more than that."

I shook my head, a mixture of fury and disbelief warring within me. "You're delusional. The rebels will never win, Kael. And you're just making things harder for everyone." I leaned forward, capturing her gaze with mine. "Do you know why I always attack in fast, overwhelming strikes with the Niothe? Because the longer you draw out a war, the worse both sides are hurt. You're doing more damage in the long run."

"We will win," Kael said, her eyes flashing with determination. "And we will do it without sacrificing our humanity, Theron. That's what sets us apart from the Empire."

I sneered at her. "They don't give a shit about humanity, Kael. If they did, I wouldn't be chained to this fucking chair. I wouldn't have had my back shredded by a whip. They only want power. To be in control, just like everyone else."

"That's not true," Kael protested, her voice rising. We must be far away from the encampment if she was yelling. "That's what elves do. I care about my people." She took a breath and held my gaze. "I care about you, Theron."

"They're not your people, Kael! *I am*." I laughed bitterly. "If you cared about me, you wouldn't have left me here to die."

"I didn't leave you to die," she said, her voice cracking. "This keeps you alive to fight another day. I captured you because I knew you were strong enough to survive."

I glared at her, betrayal and hurt thrashing in my chest like a river after torrential rain. There wasn't enough room inside me to hold it all. "You left me because I wasn't important enough to you. Because I mean nothing to you."

Kael opened her mouth to respond, but I cut her off.

"Leave," I demanded, my face hard. "I don't want to see you again."

Kael's expression fell, and she took a step back, her eyes huge. "Theron..." She trailed off, her words choked with emotion.

"I said leave!" I shouted, my voice echoing off the walls of the dungeon.

Kael shook her head, her fists clenching at her sides. "No." She looked up at me, her gaze hardening. "You're wrong. I care about you—more than I should. I hate how you're the only thing that I can think about. How I want to be near you, even though I know they could kill me for it. I hate how fucking guilty I feel all the time for what I did with you. How much I enjoyed it." She stepped closer until she was standing directly in front of me, between my spread legs. She bent down and brushed her mouth over mine. My body responded to her touch, even though my heart was urging me to punish her. "But I don't hate you, Theron. Not anymore." Her lips trailed against mine. "I hate how much I want you," she whispered against my skin.

"Kael…" I warned, and she sank onto my lap, straddling my swiftly hardening cock as she kissed me again.

She gasped at the contact and started grinding herself against me, her heat seeping into my skin.

"I'm sorry, Theron."

I groaned, unable to stop her as she kept going, her movements making it harder for me to resist her. She kissed my neck and my earlobes as she moved against me and I gave in to her touch. I growled, an indistinct sound that reverberated through the room.

"Kaella…"

"Kiss me," she murmured. She found my mouth again, and I tasted the cinnamon sweetness of her lips. Kissing her was like coming home—like being enveloped in warmth and comfort after a long journey. It was unlike anything I had ever experienced before—better than anything else I had ever felt or known.

The kiss deepened as our tongues intertwined and danced around one another, sending shivers down my spine. Kael grabbed onto my shoulders for support as she kept grinding against me—pushing us both closer and closer to pleasure tantalizingly out of reach.

"Gods, Kael," I groaned. "I need to be inside of you."

She shuddered, her breath coming in pants. "I don't know if I can."

I exhaled slowly. Of course not. After what happened, it could take years until she was comfortable again. "It's alright, *Sihaya*. We don't have to do anything you don't want."

She pressed her forehead to mine, her breath fanning my face in little gasps. "I never said I didn't want to."

I huffed a laugh, trying to will my cock to calm down. "Fair."

Her eyes softened as she looked down at me, and she brushed the hair back from my face before standing. I let out a long breath before staring in confusion as she started taking off her clothes. I watched in shock as layers of fabric fell away, revealing her pale skin beneath. Determination made her movements spare—this wasn't some sensual striptease—and she looked as if she might faint.

"Kael—*Sihaya*. You don't have to do this."

"I won't let Rhazien take this from me," she growled.

She bent down and untied my breeches, freeing my cock. I hissed at the contact with her fingers. "Kael, stop."

She peeked up at me, her silver hair falling into her face. "What? Why? Do—do you not want me because he—"

"Gods, no. I want you, *Sihaya*. You can see how badly I want you." I glanced down at my erection and her cheeks flushed even darker. "I just don't want this to be about him."

Her green eyes were almost black in the low light, wide and luminous as she leaned forward and kissed me again. Slower, sweeter than before. "You're right. It's about us."

"You're sure?"

"Yes." She kissed me tenderly, her hands cupping my cheeks. She slipped onto my lap again and I hissed as her softness brushed against my cock. Every part of me was aware of her, my skin prickling as she rubbed against me. Her skin was like silk against mine, and I needed to feel more of her, to worship every inch.

"Release me."

She shook her head, and I shuddered as she gripped my cock, rubbing the head through her wetness before notching it at her entrance.

"I need you," she whispered, sinking onto me.

"*Sihaya*," I groaned as pleasure raced through me like wildfire. She started slowly, her tight walls gripping me as her hot breath fanned against my neck. "Gods, you feel incredible."

Kael rode me faster, grinding against me as she worked to find the perfect angle. Her eyes were closed as she let out a low moan and I slipped further under her spell. Her breasts brushed against my chest with each movement and we moaned together at the feeling, sparks of pleasure igniting as she rocked against me.

"Does it feel good?" I asked, my voice low and husky. I wanted her to know it was me with her now. Only us. "When you take me so deep?"

"Yes," she breathed out. "Gods, Theron." The way she said my name was like a benediction and I hardened further inside her.

"Do you like knowing that I'm crazy for you?" I whispered, dragging my teeth over her shoulder. "That you can bring me to my knees with one twitch of that perfect ass?"

She bit her lip, nodding as she ground her clit against me. "I've never wanted someone the way I want you."

"Gods, *Sihaya*. No other women even exist anymore in my mind. It's only you. Forever you."

"Theron," she murmured, our bodies making obscene noises as she rode me. "I need you inside of me every day."

"You're so wet," I breathed, my voice raspy.

"I can't help it. I've wanted you so much," she murmured, her breath shuddering out of her. Her nails dug into my shoulders as she moved faster, harder, as if trying to get closer to me. Her tight walls pulsed around me as her climax drew near.

"Let go," I urged her, lifting my hips the small amount I could to thrust into her deeper with each word until she cried out as pleasure crashed over her in a wave, her walls gripping me like a vise. I fought not to join her; this was about her and if she needed my support. Kael slumped against me and I closed my eyes, letting the steady thrum of pleasure course through her as she pressed kisses against my neck.

She pulled away, and I opened my eyes to find her smiling at me so sweetly that it hurt my chest.

"That was…incredible," she murmured, her voice hazy with satisfaction, before kissing me again.

She shifted and realized that I was still hard and throbbing inside of her. Her cheeks flushed, and she stared back at me, the unsaid words hanging in the air between us.

"Did you?"

I shook my head, "I wanted to make sure you were alright."

"Theron," she moaned, kissing me before capturing my gaze in hers. She didn't look away as she rode me, her wetness coating both of our skin. We were connected, two souls mingling as our bodies were joined. I watched her bite her lip as pleasure coursed through her body, each thrust of her hips sending sparks of desire through me. She was magnificent, a treasure worth an empire. My sac drew up, my spine tingling as waves of pleasure grew, about to crest.

A loud explosion in the distance interrupted us and Kael shot off of me, my erection hitting my stomach with a wet slap.

"I have to go," she panted as she tugged on her breeches.

"Kael," I called out. "You can't leave me like this."

There was a pause before she came back to me, her eyes twinkling with amusement. She leaned forward and pressed a soft kiss against my lips.

"I'll be back later."

"Kaella," I growled as she fastened my breeches against my straining cock, precum weeping from my slit in an almost constant stream. "Finish me."

"No time. I have to go see what's going on."

I watched as her beautiful breasts disappeared underneath her shirt as she strapped on her—No. *My* swords.

"FINISH ME."

She shot me a grin that stopped my heart before winking and running back into the tunnels. I was left alone with a stiff cock, chained to the chair and unable to ease it. She couldn't have planned better torture. I growled and thrashed against the chains before a frustrated shout escaped me. I wouldn't be sated until I broke free and fucked Kael until she screamed out my name. Footsteps came down the hall and for a moment thought it might be Kael returning for me until Raenisa appeared at the doorway.

"Well," she drawled, eyebrows raised as she surveyed me and the chains that held me captive. "This is a first."

"Rae! Thank Atar. Get me out of here."

She gave an unladylike snort before hurrying forward and beginning to pick the locks on my chains.

"You know," she said conversationally as she worked on releasing me from my bindings, "I don't think they needed this many chains."

I laughed before wincing when one chain pulled too tight against my skin as she tugged it free.

"Almost done," she cheered after she finished freeing my arms and started working to release my legs.

"Good," I ground out, my voice strained as she noticed my pulsing cock.

Raenisa stopped what she was doing and threw me a bewildered look. "I'm not even going to ask."

"Shut up, Rae."

She opened her mouth to say something more, but before she could, more footsteps sounded from the hallway. This time they were heading towards us, not away from us.

"We have to go now." Raenisa urged, unlocking my last leg chain and hopping up off of the floor. "People are going to realize that the explosion was a distraction soon and come looking for you. There will be too many of them for us to escape."

"I need to find Kael."

"Seriously?" She snapped, her expression hard. "Stop thinking with your dick. It's just me and Zerek here, idiot. We have to run. Now."

I sighed and ran a hand over my face, knowing she was right, but still wanting to take off into the tunnels after Kael all the same. "Fine. Once I have reinforcements, we're coming back."

She rolled her eyes. "Worry about that shit later. Let's go."

Raenisa grabbed my hand and pulled me out of the room and into the winding tunnels, dodging around shadows as we tried to avoid being seen. We raced through dusty passageways and crumbled corridors, and I struggled for breath after a few minutes. I was already exhausted and my body ached from lack of food and water. All my energy had gone to healing my back. I gritted my teeth, cursing myself and Peregrine for not being able to keep up with Raenisa's pace.

Finally, we emerged from the darkness into the coolness of desert night air. Ydonja's stars twinkled in silent greeting above me, while the moons shone on my face like a beacon of hope. Until shouts drew my attention. A fire burned on the other side of the foothills, smoke billowing into the night. Raenisa whistled and two vaniras scampered to us over the ridge and I grinned when I recognized Vaernix.

"Hey, girl." I patted her side before climbing up into the saddle. A wolf howled in the distance and Raenisa let out a breath.

"That's the signal. Ride."

We took off into the darkness, Vaernix putting on speed as a second explosion went off, sand exploding all around the people attempting to put out the fire. Shouts rang out as the cloud of dust enveloped them.

Raenisa cackled. "Got the bastards."

I had to fight the urge to turn back and make sure Kael hadn't been injured. She was strong and I'd need to be too when I stole her from them.

Zerek rode out of the shadows, falling in beside me."

"Good to see you, too."

He grinned, his teeth shining white in the darkness as he tossed me a cloak. "Here."

I slipped it on. "Where are we?"

"A bit south of Sailtown." Raenisa said, "Took us a while to find you until we got a tip."

I pressed my lips together. "Then why are we going north? Adraedor is south."

"We're not going to Adraedor." Raenisa shared a glance with Zerek. "We're going to Athain."

"What? Why?"

"Orders from the empress," Zerek growled.

"I don't give a fuck what Raura says, I'm—"

"Not Raura." Raenisa's voice was odd, her gaze straight ahead. "Varzorn's dead."

A strange roaring filled my ears as she continued.

"Theodas and your mother killed him."

Chapter 13
Kael

I stood frozen amidst the carnage, my feet rooted to the sand, my heart beating wildly in my chest. The air was thick with dust and acrid smoke, choking me as sweat trickled down my back. Heat from the fire filled the underground caverns, stifling and oppressive. I scanned the surrounding devastation, and my stomach lurched at the sight of the fallen soldiers and rebels lying motionless on the ground. The pained screams of the wounded and the sound of falling debris punctuated the air as I finally made my feet move. I ran forward, pulling a man out from under a pile of stone.

I wanted to help more, to heal the injured, and comfort the dying, but despite supposedly having all this magic at my disposal, I was powerless.

Fucking useless.

Again.

Another explosion rocked the cavern, sending a fresh wave of debris raining down around me. Dust settled on my skin, leaving a gritty residue, while the taste of blood lingered in my mouth with every desperate breath I took.

"Brace!" Someone shouted, and I readied myself for elves to pour in, my heart pounding in my throat. Dirt and smoke filled my eyes, and I wiped them away with my sleeve, waiting.

And waiting.

After a minute, with no shouts of fighting or soldiers arriving, I realized that this wasn't a raid—it was a diversion. Someone was trying to draw our attention away...

Theron.

I raced towards Theron, my body still humming with pleasure from Theron's touch. *Please be there.* I sprinted towards the cave, my mind consumed with thoughts of finding him, and I cursed myself for leaving him. I should have known it was a distraction. All that mattered was tracking him down, no matter what it cost me.

As I arrived at the entrance of the cave, I stopped short, my heart thudding painfully in my chest. His chair was empty, the place where he had been sitting just moments ago was now vacant. A sick feeling spread through me like poison, and I sucked in a breath.

"Fuck!"

I hit the wall, the skin on my knuckles tearing, but I didn't feel it. I was alone in a cave with nothing but my regret for company. Self-loathing threatened to choke me as tears stung my eyes.

I stood there in the darkness, my chest hollow as if something vital had been removed.

Theron was gone.

The heat in the underground caverns was stifling, and sweat dripped down my neck as I helped Haemir pack our tent. The explosions had destroyed most of the camp and we had to leave before the elves came back with reinforcements. Haemir watched me with a sharp gaze as he worked, rolling up our bedding into tight packs.

"You don't seem upset that Theron got away," he said finally, breaking the silence.

I froze. "What do you mean?"

He shrugged. "I expected you to be the first one out there trying to recapture him."

"They said they were on vanira. There's no way I could keep up with that. And it was useless anyway."

Haemir arched an eyebrow. "How so?"

"If he stayed here, someone would've killed him. I wouldn't always be there to stop them."

He studied me, his face impassive. "Do you care for him?"

I hesitated for a moment. "He could've been a good bargaining chip. If things didn't go well, we could've traded him for the city."

He was silent, the only sounds coming from the chaos outside as the rebels worked to bind the injured to litters and salvage what they could from the wreckage.

"You must have learned a lot about him." He let the statement hang, and I took it as the question it was.

"Yeah." I stopped folding up the canvas and stared at it, unable to meet his gaze. "He—he had a hard life. The royals aren't like what we think of them. They treat each other as terribly as they treat us." I grabbed a tie, wrapping it around the pack. "He suffered a lot when he was younger. Like me," I said finally, looking up at Haemir. "Except he didn't have a Haemir to save him as a child. He had to do whatever it took to survive."

Haemir's expression softened, and I knew he was thinking of the day he'd saved me.

"He doesn't have anyone he can trust," I continued without his prompting. "Not after what his family did to him. Even his Harvestmen have duties to their families above him. Everything is political with them. He's just... alone. Has been since he was a kid."

Haemir nodded, his expression pensive. "And you understand what that's like?"

"Yeah." My brows drew together. "But I have you and Gavril. He has no one."

"It sounds like you care for him a lot."

I ducked my chin. "Um. I know it's wrong, Dad. I—"

"Never apologize for your feelings, kiddo." He patted me on the shoulder. "Empathy is a gift. I'm just worried about you getting hurt. You haven't had many relationships, and it's easy to mix up infatuation with affection."

I thought back to the way Theron had held me, brushing kisses over my hair. It may have started with an obsession on his side, but it was more than that now. Right?

I shook my head, frustration twisting up my insides as I tied the pack closed. "It doesn't matter. I'm never going to see him again."

He smiled sadly. "It's probably for the best."

I kept my eyes down, pretending to concentrate on packing, even as his words cut through me. "I don't want to think about it. Let's just focus on taking Adraedor."

Haemir sighed but allowed me to change the topic. "The explosion so soon after the raid proves the leak was on one of the teams."

I nodded, my mind whirling with possibilities. "One of them sold us out."

"And I need to figure out who."

I started to argue, and he held up a hand. "Nope. Teodosija's orders. You're to go to our home base in the south. She's looking for a teacher for you, and that's the safest place for you to learn."

"Did she find one yet?"

His eyes crinkled. "Maybe. Guess you'll have to wait and see."

"Are you not coming with me?"

He shook his head. "No. I'm going to Adraedor."

"Dad—"

"Sorry, kiddo. That won't work on me today." He laughed and wrapped his arm around my shoulders. "I know you want to help. This is how you can. Learn. Get stronger. And when you're ready..." He tipped my chin up, so I met his eyes—more familiar now than my father's.

"You can tear the entire city down."

The sand stretched on for miles, an endless expanse of shifting dunes that seemed to defy navigation. We rode on deaza, the great lumbering beasts that looked like whales with legs, their leathery skin protecting them from the harsh desert sun. They were the only thing that could eat rattleweed, their flat teeth strong enough to crush the spiky brush, so they could grow bigger than almost anything else in the desert. Despite their slow pace, they were the best way to traverse the unforgiving terrain without exhausting ourselves. They were also easy to spot and only used when traveling with large amounts of cargo, or in my case, numerous injured.

The desert wind blew, carrying the pungent odor of rattleweed, the musky scent of the Deaza, and the grime of the ragtag army that rode on the beasts. As we traveled further south, the sand changed, shifting from black to red, as if we walked on an ocean of blood. The sprawling desert seemed to go on forever, a lonely landscape that stretched as far as the eye could see. The sand under the Deaza's feet clumped and shifted, like clouds of scarlet sea foam churning beneath the landwhales' massive physique. Rage burned within me; I wanted nothing more than to find Theron and join my allies in Adraedor, but protecting our injured was my first aim.

The sun was setting, the red sky growing darker as the air began to cool. This was the other reason deaza were preferred. You didn't have to stop and camp. They were large enough to sleep on as they continued tromping through the night. I shifted in my saddle and stared off into the sunset. My thoughts kept drifting back to Theron. How was he doing? Was he safe? We hadn't gone this long apart since we met, and I couldn't shake the feeling that something was wrong.

"What do you think our next move should be?" Roza asked, her voice pulling me out of my reverie.

"In the hidden city?"

She nodded.

"Well, our fortifications are strong. Gathering more food and water for a siege would serve us best. And we can bring anything the city can spare to Adraedor to help with the attack."

"I thought the same. I'll talk to Niko and see..."

I chatted with her for a while, arguing about the best way to track ferelope. But my mind returned to Theron, and I found myself staring off into the distance again once when she dropped back to speak to someone else.

"You seem distracted," Gavril said from beside me. He knew me too well; even my practiced smile didn't work on him. "Is everything alright?"

I sighed and nodded glumly. "Yeah... just worried."

"Yeah." Gavril tilted his head, studying me for a moment. "So... are you and Roza getting along?"

"We talked it out," I told him honestly, letting out a small laugh as I remembered us brawling before that talk. "We understand each other better now."

His smile was soft, wistful. "Orya would have been ecstatic."

Her name hit me hard, and I squeezed my eyes shut to hold back my tears. No more crying.

"Yeah," I whispered. "She always wanted everyone to get along."

Gavril nodded, his expression unreadable as he gazed out at the horizon. For a moment, we just sat in silence, our deaza keeping pace with one another.

"Have you ever thought about dating again?" The words flew out of my mouth before I could stop them and I immediately regretted them; Gavril's face twisted into something close to pain and he looked away from me.

"No."

"It's been five years," I continued softly. "Orya would want you to be happy."

He hesitated before shaking his head. "I just haven't met anyone yet."

I opened my mouth to suggest that he should try, but quickly closed it, realizing how hypocritical it was for me to say that.

"It's alright, Gav. I'm sure someone will come and catch your eye."

He shrugged. "You don't choose who you love."

Theron's face flashed in my mind, his bronze eyes molten as he stared down at me, his dark hair falling around us in a sheet. I pushed the thought away, looking around as if someone could read my thoughts.

A bellowing howl cut through the air like a blade and we froze, our deaza skidding to a stop as a pack of lobaros burst over the horizon, their hundreds of sharp teeth glinting in the waning sunlight. I pulled my sword from its scabbard and raised it, assessing the situation.

"Gather up!" I shouted, urging the others to bring their deaza in a circle, making it harder for the pack to pick off our injured. The lobaros were fast, their scales blended into the swirling sandstorm that the pack kicked up, rendering them almost invisible against the background. They charged towards us in a wave of teeth and claws and sand, their snarls echoing in my ears as they leaped forward.

"Hold!"

They hit our caravan as a group, trying to knock us from the deazas' backs. Gavril fought alongside me, slicing through scales and flesh as he defended the ones behind us. Half our people were injured. They could barely stand, let alone defend themselves. I attacked with everything I had, each movement helping the group edge ahead of us, away from the battle. My heart raced as I struggled desperately to keep them alive.

"Keep moving! As a group!" I shouted, and our procession moved slowly, with Gavril and me defending the rear as Roza pushed on ahead. Bodies of lobaros littered the ground in our wake, our swords and spears thinning the pack until they regrouped, targeting one deaza at the edge of the group. The woman riding it screamed as the beast faltered, going to its knees as one lobaro managed to tear out its throat.

Gavril guided his deaza toward her. "Jump!" She leaped from the saddle onto his as her mount crashed into the sand, the lobaros swarming it in an instant.

"Keep moving," I shouted, looking back to watch the frenzied lobaros devour their kill. Hopefully, it would keep them busy until we were out of their territory.

I turned my attention to my companions; all of them were covered in scratches and cuts from fighting off the lobaros, but none of them seemed too injured or worse for wear. I let out a long breath before pressing onward into the unforgiving desert landscape, lost in my thoughts as we rode together in eerie silence.

As we approached the Bone Gap in the early dawn, I couldn't help the shiver that ran down my spine. The massive skeleton of the Sky God, Kearis, loomed above us, huge and jumbled, creating a maze of shadows and sunlight that hid the entrance. We walked through the gaps in his bones, our footsteps echoing off the canyon walls. The bones themselves were pitted and weathered, with sharp jagged edges that threatened to cut our skin. I'd offered to use my sword to carve more blades from his skeleton for the rebels, but Teodosija had looked at me with such disgust that I'd never brought it up again.

Entering the hideout was like stepping into a different world. The scent of cooking fires and sweat filled my nostrils, and the sound of laughter and chatter was almost overwhelming. Children ran around, playing games and chasing each other, while rebels and escaped slaves went about their tasks with a sense of ease that was never present in the slave quarter.

We descended into the city, winding through narrow pathways and deep crevices until we emerged in the town. Several buildings made from sandstone circled a depression that had once been a lake, each with its own unique purpose. Some were dwellings for the citizens, some held stores of food, and others served as weapons workshops. An old temple to Kearis that had been converted into a makeshift gathering place for meetings and celebrations stood in the center of it all.

The light filtered through large holes in the ceiling that used to be entrances for the winged Kyrie. Only a small section of the hidden city was in use; we hadn't freed enough slaves to fill it and the rest of the cavern reverberated with a sullen emptiness.

"Kael," Niko, an Ice Wraith Remnant, called to me, his expression unreadable as always behind his shock of blue hair. "What took so long? We expected you earlier."

"Sorry, there was a lobaros attack on the way here," I explained, hoping that would be enough to satisfy him. "We had to ride close for the night after that."

He nodded in understanding before greeting Gavril as well. "Come on, Kael. There's someone I want you to meet."

My stomach grumbled, and I almost told him it could wait, but it was better to get it over with and then crash for a few hours. "Can you take my stuff, Gav?"

"Sure, sis. See you soon." He took my pack, slinging it over his shoulder, before hurrying toward the home I shared with him and Gavril.

"Who?"

"Someone who can teach you how to use your magic."

My heart started racing with excitement. I wasn't surprised that Niko knew already. He was Teodosija's second in command; he heard everything. "What? Who is it?" How had they found a Sálfar? Were more of my kind in hiding than Theron thought?

Niko hesitated for a moment before speaking. "You'll see. Follow me."

We weaved our way through the bustling hideout, and I couldn't help but feel a sense of pride at the number of people there. Slaves and rebels bustled about their tasks, while children ran around, playing and laughing. We'd done this. Saved them from the pit, from a short and brutal life working themselves to the bone for the empire.

He led me to the meetinghouse that had once been a temple to Kearis; the doors carved with a pair of massive wings. I entered, spotting a man standing on the other side of the room with his back to me. Tall and with broad shoulders and a trim waist, his black hair almost reaching his back... Shit. Not a Sálfar. He turned, and I saw the signature streak of white in his black hair. My stomach twisted with a mix of emotions—attraction, and distrust warred within me, and I wasn't sure which one would win out.

Niko gestured toward him, smiling. "Kael, meet—"

"Xadrian?"

He walked forward with a smirk, his eyes alight with mischief as they caressed each one of my curves. His voice was as smooth and sweet as honey as he approached.

"Hello, Kael."

Chapter 14
Theron

I took a deep breath, squaring my shoulders as I walked into Hundaelr for the first time in years, the familiar luminescence settling on my skin like a touch from the grave. It was an eerie, unearthly light, emanating from the succulents that had been painstakingly planted along the walls and ceiling. Their glow illuminated the smooth, bone-like stone and cast peculiar shadows across the vast underground chambers.

Every surface had been carved in intricate detail, with elaborate geometric patterns and artistry that told stories of our history. Gold and silver filigree decorated the walls, while precious stones glimmered like stars in the darkness. Spiky spires rose from the ground, reaching for the unseen ceiling far above us, and stalactites hung resembled glittering swords.

Graceful columns and grand statues of the gods and goddesses filled any free space. Everywhere I looked, there were works of engineering genius; powered waterfalls cascading into marble pools; cleverly designed bridges crossing over meandering streams teeming with cavefish; secret doors leading to hidden chambers; nooks and crannies that beckoned to be explored; magical pathways created out of glowing stones.

This is what Atar had loved. Ingenuity and cleverness; the ability to transform ordinary stone into something majestic.

Sure, he was arrogant, believing that as the eldest God that he was the most powerful. But conquest had never been his desire. This city, though... it was the best of what the elves were supposed to be.

Despite its beauty, there was something deeply unsettling about the place now. The atmosphere was heavy and oppressive as if something sinister lurked beneath its surfaces. Shadows flickered in the corners, reminding me there was always someone watching, hidden in the darkness here. Before the Lightcurse, this place might have been only a testament to my people. But generations of Carxidor emperors had sullied it.

I hated it here. The years I spent imprisoned here by my mother, and brother had been the worst of my life. No matter how much time passed, dread settled deep in my gut, like a heavy weight that refused to be shaken off. The sense of isolation that had haunted me then still lingered in the air, and I couldn't help but feel as if I was being watched by unseen eyes.

"Prince Theron!" A servant hurried up to me, dressed in mourning clothes of the deepest red.

"Yes?"

The servant cleared his throat, obviously nervous. "You are wanted in the throne room, sir."

Raenisa stepped forward before I could answer. Her eyes narrowed in suspicion. "What's changed since Varzorn died? Where is everyone?" She gestured toward the empty streets. I hadn't realized it before, but it was deserted.

The servant glanced around nervously before answering. "Things are going well. We're in mourning," he whispered, not meeting our eyes.

"Everyone left the city to mourn?" Raenisa asked incredulously, and he swallowed, the apple of his throat bobbing.

"It must be strange to be mourning an emperor whose murderer sits on the throne," Zerek drawled, his expression neutral.

The servant's eyes flew open, and he shifted from foot to foot. "Actually," he said hesitantly, "we are in mourning for Empress Nyana's late son, Rhazien."

Bitterness rose inside me at the mention of my brother's name and had to fight to keep my expression mild. Rhazien didn't deserve to be mourned. He deserved to be tossed into the desert for the carrion crow population that he'd so delighted in feeding with fresh heads on the walls every week.

"Follow me, my lord." The servant turned, leading us toward the throne room and glancing back every few feet to ensure we still followed him. I shuddered as I walked closer to the throne room, dreading the prospect of facing my tormentors. No, not tormentors anymore. Rhazien was dead. That only left one.

My mother.

She'd summoned me here for a reason. Most likely to kill me for murdering Rhazien. In which case, at least this meeting would be brief. I'd flee, then I'd get back to what consumed my every waking thought.

Finding Kael.

The attendant brought us to the vast hall. The underground throne room was an intimidating place, a cavernous expanse of darkness and shadows that devoured the light. Its walls were ancient, carved with symbols and runes that only Atar could understand. There were a few torch-lit chandeliers in the room, and even those gave off a sinister glow that seemed to whisper secrets.

At one end of the long hall stood a magnificent throne, like something from another time. It was wrought from pure obsidian, yet a faint light pulsed deep within its core. When I was a child, I imagined that it was Atar's heartbeat. That he'd been locked away and would rescue me one day.

I scowled as I noticed Theodas lounging on the throne, one foot hanging over the armrest. He wasn't dressed for mourning, instead wearing his usual dark navy with gold trim.

"Well, well, if it isn't my new stepson," he mocked, his voice dripping with sarcasm. "Have you come to greet your father?"

"Theodas." I kept a tight grip on my composure. "I assume congratulations are in order."

A cruel glint lit his blue eyes. "Indeed, your mother and I missed you at the wedding. Such a shame that you were taken hostage and had to miss the festivities."

"How rude of me." My tone was drier than the Restless Sands and Raenisa snorted.

"Unless they did not actually capture you. Maybe you were off celebrating your own victory?"

I wasn't sure what he was referring to, but I didn't think it was good. "What do you mean?"

Theodas laughed, the sound grating on my nerves. "Oh, come now, Theron. You finally took care of your brother. That merits a few days of leave."

"I didn't kill Rhazien," I said through gritted teeth. "And I wasn't on holiday. They chained me in a cave, you imbecile."

Theodas's expression turned icy. "Be careful, Theron. You may have your mother's favor, but you're not untouchable."

My laugh was as cold as Sithos' breath. "You have no idea what you married into. If I were you, I'd flee." I held his gaze, unflinching. "I'd run as far away as I could and never look back."

The tension in the hall was palpable as his skin flushed puce, a vein pulsing in his forehead. Raenisa and Zerek tensed, ready to defend me if he attacked.

"Stand down, Theo." Tannethe slithered into the throne room, all smiles and sharp edges. She wore a sapphire sheath dress, clinging tight to her curves. "Prince Theron had a rough week."

"Tannethe." I couldn't hide the disgust in my voice. "What do you want?"

"Just to see you," she purred, her golden eyes flashing as she tossed her hair. "Where's that troublesome concubine of yours?" She glanced around the room as if Kael would materialize behind me.

"Gone."

She pursed her lips in a pout. "How disappointing. I had so many plans for her."

I shuddered at the thought of Kael in the She-snake's hands.

"You'll have to find some other form of entertainment, I'm afraid," Theodas drawled from the throne, his foot bouncing as he flipped a knife in his hand.

She grinned, her fingers tracing a line down my chest. "Theron could help with that." She leaned in close, her breath hot against my ear. "Maybe we'll pick up where we left off the last time you were here."

I took a step back, and her gaze tracked me like a viper hunting a mouse. I wasn't interested in her advances, but I couldn't risk offending her. Not when she and her family were in control of the Niothe. "We'll see."

She pouted but didn't press the issue. Theodas chuckled, the sound like gravel underfoot. "So if you didn't kill Rhazien, who did?"

I narrowed my eyes, unsure if I should tell the truth or not. Better to keep information close. "Have your spies not told you?"

"Herrath?" He scoffed, leaning back into the throne. "All his reports are about unrest with the slaves and how they're trying to revolt. He said that the perpetrator wasn't confirmed." He exchanged a look with his sister. "Though there were rumors."

I stiffened. Mirijana was supposed to have hidden with Aella, and Kael disappeared that night. That left three suspects, and only one of which showed martial capabilities.

Kael.

"I'll make it my priority once I return."

He smirked. "I'm sure you will."

"Where's my mother?" I asked, keeping my tone light.

Theodas lounged on his throne, stroking the armrest. "Ah, Theron. Always so direct," he chuckled. "She's in a war council meeting, deciding what to do about Adraedor." I nodded, already mentally preparing myself for the upcoming debate. But Theodas wasn't done with me yet. "I'm afraid she's not to be interrupted," he added, his tone dripping with honeyed menace. "Go to your suite and get settled in for a long wait. She wouldn't want you to leave before she sees you." He pressed a hand over his heart. "You know how mothers are."

I ground my teeth, familiar stirrings of anger pulsing in my temples. I wouldn't be kept prisoner here again, not by Theodas or anyone else. "Tell her I have information she'll want."

He spoke again, but I ignored his response and turned to leave, motioning for Raenisa and Zerek to follow.

But before I could make it to the door, Tannethe called out to me. "Don't worry, Theron," she said, her voice dripping with promise. "I'll come see you later. Keep the bed warm for me, won't you?"

I didn't respond as I made my way down the familiar halls to my suite. Entering my set of rooms, I took a moment to survey my surroundings. The room was opulent, with plush carpets and elaborate tapestries adorning the walls. But despite the luxury, it was still foreign to me. I had spent too much time away from this place to feel truly at home here. Or perhaps it was because something else had become my home.

Raenisa broke the silence, shucking off her armor and tossing it into an armchair.

"This is all sorts of fucked up. What are we going to do?"

"We need intel," I replied, my mind already racing with possibilities. "We can't make any decisions without knowing what's going on here."

"*The Eye that Looks Ahead*, and all that." Raenisa waved her hand dismissively as she collapsed onto my couch.

"Rae. There are probably poison needles in that thing." Zerek leaned against the doorframe, his sharp gaze taking in the room. "We should sweep the suite for traps before you get too comfortable. There was plenty of time for them to prepare for our arrival."

I nodded as Raenisa groaned, rolling to her feet and muttering about riding a vanira for days. "Good call. I'll check the suite." I turned to Raenisa. "Go to your family's rooms and use any contacts you have to find out who's aligned with whom. We need to know who's plotting against us, who can be swayed, and who's just trying to survive. Zerek, I need you to talk to the servants and the guards. See what information you can gather from them."

Zerek scowled. No doubt he was still angry about his House casting him out. He had been away from the Hollow Mountains longer than I had and I could see his desire to show his importance to his arrogant family burning in his eyes. "I'll find something," he growled before marching out of the room, his footsteps strangely silent on the stone.

When we were alone, Raenisa turned to me with a worried expression. "What if Nyana wants to kill you? It's obvious everyone here thinks you had Kael kill Rhazien—"

I placed a hand on her shoulder, trying to project confidence. "It'll be fine," I assured her. "She won't move against me until she's confirmed her suspicions. But we can't just sit around and do nothing. We need to know what's happening if we're going to have any chance of surviving this coup." Raenisa nodded, but I could tell she was still nervous. "What's bothering you?"

"I'm anxious about seeing Caelia." She muttered, looking at the floor.

Shit, poor Rae. I understood all too well the pain of unreciprocated affection, and how agonizing it was. Unfortunately, we didn't have time for diversions. "We can't afford any distractions. We have to concentrate on the job."

"You're right." She nodded as if trying to convince herself. "She might not even be here. The Sarros spend most of their time on the estate. I bet she's already back there."

I clapped her on the shoulder. "You're too good for her, anyway."

She rolled her eyes. "You suck at pep talks."

"And you suck at following orders. Go."

Raenisa shot me a lewd hand gesture before she hurried out the door. I sighed, beginning the arduous task of finding all the traps set in the suite. Starting my search from the top, I carefully made my way around the room.

I was just about to move on to the next wall when I felt something shift beneath my foot. I froze, my heart racing as I realized what it was. A pressure plate. Fuck. What would it do when I stepped off it? I threw myself to the side. A loud clunk echoed around me and a series of sharp spikes descended from the ceiling. I cursed, rolling out of the way as they slammed to the floor.

"Well. That's one down," I mumbled to myself as I stood, brushing my clothes off.

It didn't take long for me to find the rest; a few more pressure plates hidden beneath carpets and behind furniture, as well as some trip wires near the windows, poisoned darts, noxious gas—all the usual. I disabled each one, calling for servants to come clean up the mess and change the bedding. Once I was sure that everything was safe, I asked for a locksmith to be sent at once so that I could get new locks on my doors.

I slumped onto the bed, my mind filled with thoughts of my time here. From the times I'd hidden in the gardens to avoid a beating, to the dinners where I'd been forced to take part in Rhazien's cruel displays. Every corner of this palace held dark memories of the abuse I'd suffered at the hands of my family. This palace had never felt like home to me, and it reminded me of that fact now more than ever.

I held my head in my hands, my elbows resting on my knees. As a child, I'd often imagined what it would be like to have a home of my own, free from the cruelty of my mother. I'd dreamt of having an estate like my aunt's; with rolling hills covered in lush green grasses, trees heavy with vibrant leaves, and fresh flowers blooming throughout the gardens. My cousins would join me there, and when I grew older, I dreamed of having a family of my own. That was until I'd understood the truth... there would never be an escape for me.

Not while a Carxidor sat on the throne.

I stood, striding to the bookcase and removing blank paper and pencils. I needed to work out my plans, and figure out who my family was aligning with. We wouldn't be staying here for long. As soon as I had the intel I required, I'd head back to the desert, where I belonged.

And then I'd find her.

Chapter 15
Kael

I bristled at Xadrian's casual tone, my hand instinctively reaching for my sword hilt. The humid air in the temple was heavy against my skin, causing beads of sweat to form on my forehead. I took a step forward, fixing Xadrian with a fierce stare. "What are you doing here?" I demanded, my voice sharp with suspicion.

Niko intervened before Xadrian could respond. The flickering torches lining the walls cast an orange glow on his face, at odds with his blue coloring. "He's here to teach you."

Xadrian's smirk turned into a full-blown grin, the flicker of the flames dancing across his angular features. "Oh, I'll teach her all right." His deep voice reverberated through the temple, sending a shiver down my spine.

I glowered at him, assessing. He wore a simple shirt and breeches, the black fabric hugging his lean form. A silver chain adorned his neck, glinting in the torchlight. His boots were made of a supple leather that looked comfortable, yet durable.

"We're not at the palace, you can turn off the charm," I hissed before turning to Niko. "He's from a High House. His sister wants to be emperor. How can you trust him?"

Xadrian's expression grew darker, his normally flirtatious tone replaced by a sharp edge. "Caelia's ambitions aren't my own," he growled. "You know nothing about me."

Niko sighed and looked at me. "Xadrian's been in the rebellion for the last few years, giving us intel as he traveled around the empire. He'd recently come home for the competition as heir and got even more involved."

I was stunned. He was working against his sister? I thought back to when he flashed me the rebel hand sign as the emperor's entourage was leaving and how I wasn't sure or not if I'd seen it. It all made sense now—why he claimed his Sálfar heritage so openly, his insouciance and accent that differed from the other elves.

"I don't understand." I couldn't wrap my head around it. "Why didn't Teodosija tell me when I told her about my magic?"

Niko raised a brow. "You can't be serious? You disobey orders and defy her at every turn. Of course, she wouldn't inform you about our outside agents." Niko held my gaze, trying to judge my reaction before continuing. "We need all the help we can get. And Xadrian has proven himself to be trustworthy."

"I guess so." I shifted uneasily, my fingers flexing around my sword. The cool bone was comforting in my hand, grounding me in the present. To me, Xadrian was still that flirtatious courtier who seemed determined to annoy Theron. That he was a rebel sympathizer...

Xadrian stepped forward, his expression unusually serious. The flicker of the torches played across his face, casting deep shadows in the hollows of his cheeks. "I'm sorry I didn't help you more in the palace. I wasn't sure if you were a rebel or not until after you fought in the arena."

I remembered how Theron had told me that Xadrian had given him the antidote that saved me from Theodas's poison, and I nodded in understanding. "No problem."

"Not that you needed it. You did well by yourself," He added with a hint of admiration in his voice. "Using poison against Rhazien and his harem—that was quite an impressive move."

I shifted, uncomfortable remembering that night. It was too intimate to talk about with Xadrian. He wouldn't understand, hadn't seen the broken bag of bones that Rhazien had turned me into. It was something only Theron and I could share.

"Tell me more about the Sálfar," I said quickly, glancing at Niko in silent apology as I changed the subject. He nodded in understanding and excused himself, leaving Xadrian and me alone in the temple.

He leaned against the wall next to a fresco of flying Kyrie, watching me intently as I fidgeted in my seat. "What do you know about our kind?"

I scowled at him. "You're colonizing bastards who killed all the gods and turned on their own kind when they wouldn't go along with their plan. That you're Lightcursed."

He lifted a brow. "You heard about that?"

"Yeah." A knot twisted in my stomach as I remembered that day in Theron's suite as his cousin explained his research, his hand absentmindedly playing with my hair. "Oz told us the story of what he found in the libraries. He didn't know what they'd disagreed upon, though. Just that the Svartál weren't able to access Celestial metals after the betrayal."

His gaze swept me, approval in his eyes. "No one knows, but there are a few theories."

"Like how Daelor is being kept imprisoned?" I asked, remembering a story from Haechall from when I was a child.

He shook his head. "That's unfortunately only a rumor. I've seen his bones myself. Tell me what you know about our magic."

"Metals work like a conduit for your power—"

"*Our.*" He broke in. "Our power, Kael. If you want to learn to use your magic, then first you need to accept it."

I narrowed my eyes on him. "Fine. Our power. There are different types of metals. Earthborn metals affect the body and so do their alloys. Celestial metals affect the physical world."

Xadrian nodded. "Exactly. For Earthborn metals, each metal enhances a certain aspect of our physical abilities. Gold, for example, enhances strength. Copper enhances reflexes. Aluminum enhances the senses, like sight and hearing. And silver enhances speed." I listened intently as he continued. "It depends on how much metal is on your body," Xadrian explained, his tone only slightly suggestive on the last word. "If you wanted to be faster than strong, you would wear more silver than gold. The limits of what you can use are based on how well you can hold the intention in your mind as you funnel magic through the metal. Some metals are different in that you can use a stone to set the intention in it and it'll last a lot longer. Like piercings. It works better if it's in constant contact with your skin."

"What about Theron? He only wears his bone armor."

He met my eye for a long moment and I had to fight not to squirm under his gaze. "He wears that armor to show that he doesn't need his magic to best his rivals. It's intimidation. Or it would be if I couldn't crush him with a boulder." He added with a wink, and I rolled my eyes.

"What about the alloys? I've seen healing plates." I pushed away the dark memories threatening to overwhelm me.

"Electrum." He nodded. "That one is used for almost all the body enhancements as well since it's so broad in its healing abilities. There are also brass for mental acuity, bronze for endurance, and pewter for wakefulness."

I nodded, trying to commit all of this information to memory. "What about Celestial metals?"

"They're unique in that you don't have to pile it on for more enhancements like the earthborn metals," he explained, flashing the ring on his finger. "It's more about the magic you have within yourself that allows you to use it. That's why you find a lot of celestial metals fashioned into jewelry."

I nodded, fascinated. "So the more magic you have, the more you can do, regardless of how much metal?" I asked.

"Exactly," Xadrian confirmed. "That's why House Daelor and Helekian had once ruled because they had more innate magic within them than the rest of us. But that was before the Lightcurse."

My heart stopped. "What did you just say?"

His brows drew together. "What? About House Daelor and Helekian?"

The air was thick with anticipation, and my pulse pounded in my head. "That's my surname," I whispered, the words catching in my throat. "Helekian."

His eyes widened in surprise, his pupils dilating. A strange crackling energy escaped him, a current running through the room. "Atar's hammer," he breathed, his voice barely above a whisper. "You're from one of the lost royal lines."

"That's insane." I shook my head. "There's no way."

"Tell me more about your family." His breath fanned my face, warm and rapid, as he leaned in closer to me, his body crowding mine in his excitement. I took a step back, the sound of my boots echoing softly on the floor. His eyes widened, and he dropped his hands to his sides. "Sorry. Do you know which of your parents was elvish?"

I closed my eyes briefly, trying to steady myself, before opening them again to meet his piercing gaze. "My mother," I began, my voice quiet. "My father was human. He was a hunter and met my mom in Haechall—far up north near the ice fields. We lived pretty much in isolation in the forest."

"What else?" He leaned in, his onyx eyes intense as he searched my face as if checking for features that matched the rulers from long ago. Curiosity burned in his eyes, his mind working to piece together the story. "One day, men attacked our home. My mom told him to take me and run to their meeting place. She never made it, so he went back looking for her and she was dead, the cabin destroyed."

The weight of my memories was almost too much, drowning me in the new emotions welling up inside me like a flood. How could he not tell me? "He told me it was raiders..." I trailed off, lost in thought.

My eyes glazed over, unfocused, as I struggled to remember anything about my mother. The room around me seemed to fade away, leaving me alone with my memories. I couldn't remember what she looked like at all, her face lost to me in the mists of time. I had a vague impression of a woman singing, but that was all. My memories of my father were hazy, some mixing with Haemir. I remembered his big smile and his voice. He'd been a good father to me, living in the city even though he missed the forests so that he'd be able to hire help to watch me. But he'd never hinted at a secret heritage or anything that explained why my mother was murdered.

I'd wondered before why he'd run with me and not her. She had to hold them off to give him time to run with me. Gods, what had their lives been like? The room was silent, the only sound was the quiet breathing of the man in front of me and the soft rustling of my clothes as I shifted my weight and opened my eyes.

"And your father?" He asked gently.

"Dead. Died in the Fall of Caurium."

He swore, placing his hand on my arm. "I'm sorry, Kael. That's horrible."

"Yeah." My voice was hollow, and I cleared my throat before continuing. "I grew up thinking I was some sort of Remnant, probably a Fae or Siren Remnant. My dad encouraged it, telling me he didn't know my mom's heritage. But that was a lie." I reached up and touched my earlobe, where I used to have piercings that had hidden my pointed ears. "My mother must have been the one who pierced these."

"She had to make sure you looked human, so you could blend in." Xadrian clucked his tongue sympathetically. "A lot of the humans in Haechall have light hair," he mused before catching my expression. "I'm sorry. If it's any consolation, I understand what it's like to lose family."

I raised an eyebrow at him. "Do you?"

His eyes were distant. "Varzorn killed my mother."

"I'm sorry for your loss," I murmured.

He lifted a shoulder as if it wasn't worth mentioning. "We've all lost someone. That's why we're here, right?"

"Yeah." We lapsed into silence, his dark eyes studying me until I cleared my throat. "What about the Celestial metals?"

He paused for a moment before speaking, as if he wanted to continue our previous conversation. "Well, platinum is used for moving earth and stone, like telekinesis. Titanium—" He held up his ring. "Is used to manipulate stone and earth and change its shape. Iridium transforms anything into stone."

I couldn't help but be a little overwhelmed by all of this information. "What about Earthborn Iron?"

"Ah, yes," Xadrian said with a grimace. "Earthborn Iron nullifies magic. Not just our magic, but all magic."

"What about the stones?" I asked, and he held up his hand. "That's advanced. We're going to get the basics down first. When did you first notice your abilities?"

I thought back, my mind wandering to the night I had first felt something. "It was when we first met," I drew out the words as I replayed the memory of that night. "I could feel something pulling me towards you."

He smiled, flirtation creeping into his voice. "Maybe it was just love at first sight?"

I rolled my eyes. "No. Your necklace drew me in."

He nodded in understanding, his eyes twinkling with amusement. "My necklace is platinum, so that must mean you have a higher affinity for celestial metals, being a Sálfar elf."

I lifted a shoulder. "Yeah, I guess so. I never felt drawn to normal metals when I worked in the mines."

He frowned before catching my gaze once more. "You've been through a lot." It was a statement, not a question.

I hesitated before speaking, uncomfortable with discussing so much of my past with a man who was practically a stranger. "Yeah, I worked in them for ten years before I escaped."

He broke our stare, looking out the window instead.

"It must have been difficult," he murmured, not turning around to face me.

I swallowed thickly, my throat tightening at his gentle tone. "Yeah." I didn't elaborate. It almost felt like betraying Theron to share these things with another man. I crossed my arms, looking in the other direction.

Xadrian nodded and turned back towards me, his dark eyes now filled with sadness for me. He opened his mouth as if about to say something else but decided against it.

"Want to get to work?"

I nodded in reluctant agreement, the air between us thick with tension. It felt wrong that Theron didn't know these things about me and Xadrian did. I reasoned with myself that he was my teacher; he needed to know me better to teach me properly.

I shifted under his gaze and turned away, thinking about Theron instead. He must be back in Adraedor; leading his troops against the rebellion. I knew there was no chance of seeing him again, and the thought of what might happen if we met filled me with dread.

Because if we did...

We'd be fighting on opposite sides of the war.

Chapter 16
Theron

I stepped into my mother's set of rooms, scanning the opulent space. Red velvet curtains hung from the ceiling, the thick fabric draping down to the floor in elegant folds around windows overlooking the darkened city. The furniture was made of dark wood, intricately carved with scenes of battles and hunting. Despite the warmth of the colors, the room remained cold. A chill ran down my spine despite the blazing fire.

My mother sat on her throne-like chair, her long black hair cascading down her back in waves. Her golden eyes locked onto mine as I approached, her expression unreadable.

I bowed low before her, my face carefully blank. "Empress."

She studied me, her gaze sharp as a blade. "Theron," she said, her voice laced with a hint of amusement. "You've finally graced me with your presence."

I kept my gaze downcast, hiding my contempt for the woman who had murdered her brother to claim the crown. "Apologies for missing your wedding. I was in a cave being tortured." Pausing, I waited to see if she would acknowledge my kidnapping. "I'm sure you're disappointed you couldn't attend. They were quite thorough."

Her mouth curved into a cruel smile, and my stomach turned. I knew that expression well; it meant pain. "Have you come to apologize for killing Rhazien?" She lifted a goblet of wine to her lips, as dark red as her mourning clothes.

"I have not," I replied, my voice low and steady. I stepped to the side of the divan, ostensibly to peer at one of her statues, but in actuality, I wanted a barrier between us. "Another killed my brother. You're the only kinslayer in the room, I'm afraid."

"Clever," my mother mused, tapping a finger against the arm of her chair. "You've always been the worst of my two sons. Your father's soft upbringing ruined you." Her gaze was stony, assessing. "I'd almost hoped that you had murdered him. Then I'd know there was at least a drop of my blood in you. Now I have to start over."

A spark of anger ignited within me. My father had been a kind man, too honest for the politics of the court, but he had loved me fiercely.

"I see," I said, my voice dripping with sarcasm. "Well, if you don't want your disappointing son around, I'll be happy to leave."

My mother leaned forward, her eyes glittering with something dangerous. "And where will you go, Theron? To Adraedor to find your rebel concubine? That won't end well for you."

I squared my shoulders, refusing to let her intimidate me. Of course, she knew. She had spies everywhere. "Yes. I will claim what is mine."

My mother laughed, the sound cold and mocking. "You have always been so predictable, Theron. But you forget I am the Empress now. You will do as I say, or suffer the consequences."

She was a spider, patient and cunning, and I was caught in her web.

"And what is it you want?"

"We're facing rebellion in Adraedor," she said, her expression grim. "The slaves have revolted and taken over part of the city."

Adraedor was a key city in our empire, and if it fell to revolt, it could spell disaster for us. "Who holds the city?"

"Herrath Tavador." Relief rushed through me, though I kept my demeanor impassive. Herrath wasn't as loyal to his family and alliances as my mother thought.

"I can take the Niothe and crush the insurrection," I said, my mind already planning out the logistics.

"Not yet," my mother replied, her voice firm. "We need to solidify our ties to the Vennorins first. Most of the Niothe are overseas fighting the Zerkir Remnants and won't be back for some time."

"You took Theodas Vennorin as your consort. Isn't that enough for our alliance?"

"It won't be enough until I have his child," she said, her eyes gleaming with ambition.

I felt sick at the thought of another child being raised by her, growing into a monster like Rhazien did. "I'm not marrying Tannethe," I growled, knowing that she was trying to push me toward a political marriage. "I'm not interested in your alliances."

"All you care about is finding your whore," she sneered, her eyes narrowing. "She killed your brother, Theron. And all you're concerned with is her cunt."

I glared at her as I approached, rage making me heedless of the danger I was in. "You're right, Mother. She's all I care about *now*." I loomed over where she sat in her ornate chair, watching as the smallest hint of fear entered her expression. "Given our family's history of taking power, you should hope that is all that I want."

She stared at me for a moment and then smiled, amused. "You have some of my fire in you, after all. Very well, I won't pressure you to marry Tannethe." She waved her hand and stood up, walking towards the door.

"But I have another suggestion. Since you are so opposed to marrying Tannethe, why don't you wed Raura instead? Raura, come in, please."

Raura entered, wearing a dress of the deepest carmine with a plunging neckline, and I wondered how she could stand to be in the room with her husband's murderer. Then again, she'd never loved him. All she lusted for was power.

I turned away from her, my head spinning with disbelief. "You want me to marry her? Are you serious?"

Nyana nodded. "It's an excellent political move." She glanced over at Raura, who had been standing in stunned silence during the entire exchange. "And I wouldn't expect you to wed until after her period of mourning, of course."

At my mother's gesture, she stepped forward and gave me one of her practiced smiles. "Theron—"

"No," I grated out, not even looking at Raura as I spoke. "I won't marry the woman who abused me for years."

Nyana's smug expression morphed into one of confusion. "What are you talking about?"

Raura looked away, her face pale with fear. "Nyana, it was—" She tried to cut in and smooth over the argument, but my mother silenced her with a chilling look before turning back to me.

"Explain."

I fought to keep my voice even as I spoke. "When I was thirteen, Raura lured me to her bedroom, trying to get pregnant with my seed since the emperor hadn't sired a child on her. It continued for years until I realized how fucked up it was."

Nyana's face darkened as she stared at Raura. "Is this true?" she hissed, her voice cold and unforgiving.

Raura's eyes flew wide, and she backed toward the door. "It wasn't like that. I was lonely—"

My mother darted forward, fury radiating from her as she grabbed Raura by the wrist and yanked her closer. "How dare you? My son?" Wrath dripped from her words and a chill ran down my spine.

"I'm sorry." Raura held up her hands in surrender, trying to explain herself, but Nyana's face was hard as stone. With one swift motion, she pulled out a blade from behind her back and plunged it into Raura's chest as the former empress shrieked.

"Give Varzorn my best," she growled before twisting the knife.

Raura's body dropped to the ground with a thud and I watched Nyana stand over Raura's lifeless corpse, panting. She stabbed her in the torso again, tearing through the muscles and bone to eviscerate her heart.

"Mother?"

She turned towards me, her expression unreadable and her arms painted in blood up to her elbows. "What?"

I blinked. "Why did you—what about the alliance?" My mother had never put me ahead of politics...

"I had to defend our name." She shrugged and wiped the blood off of her knife. "It was a disrespect to me for her to touch my son."

Her words hit me like a punch in the gut. For one moment, I'd thought that she cared about me, but I knew better. All she valued was power.

"You damaged your alliance with the Vennorins," I muttered, unable to look away from Raura's twitching corpse. I'd wanted to kill her for so long that my mind struggled to process the information. It was strange to know that she was gone. Just like Rhazien and Varzorn. My list of enemies was getting smaller by the day. Until one day, it would only be me and my mother.

Nyana snorted. "The Vennorins need me for legitimacy. If they betray me, it will lead to a civil war between the houses and they don't have the might to stand against the Sarro-Amyntas alliance." She picked up her goblet, taking another sip of wine. "Raura had already served her purpose for us and she won't be missed."

I threw up my hands. "Then what was the point of having me marry her?"

"To lull the Vennorins into complacency. Having secured marriages to the two heirs to the throne would solidify their allegiance to us and make them easier to manipulate." She drummed her bloodied nails on the table. "Now I'll have to find you a new match."

"Unless the Vennorins have a sister I don't know about," I drawled, "then my marriage is off the table and I'm leaving."

Nyana scowled at me, her expression as ugly as the monster that lurked within her skin. She picked up a rag, wiping the blood from her hands. "I'll give you leave to find your whore, but you must take Adraedor in hand." Her golden eyes flashed, and for a moment I didn't see her. I saw Varzorn. "Crush the rebellion and get the slaves in line. We'll need fresh territory to appease these nobles, and I don't have enough armor for our soldiers."

"I don't give a damn about Adraedor."

Nyana fixed me with a haughty stare. "You will when Theodas tries to take it. Or one of his brothers. That city produces more money and metal for us than ninety percent of the empire combined. To lose it would jeopardize our power." Her gaze pinned me in place. "So retake the city, kill Tavador if you need, but don't let it fall into Vennorin hands. Understand?"

"Fine," I ground out. "I'll depart tomorrow."

"Good." She sat in her chair once more, lifting the reports that waited on her table. "Send someone to clean that up when you leave." She waved a careless hand toward Raura's corpse, not bothering to look away from her paperwork as I left her suite.

I stalked into my chambers, still reeling from the encounter with my mother and Raura. Seeing her lying there dead didn't make me feel any better. It made me worry more about Kael. She had killed Rhazien after he assaulted her, but I doubted it had brought her any relief. Just more of this strange emptiness. The need to find her built within me, a constant ache that punctuated my every thought.

A noise came from the bedroom, and I pulled my sword, silently prowling across the suite, ready to take care of whatever assassin lurked in my midst.

Tannethe lay on my bed, her long, raven hair cascading over the silken sheets, and her eyes smoldering with desire. But I knew better than to fall for her alluring facade.

"Theron," she crooned my name, her voice dripping with honey. "You took so long that I had to start without you." She let the blankets fall, revealing her full breasts. Her nipples rouged and pert as she stroked them.

I rolled my eyes and strode toward her, my gaze sweeping over her body with cool detachment. "You should know better than to be in my bed uninvited."

"We're good together, Theron. Everyone knows we'd make the perfect match." She reached a hand out, trailing it down my stomach until she cupped my cock. "Let me prove it to you."

I scoffed, plucking her hand off of my body. Not even a twitch of attraction. Nothing could rival what I shared with Kael. "I don't want you, Tannethe. You're nothing compared to what I've had."

She scowled, her eyes flashing with anger before she schooled her expression to one of desire. "What do you think you had with that whore that I couldn't give you?"

I flexed my fingers, trying to keep my temper in check. "That's none of your concern. Leave."

"You should consider what cutting ties with me does to the alliance. You could be emperor one day," she murmured as if trying to put me under her spell, her fingers trailing down her body. "We would have everything. And I would worship you." She sank to her knees and looked up at me with lust-filled eyes. "You can do anything you want to me."

"For Atar's sake, Tannethe." I stepped back and grabbed her robe, throwing it in her face before pointing toward the door. "Now leave before I throw you out myself."

Tannethe huffed and pulled on her robe, stalking towards the exit. At the threshold, she turned, her eyes filled with loathing.

"You may think you don't want me right now, but someday soon you'll regret not taking this offer."

"I'll take that risk," I growled, slamming the door in her face.

I sighed, running a hand through my hair. I didn't have time to play games with her. There was still too much planning to do. I checked the clock, wishing Raenisa and Zerek would return with their intel faster. I had the stirrings of a plan, but I needed more information. By this time next week, both Kael and Adraedor would be back under my control.

Chapter 17
Kael

My hand shook as I took a bite of breakfast; the seffa was a thick paste in my mouth and I almost gagged as I forced myself to swallow it. Gavril watched me with a furrowed brow, his eyes sharp and assessing.

"What's wrong? Are you nervous about your lesson today?"

I swallowed hard, trying to calm my racing heart, and put on a confident mask. "No. I don't get anxious."

"Sure." He chuckled, the sound a low rumble in his chest. "Don't worry, sis. You'll do great. And if you don't, I'll be there to laugh at you."

I scowled and took another bite of seffa. "You're not helping, Gav."

He grinned. "Sorry, I'm just teasing. You'll be fine. And hey, at least you have magic. I'm kind of jealous, to be honest. I think I'd be better at it than you."

"Sure you would. That's why I always beat you when we're sparring."

Gavril scoffed. "That's just because you have extra Elven strength. You're cheating."

I playfully punched him in the arm. "I am not cheating. I have natural talent."

"Natural talent, my ass. You had a better teacher and I have to deal with you."

I shot him a lewd hand gesture, and he laughed. We were still ribbing each other when a knock sounded at the door. I got up to answer it, chuckling. Xadrian leaned against my door frame as if he were an old friend. I resisted the urge to shove him out of the way. Why did he always act like he owned the space he was in?

"Xadrian. Hey." I let him in, gesturing from him to Gavril, who frowned. "This is Gavril. Gavril, meet Xadrian. I didn't know it was already time."

"This is your teacher?" Gavril asked, his brows drawn down into a line.

"Good to meet you. Are you and Kael... together?" Xadrian questioned, his gaze flicking between us.

Gavril recoiled. "Gross."

"Shut up, Gav." I laughed, shaking my head. "No, he's my little brother."

Gavril rested his elbow on my shoulder, leaning.

"Can't you see the resemblance?" he joked, and I pushed him away, scowling.

"I'm adopted. I obviously didn't inherit his terrible sense of humor." Gavril grinned when I threw him a mock glare.

Xadrian's eyes lingered on us, and I could feel the weight of his gaze on my skin like a caress.

My brother looked between us before smacking the table and standing. "Well, I have to hunt. Good luck today, sis. Xadrian." Gavril excused himself, his attitude toward my teacher a touch off, leaving me alone with the strange elf, and my pulse quickened.

He was too charming, too confident; it made me uneasy. I still didn't trust him, regardless of what the others said.

"Are you ready to train?" he asked, his eyes glinting with amusement.

I nodded, swallowing hard. "Yeah."

He smirked, his dark eyes watching the movement of my throat. "We need somewhere private. A good-sized space that won't get anyone upset if you damage something."

I thought for a moment, running a hand through my hair. "I know a place," I said. "Follow me."

"Happy too," Xadrian murmured, eying me as I shut the door. He didn't move, forcing me to stand close enough to catch his scent. Pine and musk, like the frozen mountains to the north. I blew out a breath, determined to breathe through my mouth.

"Let's go."

I led Xadrian through the winding streets of the city to an abandoned stadium that had once been used for Kyrie games. It was huge, open to the air, with half-demolished pillars and plenty of space to move around. It was so decrepit I doubted anyone would notice if I broke anything.

"What is this place?" Xadrian asked, looking around.

"It used to be an arena for the Kyrie. They would fly around here and play some sort of game. But they can't anymore."

Xadrian stepped closer to me, his eyes darkening. "What do you want to learn first? Earthborn metals or Celestial?"

I hesitated, unsure of what to say. Tactically, it made sense to learn the most dangerous magic first, but healing was also important.

"Celestial," I decided finally.

He chuckled. "You're brave. I like that in a woman."

"I have the feeling you like everything about women." I rolled my eyes, and he laughed.

"So the taciturn act was genuine?" He raked his eyes over me, appreciation in his gaze.

"More than you know."

He winked at me before he reached into his pocket and pulled out a platinum ring. It had a bat carved into it, and it sparkled in the pool of sunlight.

"It's a family heirloom from the Heliots," he said, taking my hand and depositing the ring in my palm, his fingers lingering just a touch too long. "We were the enforcers of the Helekian, keeping order amongst our people." He paused and I wondered if that was part of the reason he'd joined the rebellion. A sense of duty and connection to his lineage. "Keep it. Consider it a present."

I shifted my weight, uncomfortable with the intimacy of the gift and how close he was standing to me. It felt like a betrayal... to Theron. *Stop it, Kael.* Theron is the enemy, and I would never see him again. I needed to stop thinking about him.

"Thank you," I said, trying to sound grateful.

Xadrian leaned even closer, his breath warm against my ear. "You're welcome."

I pulled away, my heart racing as I frowned at him. I couldn't let myself be distracted by him, not when there was so much at stake.

He studied me, his eyes dark with a hunger that I ignored. "Are you ready to begin, Kael?" he asked, his voice low and smooth like velvet.

"You can turn off the bedroom voice, Xadrian."

His lip quirked up. "Are you imagining me in bed?"

"No. I'm imagining you actually teaching me something." My tone was flat, and he laughed, unaffected by my rudeness.

"Let's get to work," he said, stepping closer. "First, you need to imagine your power moving through your body and into the metal of your ring. Visualize it, whatever seems right to you."

I looked down at the platinum ring on my finger; the bat carving glinting in the sunlight filtering from above. "Alright," I said, trying to focus.

"Then," he continued, "imagine lifting the rock with your mind. Feel the energy flowing from you, through the metal, and into the stone. How you're connected, the stone's desire to be remade."

I lifted a brow. "Stones have desires?"

He grinned. "Just try it."

I closed my eyes, trying to do as he said. Warmth spread through me, like the first rays of the sun after a long, snowy night. I focused on the stone, willing it to move.

"What does it feel like?" I asked, my voice barely above a whisper.

Xadrian stepped closer, his breath fanning over my neck. "It's warm and soft. Hesitant," he murmured, his words sending shivers down my spine. "Like the first touch of a lover's hand."

I swallowed, trying to concentrate on the magic. But with him so close, it was hard to think of anything else. His scent filled my nose, and his instructions flew out of my head.

I tried to focus, but he brushed his fingertips against my arm and I jumped, startled. Power exploded from me in a rush, the stones I was trying to move flying across the room and knocking over the pillar. I gasped, embarrassed by my lack of control.

"Fuck." I winced, his gaze heavy on me. I took a step back and caught my breath. "Sorry," I said, looking at the pillar that now lay in ruins. "I didn't mean to do that."

Xadrian's eyes twinkled with amusement. "No need to apologize, Kael." He chuckled. "You have a lot more magic than I hoped. That's a good thing."

I gave him a wary look. "Is it?"

He nodded. "You're strong, just like the Helekian were. Once you learn to control it, you'll be unstoppable."

I tried to focus on his words, but his nearness made it hard. The heat emanating from his body seeped into my skin and his breath tickled the side of my face.

"Alright," I said, inhaling deeply and stepping away further. "So, how do I control my magic?"

Xadrian smiled, reaching out to take my hand, and I had to fight the urge to tear it away. "It's all about visualization and intention," he said, guiding my fingers to my ring. "Imagine your power flowing through you and into the metal. Then focus on the stone and will it to move."

I closed my eyes and tried to picture his words. White-hot stream of energy flowing from my chest and into the ring, pulsing with power. I focused on the stone, willing it to rise.

At first, nothing happened. But then I felt a faint stirring, like a breeze brushing against my skin. I concentrated harder, pouring my energy into the stone.

And then, miraculously, it moved. The stone rose from the ground, floating in mid-air. I gasped in amazement, staring at it in disbelief, and it fell, splitting with a loud crack.

Xadrian grinned, squeezing my hand. "See? You can do it."

"That was incredible." The connection to the magic, using it—I had experienced nothing like it. Like I could feel Atar himself, wanting me to reshape the stone so he could see what clever things I wrought. No wonder the elves were arrogant. They could rework the world itself. "It was like I could see it. White light."

"Your eyes turned white when you were casting." He pursed his lips and rubbed his chin, eyes lost in thought. "I wonder if they'll flood black when you use Earthborn metals."

His pensiveness reminded me of Theron and a strange homesickness struck me, remembering the way his eyes went distant when planning. I shoved the emotion away. There's no way I missed Theron. Even if my first thought had been of showing him my newfound talent. I shook my head, determined to forget about him.

"Let's keep going," I demanded, more aggressively than necessary. "I want to learn everything."

He lifted a brow, his expression amused. "Let's see how long you last."

"Careful, Kael."

Sweat slid down my neck as I strained to lift the pillar with my magic. It was heavy, much heavier than I expected, and my muscles ached with the effort. Why did my muscles hurt if I wasn't even using them? Atar was a fucking idiot, I decided. Xadrian's voice sounded far away, warning me I was overexerting myself, but I ignored him. I could do this.

I gritted my teeth and poured more magic into the pillar, lifting it higher and higher into the air. But my grip slipped, and it came crashing down with a deafening boom, sending chunks of stone and metal flying in all directions.

I winced at the sound of shattering seats as I surveyed the destruction. Xadrian's irritated voice broke through my haze of pain.

"Atar, save me from stubborn women," he muttered. "You need to take a break, Kael."

I nodded, conceding defeat. My magic was drained, and I could barely stand. I sank to the ground, resting my forehead against the cool stone beside me. Xadrian came to sit beside me, his eyes wide with concern.

"Are you alright?" he asked, placing a hand on my shoulder.

"I'm fine," I mumbled, even though I wasn't.

He offered me his canteen, and I shook my head, unwilling to drink from his cup. "Mine is over there."

He retrieved it and passed me the canteen. I took a drink, savoring the lukewarm water. It wasn't like the iced jugs of the palace, but I was learning to appreciate it all the same.

"Stubborn women, huh?" I chuckled, and he joined me after a moment. "Spoken like a man with two sisters."

"They're both as bullheaded as you," he laughed. "Aracel can sweet talk her way into anything she wants. Caelia, on the other hand, is like a hammer. She'll beat people into submission if that's what it takes."

I scowled. "I wish Caelia would stop hammering Raenisa. She keeps stringing her along."

"Their relationship is their business." He held up his hands in surrender. "I'm out of it."

I rolled my eyes. "I'm just saying it's inconsiderate. Raenisa deserves better than someone who'd abandon her for a crown."

"Caelia has reasons for her ambition," his voice was strange, but I didn't pick up on why.

"And Raenisa is worthy of a person who'd love her more than ambition."

"Why do you care?" he asked, his eyes narrowing. "Don't you hate them all? They treated you like a pet."

I paused, surprised by the question. "I... I don't know. I thought I hated them all, but now... I'm not so sure."

Xadrian studied me for a long moment, his gaze searching. I knew what he was about to ask, and I stood up before he could ask anything about Theron.

"Thanks for the lesson, Xadrian," I said, trying to sound casual. "I need to get home."

He stood too, his expression unreadable. "Sure. I'll see you tomorrow."

I nodded, turning to leave. As I walked away, I could feel his eyes on my back, and I wondered what he was thinking. Did he know how I felt about Theron?

Did I?

Chapter 18
Theron

I gripped the reins of my vanira, watching as the walled desert city of Adraedor came into view. Vaernix chittered, no doubt excited to return to her cave with fresh ferelope and cool darkness. Raenisa and Zerek flanked me on their mounts, crouched low on the mountainside, hidden from sight.

The city teemed with activity, even in the dead of night. The outer ring was filled with slaves and rebels who huddled together in makeshift tents and shanties. Smoke and sweat saturated the air.

As we crept closer, we could see the royal guard patrolling the inner ring, their golden armor glinting in the moonlight. The palace loomed in the distance, the wide expanse of the sandy courtyard open and empty. The killing field ready to be put to use.

"We'll have to be careful," Raenisa whispered, her voice barely audible over the rustle of the wind. "But I think we can climb past."

"Agreed," I said, nodding. "The Remnants don't have as good of night vision as us. It should be alright if we have cloud cover."

They nodded in agreement, and we set off, skittering down the rocky mountainside, our vanira moving gracefully over the uneven terrain.

I stayed low, sticking close to the shadows, keeping my movements small and slow. It seemed like an eternity, but we reached the outer ring. We slipped past the rebels and slaves with ease, their tired eyes hardly glancing our way as we went deeper into the city.

The inner ring was more heavily guarded, and we had to move with even more caution. I kept Vaernix in a low trot as Raenisa and Zerek took turns scouting ahead. My heart thumped against my chest as I watched them disappear into the darkness. The rebels weren't in this area, but it didn't mean it wasn't booby-trapped by my soldiers.

Just as we neared the palace, a shout rang out. Guards emerged from the shadows, weapons drawn.

"Stop," I commanded, my voice ringing out in the night.

They stopped in their tracks, shock visible on their faces as they recognized me. The leader stepped forward, bowing low.

"Your Highness," he said. "We didn't know you were coming."

I smiled, trying to quell the fear I saw in his eyes. "That was the point. Our enemies weren't expecting me, either."

The soldiers exchanged a glance, but they kept silent and watched as their commander straightened and motioned for the troops to stand down.

"Thank Atar for that. We need help with the rebellion. They're wily, sir."

Murmurs of relief filled the night air as the royal guard realized who we were. They chattered excitedly about our return, and how we'd put down the revolt.

"Come now, it's barely an uprising. We can manage it with ease," I said, cutting off their speculation with a chuckle. One of the most important things a leader can do is project confidence. "But I will need your help."

The commander nodded eagerly and at my command, he organized extra patrols on the hillside overlooking Adraedor—just to be safe. He promised more security around the palace as well.

We hurried towards the gates, eager to get inside before dawn broke and rumors of our arrival spread throughout the city. The heavy gates opened with a loud creak and we rode in.

The stable was my first stop. Vaernix chittered as we entered the web-shrouded cave, seemingly happy that they were home. I called for an attendant to take care of her, too exhausted from crossing the Burning Frontier to do it myself. I'd led them at a brutal pace, determined to return to the desert as quickly as possible, but no one had complained.

"Come on, let's get some food and clean up."

A pang hit my chest as I walked past the dungeon where Kael had freed her fellow rebels under my nose. Would everything here remind me of her? The scent of spice in the air, the moons as pale as her hair. She'd delved deep into me and I'd never be free. Just one more reason to find her.

I strode into the indoor courtyard, scowling at the water splashing in the fountain. It was obscene in its wastefulness. After staying in the desert and seeing how little they had to survive on, it was galling. I understood Kael's disgust with us now.

Herrath's arrival yanked me out of my thoughts as I ran forward with a wide grin on his face. He wrapped his arms around me in a back-slapping hug.

"Theron." He stepped back to look me over. "Glad to see you're still in one piece."

I gripped his shoulder. "You got my message?"

"I did. Mirijana and Aella are safe. Miri told me what happened, and I sent off sentries for you the moment I realized something was wrong."

"Good man."

Raenisa and Zerek looked at us in shock. She raised an eyebrow and quipped, "What? Do we like Herrath now?"

Herrath shot her an annoyed glare before I cut in. "Yeah, we do," I said with a chuckle, patting him on the shoulder. "He had his reasons for doing what he did. It's in the past. He's one of us."

Herrath smiled, standing up a little taller as he began his report on what had been going on while we were gone.

"The rebels are regrouping and preparing to launch another major assault soon. Most of their forces have been driven into the slave quarters—but they've left behind some of their toughest fighters." He took a breath. "We've managed to keep the noble quarters relatively safe. But it's far from secure."

I nodded, taking in the details as he continued while I studied my surroundings once more. The scent of spice still hung heavy in the air, mixed with the sound of rushing water from the fountains nearby. In the faint moonlight, I could make out the faces of soldiers in the courtyard outside here and there, reflecting their worries as they completed their rounds.

"You've turned off the water to the outer forums?" I asked.

He dipped his chin. "Days ago. They should run out soon."

"Good work."

He hid a pleased grin. "What is going on in the palace? What are our plans?"

"Raura's dead. Nyana killed her."

A vicious smile spread across Herrath's face before he nodded. "That would explain some messages I've been ignoring from my parents."

Raenisa exchanged a look with Zerek, no doubt shocked that Herrath had such little regard for his family's alliance. A servant brought a plate of sandwiches with a jug of water, which Raenisa and Zerek pounced on.

"Most of the Houses are withdrawing their families from the court to their country estates," Raenisa began, taking the meat out of one sandwich and piling it onto another. "It's a measure to protect their bloodlines, in case there's another coup. A lot of members have gone into hiding. No one has seen Xadrian since he left Adraedor. And there's been several alliances formed through marriage pacts that are not being disclosed to the Empress." She paused to take a bite of her sandwich and groaned. "So good. The sandwich, not the situation. My parents said that the Amyntas-Sarro Alliance has approached them." She glanced at Zerek, who looked away, no doubt unhappy to be reminded of his family.

"What did the Taelyrs say?" Herrath asked, and her shoulders slumped.

"They said no. They think Caelia wants a civil war."

Zerek nodded. "She's not the only one. Xavier does too, and more of the high houses are shoring up their alliances. It'll be harder to gather information."

"What about the empress?" Herrath cut in, and my stomach growled. I grabbed a sandwich, taking a large bite. "She'll want to come here soon."

"Almost makes you happy there's a rebellion," Zerek muttered.

I snorted before running a hand through my greasy hair. "Later. First, we need to bathe and eat. Send more food to my suite and meet me there in an hour."

I entered my suite, relieved to find that nothing had been disturbed in my absence. Everything was in place. Except for Kael... That one detail felt like too glaring an omission as if the room somehow knew it should have something there but didn't know what it was missing.

I stripped off my armor and undressed, stacking it neatly before sinking into the warm water of the tub. As I laid back and closed my eyes, images of Kael flickered in front of me—her pale skin and silver hair; her cutting smile and sharp words; the fire in her gaze when she finally gave in to pleasure.

It felt like a lifetime ago that I'd held her here in this very room while she bled out, desperate to heal her. The couch was still there; no bloodstains to be seen or any evidence to show what had happened here only weeks ago. It was surreal how mundane everything appeared now—as if nothing had ever happened at all. The entire suite was stained with my last memories of her here, and I almost wished they were visible. Then at least it would seem real.

I could still feel the warmth of her lips against mine before she raced out of the room. To who knows what fate.

The thought of her being caught up in the explosion sent a chill down my spine. What if something had happened? What if she was hurt? The need to find her grew within me like an itch constantly nagging at me, urging me to get up and go after her. What if she was going through her change right now, and I wasn't there to see her through it?

I growled, throwing myself out of the tub and dressing, already planning where I'd start my search.

The door opened, revealing Herrath followed by Mirijana carrying a tray of food.

"Lord Marshal." She smiled warmly at me as she entered. She stole a glance towards Herrath, who was watching her with an intensity that made me pause.

"Is it true?" She asked, her gaze meeting mine. "That Kael betrayed you?"

I took a deep breath and nodded. "Yes," I said after a moment. It seemed less important now compared to my need to find her.

"I can't believe it." She shook her head. "She was nice once you got to know her."

Herrath snorted. "Kael was never nice. She's dangerous," he replied coldly, his eyes still fixed on Mirijana as if daring her to challenge him. "Even more so now that her cover is blown."

"I won't have this argument again," Mirijana glared at him.

Herrath opened his mouth to retort, but I cut him off.

"What do we know about the palace's ability to withstand a siege? The rebels could still break through the outer gate."

Herrath moved away from the wall he'd been leaning against and crossed his arms over his chest, considering my question for a moment before responding. "The walls are fully manned. I have plenty of pikes at the ready and oil is constantly simmering. They'd have a difficult time breaching it." He paused before adding, "As for the palace, we're stocked with food from the visit and able to withstand a siege for six months at the least."

"Good. But we still need to be vigilant. The longer they go without water, the more desperate they'll become. The boiling oil won't seem as daunting in the face of dehydration."

He nodded. "I'll have the guard ready."

"Have you secured the tunnels?" Herrath shook his head. "That should be our priority in the morning. They've used the tunnels to move around before. I wouldn't be surprised if they were again."

Herrath swore. "Sorry, Theron. I didn't—"

I held up a hand. "You've done well. No need to apologize. I'm just glad it's you here and not Theodas or Trevyr Vennorin."

He shrugged as Raenisa, and Zerek entered. "They told me to hold the city. They just didn't know I was holding it for you. Not them."

I patted his shoulder, and Raenisa stared at him for a long moment before flopping onto the couch. Zerek grabbed food from the tray Mirijana had set down, leaning back. "So what's the plan?"

I sighed, pushing my worries aside for the moment. This was a conversation we had to have. "I'm leaving tomorrow. I'm going to get Kael back."

Raenisa's expression soured. "You should let her go. We need you here to handle this rebellion."

"You're my second-in-command. This is your chance to lead our soldiers in combat."

She narrowed her eyes at me; her tied-up hair making her features appear more severe. "Don't try to distract me. Your obsession with her is going to get you killed." She turned to Zerek. "Back me up on this. He was torn to shreds when we found him."

Zerek shrugged, tossing a piece of fruit into the air and catching it with his mouth. "He also smelled like sex and Kael. I'm not touching this situation at all."

"I agree with Raenisa," Herrath put in, and she eyed him before nodding.

"See? Even Herrath gets it." She leaned forward, her expression earnest. "I understand, Theron. I liked her too. But it's not worth it to chase after someone that doesn't want to be caught, remember?"

I shook my head. "Sorry, Rae. I have to do this—"

"Untwist your sac and—"

I cut her off. "She's an elf. Sálfar."

Everyone froze, shock filling the room. Raenisa was the first to break the silence. "Are you serious? How did you find out?"

I let out a tired laugh. "It's complicated—"

"And Kael didn't know she was an elf when she was here?" Herrath questioned me, glancing at Mirijana, who lifted a brow.

I shook my head. "No. She thought she might be a Sálfar Remnant."

Raenisa snorted, shaking her head. "That makes no sense."

Herrath nodded thoughtfully before turning to Zerek and Raenisa. "This changes things."

"We can't let her stay in rebel hands. She's too dangerous, especially if she ever finds out how to use Celestial metals." I explained, not wanting to go into my personal reasons for finding her. They wouldn't understand. "She'd be able to level our walls by herself."

Zerek whistled low under his breath. "Fuck. I didn't even think of that."

"This information doesn't leave the room. If my mother or any of the other high houses realize a Sálfar is running around, there's no telling what they'll do."

"Kill her, break her, or breed her," Herrath muttered, and my stomach flipped.

"Exactly. I need to move fast to find her." I grabbed a piece of paper and sat at the table, beginning to write. "Here's the plan..."

Chapter 19
Kael

I woke up to someone pounding on my front door. For a moment, I was back in the mines, hammers striking the stone as the sound reverberated through my skull. I groaned and rolled over in my bed.

"Get the door, Gav!" I shouted, burying my face in my pillow.

My brother grumbled as he shuffled down to answer the door. I was almost asleep again when I heard his surprised exclamation.

"Roza? What are you doing here?"

Dragging myself up, I ran a hand through my hair, still groggy but already worried. I rolled myself out of bed, the cold air biting at my skin. If Roza was here this early, then something was wrong.

Walking downstairs, I saw Kadir standing there, looking like he'd seen a ghost. Roza stood next to him, frowning as usual.

"What's going on?" I asked, rubbing my eyes.

Kadir exchanged a look with Roza. "The Emperor is dead."

"What?"

Kadir nodded. "I had it confirmed from more than one source. His sister killed him with Theodas Vennorin and she declared herself Empress with Theodas as her consort."

"Vetia's horns," Gavril muttered.

"This might not be a bad thing." I yawned, pressing the back of my hand to my mouth. "They'll be more unstable now. New alliances forming."

Roza frowned. "That's not all." She looked toward Kadir, who continued.

"The Marshal is back. And he's hunting for you."

A jolt ran through me; not fear, but something else. Something dark and urgent that I didn't want to name. I pushed it away, worried about what they'd see in my expression.

"What else?" I asked, trying to keep my voice steady.

Roza stepped forward, kicking the dust off her boots in the doorway. "There's trouble in Adraedor. The tunnels have been compromised, and people are dying of thirst. They're getting desperate, and it's only a matter of time before they do something reckless. I get the feeling that Haemir and Teodosija aren't agreeing on much right now."

My heart pounded in my chest. Adraedor was the key to everything. If we lost it, we lost the war.

"Have they tried firesetting?" I asked, racking my brain.

Kadir shook his head, his vibrant hair similar to Roza's. It was strange seeing them next to each other, like siblings from a distant past. "The walls are magically reinforced. It won't work."

"Even if we could damage the walls, we don't want to." Roza idly flipped her knife, something she'd once done with her hammer in the mines. "If we can take the city, we'll need the walls to hold it when the elves try to take it back."

Thoughts of using my magic to take down the walls fizzled out. She was right.

Turning to Kadir, I said, "We have to figure out a way to get through those walls. Do you have contacts on the inside that can be swayed?"

Kadir lifted a shoulder. "Possibly. It'll be difficult to get word to them. Especially if I don't have anything to bribe them with."

I turned to my brother. "Gav, can you help with that?"

"I'll start working on it. But what about the Marshal?" He glanced around the room as if worried that he'd come out of the shadows.

Closing my eyes and taking a deep breath, I said, "I'll figure it out. I always do."

He didn't respond, just nodding, his expression pinched. A pang hit my stomach. I had to tell him the truth about Theron. I couldn't let him be this worried.

"Let me know what I can do," Roza said, heading toward the door. "I need to find Andreja. She just got back from Adraedor, and she's supposed to leave again soon."

"See you later."

Roza left with a wave, taking off at a slow jog, and I shut the door.

"Not even one insult. Perhaps we have turned a page," I joked before I realized no one was behind me anymore. I faced Kadir and Gavril, who were both sitting at the table, looking grim. Neither had laughed at my poor attempt at humor.

"What's going on?" I asked, narrowing my eyes.

Kadir leaned forward, his eyes locked on mine. "There's something off about Andreja," he said. "I've been in the spy game long enough to recognize a compromised asset when I see one. She's acting strange."

I frowned. "What do you mean?"

Kadir shrugged. "Andreja's just... different. She's been avoiding me, disappearing in the city from the safe houses."

My stomach sank. "Do you think she's working for the empire?"

Kadir nodded. "It's possible. Someone has been feeding the elves information."

Gavril crossed his arms, leaning back in his chair, but didn't comment.

"It's possible that she's doing special missions for Teodosija. Like me," I pointed out.

Gavril snorted. "Missions on her back." Andreja had a reputation for getting what she wanted with her looks, something that I threw in her face whenever she and Roza went after me.

Kadir shot him a withering look. "That's not what this is about. There's nothing wrong with a cactus honey scheme. I'm just worried about the hidden city. She returned from Adraedor with me today and already wants to go back. Teodosija didn't ask for us to return that soon." He shook his head. "I'm not sure what to do."

"We need to tell Dad and Teodosija," Gavril put in. "They'd want to know."

"I don't have any proof."

"You have good instincts. Our dad will trust that. Just tell him your suspicions and he'll put an eye on her."

Before anyone else could speak, another knock came at the door. Gavril grumbled as he got up to answer it, and Kadir's shoulders stiffened.

Xadrian stepped inside, glancing around the room with a puzzled expression. His gaze flicked to Kadir, and I could tell by the look in his eyes that he didn't trust him. I didn't blame him; Kadir was secretive about his past, and Xadrian was an enigma that no one was sure how to handle. Neither of them had opened up much.

"Ah, who do we have here?" he asked, his voice light but cautious. He stepped forward, holding out his hand. "I'm Xadrian."

Kadir nodded in acknowledgment but didn't take the offered hand. "Kadir," he said shortly before turning back to me. "I need to get some sleep so I can leave for Adraedor tomorrow. Do you want me to bring any letters for you?"

"That would be great. I'll drop them off tonight."

Kadir dipped his chin before heading towards the door without another word. He paused for a moment in the doorway before slipping out into the gray morning, leaving a long silence behind him.

Xadrian watched him go with an unreadable expression before turning back to us with a raised eyebrow. "Friend of yours?"

Gavril shrugged as he moved back to his seat at the table while I crossed my arms over my chest.

"Something like that," I muttered. "What's up? You're here early."

"I found a new place for us to work on your metals," Xadrian said, his eyes raking over me in my night shift.

A flush crept up my neck. "That's great," I said, trying to sound nonchalant.

"But it's a bit of a walk," Xadrian continued. "So we need to leave early."

"Right."

I excused myself to dress, feeling his attention on me as I went. I squirmed, unsure if I liked it or not, as I hurried upstairs and away from the awkward situation.

My nerves were on edge as Xadrian led me deeper into the highlands. His constant flirting had been confusing me for days, but I couldn't deny the thrill of being out here with him, in the quiet.

We had been walking for hours, and as the sun crested the horizon, it illuminated a wide canyon ahead of us. I paused in awe, my breath caught in my throat as I gazed out at the beauty before me. The towering walls were painted in hues of golden yellow and deep reds and oranges that blended to create a stunning picture.

The air was cool and crisp but carried with it a hint of something sweet-smelling like cacti flowers or honey. Bushes full of bright purple blossoms lined the sides of the rocky path we followed down into the depths of the canyon.

As we descended further into it, I noticed dark alcoves carved out along the side walls that were filled with ancient artifacts from a long-forgotten time, offering glimpses of Kyrie culture from before the Godsfall.

Finally, he stopped at a thin crevice. "It's right through here." He squeezed through the narrow gap, shuffling to make his bag fit. I followed him warily, scraping my skin as I slid through the gap. The crack opened into a clearing.

I gasped in surprise. He'd found an oasis. An emerald paradise surrounded by rocky crags high on all sides. The air was strangely still and silent like a secret only known to us. A clear pool shimmered in the center of the clearing, fed by a trickling waterfall that cascaded down from the crag above. Fragrant flowers bloomed all around, creating rainbow hues that enticed me further into their embrace. On one side of the pool was a large tree with branches so thick they blocked out most of the sky, providing an intimate hideaway from the sun's harsh rays. All around us were birds chirping and small animals scurrying about, basking in their newfound freedom and safety.

"How did you find this?" I murmured, running my fingers over the velvet soft leaves.

"I asked some elders. They know there's a spring here, but since it's so far away, it's not used much. I investigated and found this." He grinned at me. "I thought you'd like it."

My stomach flipped, nerves filling me. This wasn't just flirting or teaching me. This was more...

"It's beautiful." I took a step closer to the water, putting more distance between us. "Should we get started practicing?"

He watched me for a long moment. "I brought some food and drinks. I thought we'd have a picnic."

A strange sensation filled me. Something akin to dread as I picked at my shirt, fighting the urge to run.

"We should practice first," I said with false brightness.

His jaw tightened, and I sensed his disappointment. But he nodded. "Try to lift that rock?" He gestured to a boulder near the water's edge.

I swallowed, my mouth dry as I took a deep breath. I stepped next to the water, Xadrian behind me. With trembling hands, I reached out with my magic for the stone and clasped it in my telekinetic grip, focusing all my energy on lifting it off the ground and turning it in careful maneuvers until I had it perched on its edge.

"Good. Now lift the one next to it."

I tried, keeping the first balanced as I sought the other one. It came slowly, and I lifted it beside the first, sweat beading my forehead that I didn't dare to wipe away and break my concentration.

"Add another."

I ground my teeth, casting about with my magic for another. It was a strange sensation—like groping in the dark. I felt suggestions in the stone, flecks of metal asking to be forged into something new. To create. The stone called to me and I pushed it away, focusing on my task. The third boulder shook, lifting from the ground before all three fell in a rumble that echoed around us.

Xadrian turned to me, his eyes glinting with a fierce intensity. "Kael, you need to let go. Stop being afraid of your magic. You're holding yourself back."

I bristled at his words. "I'm not scared. And I'm not blocking myself. Maybe I just don't have as much power as you think."

Xadrian shook his head, stepping closer to me until we were almost touching. He lifted at hand and all three boulders rose into the air at once. "Compared to you, I have a drop of Sálfar power. You could reshape the canyons, the mountains themselves if you wanted to." He tipped my chin up with his fingers, his skin soft on mine. Not the callous-roughened ones I longed for. You have to learn to have faith in yourself, Kael. Trust your instincts, let go of your fears, and embrace what you are."

"Xadrian…" Heat rose in my cheeks and a massive boulder exploded, sending fragments flying that he blocked with a wave of his hand.

"See?" he said, a triumphant smile on his face. "Your power is strongest when you're not thinking about it. Let go and welcome it. Feel it."

He leaned forward, his eyes locking with mine. His breath was warm on my skin, his lips were dangerously close. Too close. My pulse fluttered wildly as he pressed his mouth against mine, his tongue tracing the seam of my lips and beseeching me to open for him. Warmth radiated from him and the rapid thumping of his heart against his chest mirrored my own.

I took a small step back, my nerves filling me like a wildfire raging through me. "I-I'm sorry," I stammered, pressing my fingertips to my flushed cheeks as I looked at the ground, shame and guilt settling in my stomach like a stone. "I—I can't."

"Why? I thought we—" His eyes searched mine with unspoken questions and I swallowed hard.

"After everything with Theron, I—my head's a mess." I groped for the right words—how he would've been perfect for me if my heart hadn't already been stolen—but I couldn't find them and I finished lamely. "It wouldn't be right."

Xadrian exhaled, his breath ruffling my hair. "I understand," he murmured. "It can't have been easy for you in the palace. I'm here for you. You don't have to tell me what's bothering you if it's too difficult." He stepped back, giving me space and allowing me to breathe again. A lump formed in my throat at his kindness. "But when you're ready, I'm here."

I nodded, my heart breaking at the thought of hurting him. But... I couldn't give him what he wanted. I couldn't deny the feelings I had for Theron. Xadrian was everything I should want—handsome, fun, and part of the rebellion. But when he touched me, all I could think about was Theron. How Xadrian's lips were too full and gentle, his hands too soft. I needed Theron's hard edge; the way he kissed me like I was water in the desert, air he was desperate to breathe. And... I felt the same.

I didn't want anyone but him. Even if I wanted to, there was no denying how Theron looked at me and how his eyes seemed to pierce through my soul.

Yet we remained on opposing sides of the war. It was a cruel joke.

Xadrian's voice cut into my thoughts as he said, "We should probably get back to practicing now." His tone was gentle and understanding, sending a fresh wave of guilt through me. He still had hope, and I was a monster for not crushing it now. But I didn't. I just nodded and followed him back to the tree, the thought of being honest with him nagging at the back of my mind. It was so tempting to tell him everything—to be as sincere as he was with me. But if I did, would he even want to teach me anymore? Would it change our friendship?

My chest ached, but I swallowed my pride and said nothing. Maybe when we took Adraedor, I'd talk to him about it and express my feelings without putting our friendship at risk. Until then, I kept my mouth shut and focused on doing what I needed to do for the rebellion. I steeled myself, pushing thoughts of Theron from my mind.

"Yeah. Let's get to work."

Chapter 20
Theron

The sun beat down on my back as my Vaernix skittered across the black sand, leaving a trail of dust in our wake. Zerek rode beside me, his vanira clicking its mandibles in the heat. I pointed to a rock formation jutting up from the desert.

"Think that's it?"

He shook his head. "No, not big enough. And our informant said the skeleton is in a canyon."

I took a swig of water from my canteen, the liquid hot and stale in my mouth. Zerek glanced behind us at the twenty soldiers trailing at a slower pace, slumped in the saddle after days of fruitless searching. "Maybe we should go back for more men. These are flagging."

I shook my head, the desperation to find Kael pulsing through me. "No, we can't lose time. I need to hunt her down as soon as possible. I pulled out a handful of medallions. "Here. This will help them."

I wore more alloys and earthborn metal than I ever had before, piling it onto my body. Only sympathy for Vaernix made me stay at a reasonable amount.

"Why are you so determined to get her back?" Zerek asked, his voice laced with skepticism. "She betrayed you. Tortured you."

I paused for a moment, considering my answer. She hadn't tortured me unless you count her leaving me with a cock stiff enough to tear through my breeches. And the betrayal... Well. I had a plan to get even for that. "She's a Sálfar—" I began, but Zerek cut me off.

"None of that bullshit you fed Herrath and Rae. You've been obsessed with her from the moment you saw her," he said, his tone matter-of-fact. "Why?"

I lifted a shoulder, looking off into the distance. I'd once hated the desert, but now I could appreciate its austere beauty. "At first, I was drawn to her fierceness, her strength. She didn't hide and cower like other women. And she's gorgeous." I paused, remembering how she had argued with me instead of simpering. "She was a challenge, and I liked that. But then I got to know her, to understand her. We're similar. She's had a hard life, one that I contributed to. But she understands me, and I her." I met his eye. "I know that with her, I don't have to pull back. She's more than strong enough to take anything I throw at her. She's ruthless, vengeful... and unapologetic." I smiled to myself. "Kael's everything I'd hoped to find."

Zerek raised an eyebrow. "That's not what I expected you to say."

"Did you think I was going to sing you an ode to her cunt?" I chuckled. "I could, but that's not why I want her. If I just wanted somewhere to shove my prick, I would have stayed in Athain with Tannethe."

He made a face. "I don't see how someone who betrayed you is much better than the She-snake."

"Kael had her reasons. In her position, I would have done the same." I shrugged. "She makes me want to be better. I only stood up to my family because I wanted to protect her," I continued, ignoring his skepticism. "But really, it comes down to one thing."

"What's that?"

"I need her." I closed my eyes, the memory of her face flooding my mind. "The idea of what the Vennorins would do to her if they got their hands on her..." I clenched my jaw, rage filling me.

"They'd force her to marry Trevyr and breed her like a prize mare."

My anger boiled over, and I gritted my teeth. "That's why we have to find her. The rebels know she's an elf, and it's only a matter of time before that news gets back to Athain. Everyone will try to get their hands on her."

Zerek tried to lighten the mood with a joke, "Seems like you want to get your hands on her, too."

I chuckled despite myself. "After what she did, I'm going to make her pay for it."

He raised a brow but didn't respond.

We rode on in silence, our mounts moving in sync over the shifting dunes. I couldn't stop thinking about Kael, about how she had stolen my heart even as she fought against me. I would stop at nothing to get her back. The need to find her beat within me like a drum and I knew I wouldn't rest until she was by my side.

Where she belonged.

We stopped to rest in the shade of a rocky outcropping deep into the southern desert. I leaned against the rough stone and took a breath of the hot, dry air. Grit caked my throat, and sweat ran down my back. Zerek pulled out some dried meat and passed it to me. I took a bite and chewed slowly, the salty taste making my mouth water.

One of the soldiers, a young man with red hair, wandered off to a dune to pick an Areca flower, laughing to his comrades.

"Don't touch that," I warned, my voice low as I approached him.

He gave me a look of surprise but withdrew his hand. I drew my sword and poked the flower with the tip. In a flash, the petals disappeared, and a venomous insect clamped onto my blade.

"*Sihaya*," I explained, thinking of Kael. "False flowers. Get back to the rocks. Areca smoke isn't worth losing fingers."

The soldier laughed nervously and walked back to his comrades, who ribbed him mercilessly. As we ate, I couldn't shake the feeling that something was watching us, waiting for its chance to strike.

"What's wrong?" Zerek asked.

I squinted, looking over the highlands. "I feel like we're being watched."

"Perhaps we're close."

I nodded, gesturing to a break in the rock further on. "Looks like an opening to me."

A roar echoed around us, and we scrambled to our feet, weapons in hand. A massive creature lumbered out of the shadows, its scales glimmering in the pale moonlight. Fuck. A koracuda—an armored beast that stood fourteen feet tall, with a saber-toothed maw and a tail like a giant club. Its eyes blazed with hatred as it charged straight for us.

"Scatter!" I shouted, diving out of the way. The creature's tail caught several of the soldiers off guard and sent them flying into the dunes. I ducked beneath its flailing appendage and lunged forward with my sword. The blade bit deep into its scaly hide, and it spun, its tail hitting me in the stomach with enough force to send me into the rocks. The creature howled in agony and swiped at me with its claws, missing my face by inches.

Fear radiated from my soldiers as they slashed at the beast with their swords and pikes, trying to drive it back or distract it long enough for me to land a killing blow. But the koracuda was too strong, and we were losing the fight.

"Theron!" Zerek appeared next to me, a long pike in his hands. He jabbed it into the beast's flank, causing it to shriek and turn towards him. Taking advantage of its momentary distraction, I charged forward and plunged my sword deep into its throat. A roar filled the air as it staggered back and fell to its knees, its blood staining the sand beneath our feet to a midnight black.

"Atar's hammer," I blew out a breath. "I've never seen one so big."

"Second time I heard that this week," Zerek said with a tired chuckle, and I burst out laughing. Every time I tried to stop, I'd start again until my stomach hurt.

"Gods. I'm so tired even you seem funny." He rolled his eyes and grinned as I sat down next to him. The same soldier from before was busy cutting free a scale from the magnificent beast. He reminded me of when I'd first joined the Niothe; I'd kept souvenirs of my adventures as well, so happy to be free of my mother and brother. Until the grind of the war wore me down and I stopped finding things to be amazed by. I picked up a pale stone from the dark sand and held it up to the light. It was almost clear, with iridescent white swirls with flecks of green. I slipped it into my pocket, thinking of Kael.

A chorus of howls went up in the distance—far more menacing than the first.

"For Atar's sake." Zerek groaned. "Lobaros?"

"Yeah. If we're lucky, they'll stay with the kill and leave us alone." I stood, brushing sand off my breeches. "Move out!"

The men scrambled to mount their vaniras, eager to get away before the lobaros joined us. I had come too far to give up now. Kael was out here somewhere and it was up to me to find her.... I pointed forward, leading the group into a narrow cleft in the mountains. The air grew cooler as we rode on, and the walls seemed to close in around us. We were getting close now—I could feel it in every fiber of my being. The wind whistled through the rocks and I swear I heard something calling out from behind them—like a hidden voice beckoning for help.

"Hold," I called out, bringing our line of vaniras grinding to a halt. "We'll go on foot from here."

"What's wrong?" Zerek murmured, looking over the narrow walls of the canyon.

I shook my head. "I don't like this approach. It's a funnel forcing us together where our numbers won't matter."

He nodded. "It's how I'd fortify a desert base."

"Exactly. We're close to finding their hideout, and I don't know if brute force is the best option."

"What do you suggest?"

"We'll camp here for tonight," I said, sliding off my vanira. "Zerek, take the first watch. I'm going to scout ahead."

He dipped his chin and pulled his crossbow from where he'd been carrying it on his back. The others set up camp for the night, eager for a rest. I set off at an easy pace. There was no way I could relax, and burning off this energy helped. There was something about being so close to finding Kael that made it impossible for me to stay still.

The sun had just set when I heard voices. Two sentries talking casually as they patrolled this area. I ducked into a crevice in the rocks and watched as they passed by. My heart pounded in my chest—if people were watching, then I must have been close to my destination.

I waited until their voices faded away before emerging from my hiding spot and continuing up the canyon. I kept my eyes and ears alert as I trekked through the gulch, searching for any signs of the sentries. The sky was clear and stars glittered in the night.

I followed a winding path up the side of the canyon and stumbled upon an enormous skeleton lying in pieces on the ground. It was immense—with long ribs arching outwards like curved blades jutting from its back. One massive arm was missing entirely; the skull lay on its side—the jaw lost in the pile of bones.

I watched from the shadows as one sentry walked through the bones and into a hidden crack in the canyon. His torch cast eerie shapes onto the walls, illuminating small parts of the cave at a time. I held my breath, hoping he didn't see me. He stopped for a moment and looked around, but then continued on his path.

I watched him until he disappeared down a narrow crevice underneath the ribcage, leaving me alone in the canyon. My heart beat so hard it was all I could hear. This must be it.

I had found her.

Chapter 21
Kael

Sitting among the rebels gathered around the crackling bonfire, I couldn't shake off the sense of unease that settled over me. We were celebrating tonight, the hunting team having taken down half a herd of ferelopes, and the scent of roasted meat filled my nostrils, mingling with the smoky aroma of the fire.

Even amongst the melodious laughter of the gathered crowd, I couldn't help but think of all the people who weren't present here with us. Most of them were away in Adraedor, about to storm a city with little more than hammers and picks. When we managed to steal moments of peace like these, it was always in stark contrast to what our fellow slaves were going through beyond the sand-strewn dunes.

The children, far too young to understand what was happening, ran around with smiles on their faces and laughter ringing out through the night air. The women joined in too, singing songs they had learned from generations past; melodies from before the Godsfall, when they'd worship their gods in their presence.

I sighed, leaning back against the wall, only half-listening as Gavril regaled Roza and Cithara with his tales of his hunting prowess.

Gavril gestured wide, his eyes glassy from Areca smoke. "I'd buried myself in the sand so the herd couldn't smell me—"

"Sand isn't enough to cover that up," Roza interrupted with a laugh, and Gavril covered up his heart in mock pain.

"I don't stink."

"Yes, you do." Cithara put in, her mismatched eyes squinting in confusion. "You smell like ferelope. And sweat."

Roza cackled and leaned back, sneaking a drag off a pipe that she hid as one child ran past. They'd offered me some, but after what had happened to me in the palace, the scent of it turned my stomach. At least I'd killed the bastard. And Theron had found me, saved my life... I clenched my fists, only looking up when I realized the group had quieted.

"Kael?"

"What? Sorry, I was just lost in my thoughts."

Cithara nodded. "You're thinking about him again."

I looked at her, alarmed. Fae Remnants couldn't lie and could discern truth sometimes, but they weren't mind readers. "No, I'm not."

"Lie," Cithara said in a singsong voice.

Gavril stared at me for a long moment before he waved the others off. "Give us a second."

"But I want to hear about her Elven lover—"

"Roza?"

"On it." Roza nodded and dragged Cithara away as the Fae Remnant tried to explain how she just wanted to know how the sex was.

"For Vetia's sake." He shook his head before he scooted closer to me. "What's wrong, sis?"

I swallowed hard, not sure if I wanted to tell him. But Gavril was my brother... And I needed to trust him. To believe that he and Haemir wouldn't abandon me over something like this. Not only that, I didn't want him to fear Theron.

"It's just—I have feelings for someone and I think I shouldn't."

He didn't immediately react, instead, he nodded slowly after a moment. "Why do you think you shouldn't?"

"Lots of reasons. You and Dad wouldn't approve of him."

Gavril exhaled, slouching against the wall. "Look, I know Dad can be a bit of a hard-ass. But he loves you, Kael. And if this guy makes you happy and respects you, then that is enough for us to accept him."

"Really?"

He rolled his eyes. "Of course, idiot. I may not have liked him much at first, but I can see how much he cares about you. And you're both elves, so you don't have to worry about anything there. It makes sense."

"Thanks, Gav." I put my arm around his shoulders and leaned into him, relief flooding through me. "But it's not that easy. I can't even see him without risking my life."

"What do you mean?" He asked confusedly, jerking his chin toward the dance floor. "Xadrian is right there."

"What? I wasn't talking about Xadrian." I looked over to see him dancing in a circle with Cithara and her sister, laughing as he fumbled the steps. He looked up, catching my eye, and smiled, his gaze lingering on my lips. I ducked my chin and looked back at Gavril, whose brows had drawn together.

"Then who did you mean?"

I took a deep breath, ready to tell him everything—

"Kael, care to dance?" Xadrian stopped in front of me, his hand outstretched. The firelight played over his golden skin, gilding him like the statues of the gods in Adraedor. Tonight he looked it; like women had once danced for him in the moonlight, content just to worship him.

My heart skipped a beat, a mixture of nerves and discomfort washing over me.

"Uh..." Flustered, I glanced at Gavril, whose face had darkened as he stared at me, slack-mouthed. Fuck. He'd figured it out and definitely did not approve. So much for accepting anyone I chose.

"You can't be serious?" Gavril growled, and I jumped up, grabbing Xadrian's hand.

"Come on, let's dance."

I pulled him onto the dance floor with a forced smile, fleeing before Gavril said anything else.

"Kael?"

I shook my head, catching sight of Gavril stalking away from the bonfire into the dark streets. "It's alright. Just family stuff."

His grin faltered. "Yeah. I know all about that." He pasted on another smile, his flirty facade back in place as he leaned closer to me. "I thought you might be remembering the last time we attended a dance party together."

My mind cast back to the night that Varzorn had invited Theron to the rooftop party that had begun with such sensual dancing before devolving into a night of debauchery. I'd watched Xadrian dance with another woman, unsure if he was inside her or not before Theron had claimed all of my attention. The memory of that night, my dress of pearls rolling between our bodies as I rode him... I shivered and Xadrian grinned, his eyes heavy-lidded as he gazed at me.

"No," I said, shaking off the memory and narrowing my eyes at him. "This isn't that kind of party."

He quirked an eyebrow. "We can turn this party into whatever kind you want. I'm ready to leave whenever you are," he said, his voice low and suggestive. His hand rested on my lower back and I hesitated, torn between wanting to flee into the night and telling Xadrian the truth. I decided on the latter.

"Xadrian... I just want to be friends," I breathed. "To have fun." A flash of disappointment passed through his eyes, gone in a moment. He nodded and took a step back, allowing me the space I needed. "I know that you want more. But I can't give it."

"Friends sounds good." Xadrian's eyes softened, crinkling at the corners as he smiled. "It's been a while since I had a friend."

"Me too," I admitted, peeking up at him.

"Come on. Let's dance." He grinned before leading me in a joyful dance around the crackling fire. The flickering flames illuminated the night, casting a warm glow over the gathered rebels. The rhythm of the music seeped into my veins, and I loosened up, allowing the worries that burdened my mind to drift away.

We twirled and spun, laughter bubbling from my lips as Xadrian teased me. "You call that dancing? I thought the Sálfar were known for their grace?"

"Oh, shut up." I laughed, content to let the music carry me away.

For a moment, it felt like the weight of our world had lifted, leaving only the sound of music and the pulsing beat of our feet.

The warmth of the fire seeped into my bones, and I couldn't help but smile at the sheer pleasure of being amid such camaraderie. This is what I should be fighting for. Not revenge. Not the need to prove myself. But for moments like this.

A sudden commotion erupted nearby, accompanied by a sharp shout and a chorus of screams. I turned, my heart skipping a beat as I saw Theron standing there, flanked by a contingent of his soldiers. A jolt of joy went through me before I registered his expression.

His face was twisted in rage, eyes darting between me and Xadrian.

"Attack!" Zerek commanded from beside him, rushing forward toward the fire with soldiers streaming behind him like ants.

The music cut out abruptly, and children shrieked as their mothers yelled for them to run.

"Theron, no!" I shouted, running over to scoop up the swords I'd left where I'd sat with Gavril, who was still nowhere to be seen.

I charged at the soldiers, screaming as I swung my sword at them. Roza appeared beside me, her weapons a blur as she fought. Xadrian used his magic to toss boulders at Theron's soldiers, forcing them back toward the entrance. I stabbed one in the chest before spinning with a backhand slice at the soldier who rushed in behind him. They were targeting me, careful in their strikes, but I didn't pull mine.

"KAEL!" Theron bellowed as he approached, his expression thunderous. Fuck. Once he had me, the others would go for the women and children. Roza dove in front of me, batting away Zerek's sword as I turned to look back.

"Xadrian!" I shouted, and he spun toward me, his eyes finding mine in the confusing melee. "Protect them!"

I reached for my magic and it came with barely a thought. It moved as if in slow motion, heat rushing through me and my ring, and all around me. I felt the surrounding stone, how it connected to the mountain range, how deep it ran under my feet. All of it. Connecting to the stone above, I yanked, collapsing part of the cave so that Theron's soldiers couldn't go any further into the hidden city, Xadrian's face disappearing behind a wall of stone.

"Cetena's scales," Roza breathed before Zerek charged her again. She turned her back to mine, and I did the same, guarding her as Theron's soldiers surrounded us. Theron stood there, his bronze eyes flashing in anger. He wore a suit of armor I'd never seen before, adorned with intricate symbols and patterns of silver and gold. His black hair was tied back, pieces around his face falling loose. He radiated strength... power. The need to dominate him, to fight him until he proved strong enough to take me, filled me and I had to shake my head to clear it. Not the time.

"How could you?" I growled. "There are women and children here."

He stepped forward, each footstep echoing through the cave like thunderclaps. "You thought you could come here and do whatever you wanted?" His eyes blazed as they locked on my hand. "Wear his ring?"

"Oh, this ring?" I shot him a lewd hand gesture that flashed it before murmuring to Roza. "On my move, break right. I'll meet you at the spring." She tapped me once in acknowledgment. "This is what I can do with it."

I pulled more magic, throwing a boulder from the side and clearing a path for Roza as it bowled over Theron's men. She darted forward, and Zerek cursed and charged after her.

Theron was magnificent in the flickering firelight, his dark hair and bronze eyes standing out against the metal of his armor. A low rumble escaped his throat, his attention never wavering. "I'm not leaving here without you, Kael."

"You want me? Come and take me." I snarled, smacking my swords against each other as he charged.

His sword met mine, the jarring force of it sending vibrations up my arm, sparks flying between us as we clashed in a dance of blades. The men around us paused, the clang reverberating through the cave like a war call. We circled each other, swords drawn and glinting in the light from the fire. He was testing me—seeing how far I'd go—but I had no intention of giving in to him.

He moved easily despite the bulk of his armor, ducking and dodging each blow I meted out. I watched as he parried each attack with practiced ease, muscles rippling across his body as he struck back with more strength than I possessed.

I pulled my magic, throwing a handful of rocks at him that bounced off his armor. He growled, "That's a dirty trick."

"I thought you liked it dirty," I shot back, smirking.

I struck, and he blocked, putting me on the defensive. He pushed forward, and I tripped, looking down to find one of the guards on patrol tonight bound and gagged. Theron used my distraction, his sword pressing against my neck as he leaned in close, his hard armor digging into my skin.

"YOU. ARE. MINE," he growled, ripping Xadrian's ring from my finger and throwing it into the sand. He towered over me, looming like a giant in the dim light of the cave. My breathing quickened, and I clenched my thighs together as his eyes bored into mine.

He moved closer until his lips nearly touched mine. "You won't escape me this time," he breathed before stepping back, binding my hands tightly with rope from one of his guards.

My heart pounded in my chest as I glared at him. I could feel the anger radiating off of him, and I knew that if he could have taken me then, he would have done it with a vengeance.

And I would have loved every second.

Swearing drew my attention, and I turned to see Roza struggling as Zerek bound her hands, throwing her head back and smashing his nose.

"Let her go," I demanded. "It's me you want. I'll go with you and I won't fight anymore if you let Roza go."

He gripped me by the hair, tipping my eyes up to meet mine. "As if I'd believe a word that comes out of your traitorous mouth. You were in league with Xadrian all this time." He spat. "I won't be fooled by you ever again."

I shook my head. "It wasn't like that—"

"Enough," he growled, forcing a length of leather between my teeth. "Your faithless heart will be your undoing, Kaella."

My shouts were muffled as he tightened the strap, and I glared at him. He grabbed my swords from the ground and strapped them onto his back with practiced ease.

"Finally, I got these back where they belong." He smirked as he regarded me.

"Just like you."

Chapter 22

Kael

I glared at Theron as he spoke to his men, checking over his shoulder.

"Injuries?"

"We have nine injured, no deaths," Zerek answered, stepping aside as Roza thrashed, trying to trip him. "Nothing that can't be healed."

"Good. Let's move out." He turned back to me, his eyes hard. "We'll need to put distance between us and Xadrian when he comes after her."

Theron looked like he hadn't slept since I'd last seen him, his bronze gaze dull with exhaustion and his face lined with weariness. He was covered in alloys; strips of pewter and bronze to keep him moving. Despite this, he still looked angry as he wrapped an arm around me and swept me up into his arms, easily carrying me even with the weight of his armor.

I yelped when he pressed me against his hard chest plate and he relented, positioning me so I wasn't in pain anymore before scowling and looking away.

Roza's muffled curses grew louder as Zerek picked her up. She kicked him once before he threw her over his shoulder, holding her behind her knees.

"If you keep fighting me, I'll drop you," he hissed, but it did nothing to cow Roza and I watched as she continued to squirm, guilt filling my chest. It was my fault Roza was here.

Zerek followed close behind us, shooting a glance toward the sentries tied up and laying near the entrance. "What should we do about them?" He asked as Theron kept walking without breaking stride.

"Leave them." He growled, looking back at Zerek and adjusting his grip on me slightly as if to reassure himself that I was still there.

The sky was dark and the air was cold against my skin as we moved through the canyon. The only sound was our footsteps and the occasional whisper of 'Sálfar' between Theron's men. His breath fanned over my neck, his heart beating steadily against my back, and it somehow made me feel a little more secure despite being bound.

His group raced through the darkness. Competent soldiers who'd been trained for years in the Niothe, no doubt. And now they knew where our primary base was. A distant howl filled the night air, and a chill skittered down my spine; something was hunting us out here in the dark. I shivered, thoughts of Gavril filling my mind as I prayed he was still safe.

Theron seemed to sense my unease and tightened his grip on me, pushing even faster toward wherever he was taking us. Finally, after what felt like an hour, we reached our destination—a small clearing where several vaniras had been tethered to hastily erected posts.

"We ride until the sun is high, then we'll break for camp. I want to be in Adraedor by nightfall tomorrow."

His soldiers grunted in agreement, crawling onto their vaniras with relieved sighs. The men looked almost as tired as Theron. He'd been pushing them hard, no doubt.

Theron mounted his vanira and pulled me up in front of him before taking off again. I still disliked riding on the beast, but it was a strange comfort being so close to him, feeling his nearness despite the armor separating us. The sense of homesickness I'd had since his escape fled and I finally relaxed. His breath hitched as I leaned back into him, settling in for a long ride.

"Kael." Theron's voice woke me from my doze and I opened my eyes to see the contingent had stopped. We had reached a rocky mesa with small caves scattered about.

The men were already setting up camp, and in no time tents had popped up around us with practiced ease as others claimed caves. Theron lowered me to my feet and I stretched as best as I could with my hands bound. I turned in time to see Roza making a run for it the moment her feet hit the sand.

"Fucking hells," Zerek swore before sprinting after her and tackling her. She rolled like a wild beast trying to free herself. He managed to pin her legs, then tied them as well. "At this rate, I'll have to tie you to a rock."

Roza's muffled swears were still discernible when she told him to go fuck himself. He looked at her with an amused expression, shaking his head before standing and tugging her to join him and the others in setting up camp. "Up you get, you little sea wasp."

She glared at him as he scooped her into his arms once more.

"Come on," Theron growled, guiding me toward the largest cave that he'd claimed for himself. Roza shot me a look of pity as I followed him into the shadows, no doubt believing the worse.

Once inside, Theron gestured for me to sit down on the bedroll he'd placed against the wall. I watched as he began taking off his armor, more mesmerized by him than I wanted to admit. His large, capable hands moved with practiced ease around the straps and buckles, slowly revealing his muscled frame beneath. My breath caught in my throat as he removed the last of it, standing shirtless in front of me—all smooth skin and powerful muscles.

He looked at me then, eyes blazing with determination and something else that made my heart flutter in my chest. He noticed me staring, and I brought my hands to my mouth to remove my gag.

Theron glared, his bronze gaze flashing. "Leave it. I don't want to hear any more of your lies."

I narrowed my eyes at him and didn't stop trying to pull it free. My nail scratched my cheek, and he hissed, stilling my movements.

"Stop."

He stepped closer and reached down to untie my gag, his fingers brushing against my neck as he untied it. His gaze softened for a moment before hardening again before he tossed me a canteen. I took a grateful swig before speaking, the warm water soothing my dry throat.

"What the hell, Theron?" I growled, and his eyes widened. "I told you I wouldn't fight if you left Roza. You didn't have to bring her into this."

"And I'm supposed to believe you?" He snarled. "All you've done since I met you is a lie. I can't trust a word you say."

"That was my mission—" I began, and he cut me off.

"How long have you been fucking Xadrian?" He growled, invading my space. His citrus and leather scent filled my nose, and I had to fight not to lean into him again.

I rolled my eyes. "Seriously? It's not like that."

Theron yanked me to my feet and pulled me to him. His hand burrowed into my hair before it tightened as he tipped my head back, exposing my throat. "Then what is it like? You've been with him for months, haven't you? Both of you playing me like a fool?"

"No!" I protested, shaking my head again. "I swear I haven't had sex with Xadrian or anyone else since you. Which I'm regretting now since you're being a jackass." He raised a brow, and I continued. "I didn't meet Xadrian until the palace. And I'm not fucking him, so you can calm the hell down."

"Stop treating me like an idiot, Kael," Theron growled, his hand spasming in my hair. "I saw the way he looked at you. How you smiled at him when you were dancing."

Theron's face grew dark and his jaw clenched as if he were trying to contain his fury. He stepped away from me and turned his back to hide the emotion on his face, but I could still feel the jealousy radiating from him.

"I was smiling because I was happy, Theron. I'd just told him I wasn't interested in him that way and he'd agreed to be friends. It was just a dance." I let out a breath, waiting for his response.

He shook his head. "It wasn't for him." He stepped closer, invading my space. "You want me to believe that he never touched you?" His voice roughened as he leaned closer, his lips whispering over my skin. "That he didn't put his hands on what's mine?"

"I don't belong to you."

"You do." His eyes bored into mine. "Every sigh of pleasure, every moan that comes out of your mouth belongs to me." He pushed me up against the wall of the cave, the length of his erection pressing into my stomach. "So tell me, Kaella, did he take what's mine?"

I glared up at him. "He kissed me once." His gaze burned into me, and my heart raced in anticipation. "But he took nothing that's yours. I was silent before I stepped away from him because he isn't the man that I want."

Theron's gaze softened, and he pressed his forehead to mine. His hand moved to my neck, caressing the skin there before he gripped my throat. He didn't tighten his hand, but the threat was there.

"I wish I could believe you… but his ring on your finger says differently." His lips firmed into a thin line as he stepped back from me, his gaze heavy.

My mouth fell open. "Are you fucking kidding me?" I pushed away from the wall. "You attack a compound full of women and children and you're angry at *me*? You accuse me of being unfaithful to you?"

"They were rebels—"

"So am I!" I shouted as I raised my chin and took another step closer, searching his face. "This isn't about you and me at all, is it?"

He blinked as if he hadn't expected me to be so angry. "What are you talking about?"

I cut him off, my voice rising with each word. "You didn't come after me to steal me away for yourself. You were coming here to make sure no one else did!"

I closed my eyes, my throat tightening with emotion. "I heard your men discussing finding the 'Sálfar' before anyone else did," I snapped. Theron's jaw tensed, but he said nothing. He wanted me, not for who I am, but for what I could do. I shook my head in disbelief. "If there's a fool in this room, it's me."

He wanted me so that no one else could use my power against him. Tears welled up in my eyes and I retreated from him.

"Kael—"

I turned away, taking deep breaths as I willed my tears not to fall. I'd already cried for him too much.

"*Sihaya*," he growled, pulling me toward him. "Let me remind you of something you seem to have forgotten." He crowded me, pressing his body against mine. "That no matter where you go, no matter what you do. I will always come for you."

His lips crashed down onto mine. The kiss was hard and unforgiving—I could taste the anger on his tongue. Our teeth clattered against one another as our tongues intertwined in a frantic dance. I wanted to pull away but couldn't bring myself to do it, wanting him too much.

Theron pulled back, panting heavily as he searched my eyes. "You are mine," he growled. "And I won't let anyone else take you away from me." His hands moved possessively over my body, sending shivers of pleasure through me despite my anger at him. I trembled beneath his touch and he smiled before claiming my lips again in a desperate kiss that promised pleasure and punishment in equal measure.

No matter how much I wanted to deny it, I was his. No one else would ever have my heart the way he did.

Theron leaned down and kissed my neck, the warmth of his lips sending a thrill through me. His hands moved up to my shirt and with one tug, he tore it open, revealing my breasts. "They're perfect," he murmured, his voice full of awe as he licked and caressed each nipple with his tongue as if to make up for how Rhazien had treated them before. "So much better than Carita's creations."

"Theron." My back arched off the bed involuntarily, and a moan escaped my lips.

He chuckled against my skin before pushing me down onto the bed and pinning my hands above my head. His lips found mine again, possessiveness making his movements rough. I gasped as his mouth moved away from mine and down my neck, his teeth grazing my sensitive skin.

His fingers slid down my stomach, teasing and tantalizing me as they moved lower.

He cupped my sex, tipping my head back, so I had to meet his eye. "This is mine," he growled as he dipped his finger into my wetness.

I gasped in pleasure as he found my clit. He moved in circles, each stroke bringing me closer and closer to orgasm before pausing.

My eyes flew open as I looked up at him in confusion. He smirked at me before leaning down and whispering into my ear, "Did you really think I wouldn't punish you for betraying me?"

My cheeks flushed with anger and arousal as I realized what he meant. "You call this punishment?" I panted, trying and failing to hide the quiver in my voice. "I don't care. Do whatever you want."

He laughed at my defiance before pressing his lips against mine again. His fingertips moved lower, slipping inside me as he began to move them in and out of me. His voice deepened as he whispered against my lips, "So tell me, Kaella, do you care when I do this?"

He crooked his fingers inside me, rubbing that spot that made my legs jerk.

"N—no." I met his gaze and refused to look away as he pressed my clit with his thumb. "Barely feel anything."

A smirk appeared on his face as he increased the pressure, my body writhing beneath him. I gasped and moaned as waves of pleasure began to wash over me once more. I was so close...

"Do you want me to let you come?" He asked, a mischievous glint in his eyes.

My breath came out in shallow pants as I shook my head. "No."

He laughed before increasing the pressure, sending shocks of bliss through my entire body. I bit my lip to keep from screaming out in pleasure as he continued to tease me with cruel precision, pulling back each time I nearly crested.

"You can beg for it, Kael," he murmured against my skin before pressing a soft kiss against my lips. "But you won't get it until you accept you are mine."

I growled, fighting my hips as they rolled of their own volition.

"Bring it on."

Chapter 23
Theron

Kael's body shook as I teased her, sweat glistening on her skin. Not from the sun beating down on us, but from the tortuous pleasure I'd been inflicting on her for hours. I'd pleasured her in the cave, bringing her close to orgasm over and over again, only for her to refuse me, too stubborn to beg. She heaved a sigh of relief when I'd said it was time to leave, not realizing I had no intention of stopping until she gave in to me.

Her legs shivered, spread wide on Vaernix's back, and pressed against mine. I traced the seam of her cunt, teasing her swollen, delicate flesh as I had been for hours as we traveled.

I dragged my teeth over her neck and she groaned, too lost in need to school her reactions.

"Just tell me you're mine, *Sihaya*. And I'll let you come." She rolled her hips, trying to grind against my hand and I tsked. "Ah, ah. Not without permission."

Kael moaned and shook her head, determined not to give in. She kept her eyes focused on the horizon, where Adraedor could be seen coming closer with every minute. Her lips were set in a thin line and she refused to look at me despite my relentless teasing.

The soldiers had been following us since the cave, keeping their distance but never leaving our sight. I ordered them forward, and they rode their vaniras up the mountain, rather than carrying on to the city walls. Kael tensed when they passed by but she made no sound even as I continued to stroke and tease her body with my hands and lips.

The sun was setting now, casting deep shadows over the surrounding landscape. Kael's body trembled beneath me as I increased the pressure of my touch, running my fingers along her inner thighs until she gasped with pleasure even as her resolve remained strong. My cock was an iron rod pressing into her back, aching for release.

But I wouldn't stop until she begged, no matter how hard it might be for both of us.

She shuddered when I removed my hand from her breeches to grasp the reins as Vaernix followed Zerek's mount, taking up the rear position.

"Sneaking into your own city," Kael taunted breathlessly, and I nipped her neck.

"If you still have enough energy to sass me, then you'll have enough to ride me when we get home, *Sihaya*." She looked over her shoulder at me, glaring, and I smirked. The vanira traversed the mountain easily and before long, we'd descended into the courtyard.

The soldiers had already dismounted and gathered around, awaiting orders. I signaled for them to remain at attention as I reached for Kael and helped her down from the vanira. Her legs wobbled unsteadily, but she managed to stand on her own, though she was still shaking from the pleasure I'd denied her.

I smirked at her slight blush before turning to address my men. "Take care of your vanira, then get some rest," I ordered. "We will take back this city soon enough."

Zerek moved forward, ready to lead Roza away to the dungeon, but I stopped him with a hand on his shoulder. "No," I said firmly. "Kael's friend stays with us in the palace."

He glanced at me, incredulous. "Do you think that's a good idea? She's practically feral."

Roza lunged forward to take a swing at him. He deflected easily and held up his hands, gesturing towards her in exasperation. "See?"

"Perhaps she needs a muzzle," I suggested, and Kael jabbed an elbow into my ribs.

She stepped between us, her eyes pleading with the angry Sirin Remnant. "Please trust me," she whispered. "You'll be safe in the palace. I can protect you there."

Roza's eyes darted between me and Zerek. "I'm not fucking either of you."

Zerek snorted. "As if I'd be interested in a sea whip like you. Your cunt is probably poisonous."

Roza snapped back at him, but I tuned it out, too focused on Kael's expression. She looked... jealous. A spark of hope lit in me. Seeing her with Xadrian had snapped something inside of me and I'd behaved... badly. The idea of him touching her, the way she smiled at him, made red pulse around the edges of my vision. She'd seemed like she was telling the truth when she said that she didn't have feelings for him, but then again, she was a masterful liar. How was I to know how she truly felt if I couldn't trust her words? But maybe I could trust her reactions... I led her inside, a vague plan forming. Something settled into place inside of me when she was back in my space.

Where she belonged.

We stepped into the palace, and my shoulders relaxed as we entered the internal courtyard. It was huge, filled with lush gardens and a large pool in its center. Gilded fountains sprouted from the walls, dotting the landscape with sparkling droplets of water that caught the light of the setting sun. The air was heavy with humidity and after so many days spent in the desert heat, I could feel it settle into my skin like a balm.

Plants from Athain filled the garden, flowers cascading over white stone pathways that ran throughout the courtyard. Ornate sculptures depicting the gods and goddesses, gleaming under their protective coating of gold leaf, dotted the space.

The pool in the center was illuminated by a ring of torches around its edges, reflecting off its surface like tiny stars against a dark sky. Its waters sparkled blue in the evening light, inviting us closer to take a dip from our long journey across the restless sands.

Raenisa and Herrath approached, their expressions stormy. While they had every right to be mad at me for putting them in this position, their glares were directed at Kael, who stood beside me, squaring her shoulders as if preparing for a fight. Roza watched them approach, silent and wary.

"Thank Atar, you're back. Things have been insane here and Tavador is no help." Raenisa started without a preamble.

Herrath glared at her. "Seriously Raenisa? I've been doing just as much as you."

"Yeah, right. In between playing grabass with Mirijana and chatting on the speaking stones." Raenisa snorted, and Herrath shot her an exasperated look before turning back to me.

"The Vennorins have been asking a lot of questions and I don't know how much longer I can hold them off from coming here."

Herrath ran a hand through his hair, mussing a few hairs out of place that he immediately fixed. "And the Empress has sent you messages daily. She awaits your response."

Great.

I blew out a breath. "I'll handle that later. What news do you have, Rae?"

"We've been holding down the rebellion, but the rebels are gaining ground," she said grimly. "It's gotten harder to push them back. They have this big fucking Inferi Remnant leading them now."

"Vetia's horns," I swore.

Roza smirked, sharing a glance with Kael, who huffed a laugh. Raenisa saw it and scowled. "What's so funny?"

Roza sneered at her, tossing her shorn magenta hair. "That's Kael's father. Good luck beating him, because once he finds out she's in the palace, nothing will stop him from breaking through those walls."

Herrath looked alarmed at the suggestion, but before he could respond, Raenisa spun around to face me. "One back-talking concubine isn't enough? You had to get another one?"

Kael growled under her breath beside me, and I had to fight off a grin. "She's not a concubine. She's a—"

"Hostage." The Sirin Remnant interrupted me and I shrugged.

"I was going to say, 'guest.'"

"Guests can leave," she snarled at me, and Zerek stepped between us.

"I'll take her upstairs and get her settled."

"I'm not an infant to settle," she snapped, sharing a look with Kael as he pulled her away.

I watched them go before turning back to the others. Raenisa was looking at Kael with a mixture of anger and betrayal, but Herrath's expression was cold. Calculating. I tugged Kael to me before Raenisa could start into her.

"I need to bathe. Can you have Mirijana send up some food, Rae?"

"You should have Herrath do it since he's with her all the time." Raenisa raised a brow.

Herrath rolled his eyes. "I'll do it. Glad to have you back, Theron."

I clasped him on the arm before he left, ignoring Raenisa's sour look. "Come on, Kael."

"I wanted to go over battle plans—" Raenisa began, and I cut her off.

"Tomorrow. I'll be busy tonight."

Kael stiffened beside me, glaring at me, and I grinned at her. If she thought I was finished with her, she was mistaken. Raenisa grumbled about idiotic men as she stomped off, no doubt to terrorize one of my soldiers.

"Come on." I took her small hand in mine, leading her to my suite.

As we entered my set of rooms, Kael let out a sigh, her tense posture relaxing. She ran a finger along one tapestry as she looked around and I couldn't help but notice how much more alive this room felt with her here. It was almost like being reunited with a part of myself—something that had been missing for so long was now complete once again.

I set my swords down on the side table and watched as Kael's gaze drifted back to them. "Don't even think about touching my swords again."

"You mean *my* swords."

A smile tugged at my lips. I'd missed playing these games with her.

I moved towards the bathing tub, unbuttoning my tunic as I went. "Come on. Let's take a bath."

Stepping over to the tub that had been prepared for me, I undressed, removing my clothing slowly and setting them aside to be washed. I watched her out of the corner of my eye, gauging her reaction. Was there a spark in her eyes, or had she become immune to my body? Either way, I would have to try harder if I wanted to see if Kael had true feelings for me.

I stepped into the steaming water and beckoned to her. "Join me."

Kael held up her hands to show that she was still bound. "I can't."

Motioning her closer, I held her gaze as I untied her, unable to decipher anything in those emerald depths. She stripped off her clothes, her curves supple and dangerous. She wasn't some soft-bodied concubine. No, she was a warrior, with proud shoulders and strong thighs, and all the more attractive for it. I sucked in a breath as she joined me in the water, sinking down until the warm liquid engulfed her body.

Her skin glowed like pearls in the candlelight, sending a wave of desire through me. She groaned as she washed her hair, taking time to scrub every inch of herself as if she hadn't bathed in weeks.

"Wash me," I commanded, and she huffed a laugh.

"This seems familiar." She raised a brow in challenge and I sent her a lazy grin, one that I knew irritated her.

Her fingertips were soft as they moved across my body, tracing lazy circles around my muscles as if mapping them out. Every stroke sent sparks of pleasure coursing through my veins like wildfire. My erection bobbed between us, stiff and aching each time she brushed it. She eyed it as if debating whether or not to take me in hand.

I pulled her closer, pressing myself against her slick body as I murmured in her ear, "Do you want to touch me, *Sihaya?*" She shivered, her skin prickling against mine, and I continued. "I seem to remember you leaving me aching and unfinished."

Kael leaned back and looked up at me with a smirk. "Couldn't find someone else to take care of it?"

I let out a low chuckle. "What if I did?"

Her eyes flashed white, with no pupil or iris visible anymore. Her hand darted out and tightened on my cock almost to the point of pain.

"Mine," she growled before kissing me hungrily. Claiming me. I had an answer to whether or not I could make Kael jealous. *Gods almighty.*

She stroked me in time with the movements of our tongues and I shuddered, lost in the pleasure. It felt like coming home—like I had been searching for something for so long, only to find it here in Kael's arms. She broke away from the kiss and backed up, smirking as she left me with a cock teetering on the abyss of pleasure.

Again.

"Kael…"

"Turnabout is fair play." She smirked. "You tortured me for hours. Now it's your turn."

I groaned, my cock throbbing in anticipation. "Is that right, *Sihaya*?"

She bit her lip, her pupils blown wide. "Yes."

"There's a problem with your plan, Kaella." I pulled her closer, my breath ghosting over her skin. "Because I can finish myself." She sucked in a breath and I continued. "While you watch."

I took my cock in hand and stroked it, groaning as she watched me with wide eyes. I wanted her to watch, wanted her to see just how she made me feel.

"Do you know what I did in that cave?" I murmured, pulling her to my side and whispering into her hair. "How I kept myself sane?"

She shook her head without moving her eyes from my cock as I stroked it, running my thumb over the head. "No."

"I imagined everything I'd do to you once I escaped." I ran my teeth over the tip of her ear, and she shuddered, her nipples hardening. "How I'd fuck your perfect mouth, pushing deep into your throat." She gasped, grinding against me. "You'd suck down every drop of my seed as I came, begging me for more."

She moaned along with each stroke of my hand, rubbing her body against mine. "Theron..."

"I'd fuck you next, out on the balcony for all to see. Until you screamed my name over the dunes." My breath stuttered out of me as her hand joined mine, stroking me faster. "So everyone in this godsdamn city knows you're mine."

"Gods yes," she moaned, taking over for me and moving her hand faster.

"Fuck." I groaned as her grip tightened. My orgasm ripped through me, exploding in a million stars behind my eyelids as my cock jerked in her hand. I kissed her, moaning as she kept stroking, wringing every drop of seed from me. "*Sihaya.*"

She pulled away, her eyes soft as she searched my face. I tilted her face up, brushing my lips over hers. "Come here."

I stood, my cock in her face before I stepped out of the water and slung a towel around my waist. Exhaustion tugged at me now that I'd removed all of my alloys. "Time for bed."

She narrowed her eyes on me. "So you can torture me more? No thanks."

"No. Just rest," I said softly, guiding her out of the tub and handing her a towel. "I haven't slept well since the night I held you in the cave."

I wanted—no, needed—her in my arms again, just to feel secure once more.

"Oh." Standing before me with water dripping from her body, she looked so vulnerable that I growled. "Me either."

I took her hand in mine to lead her to the bedroom, running my thumb over where Xadrian's ring had sat on her finger. She might have thought it was only a gift for her magic, but I knew better. I'd almost lost her once; I wouldn't let some half-rate pretty boy take her from me again.

"We should get some sleep," she whispered, turning away from me and padding off towards the bedchamber.

I watched her go, still angry about Xadrian but mostly afraid that I would lose her again somehow—tonight or tomorrow or in the days to come when I crushed the rebellion. No matter what I did, I'd lose her...

Never.

Stalking across the room to the weapons rack, I grabbed a chain and manacles. I didn't care if she hated me. I wouldn't lose her again.

Not when I'd just gotten her back.

Chapter 24
Kael

I woke to Theron's face buried between my legs, nearly on the verge of orgasm. I shook, my thighs tightening around his ears.

"Theron," I moaned, arching into his touch as his hand found my breast, tweaking my nipple and causing me to cry out. "Are you going to let me come this time?" I asked, already breathless with anticipation.

He looked up at me, his eyes glittering. "Yes," he said, taking my hand in his and planting soft kisses along my knuckles to the manacle that encircled my wrist. He wasn't angry anymore. This was the same Theron as before, playful and teasing, as if by having me physically bound to him something inside him was finally secure.

I'd have to convince him to untie me soon, but I was too lost in lust to bother now.

I gasped as his tongue found the spot that sent sparks of pleasure through me and I was on the brink of orgasm, my hips thrusting towards him instinctively. After so many hours of torture yesterday, my body was desperate for release. I cried out as I reached the peak, shaking with pleasure as I came undone.

He moved up my body and entered me in one smooth motion, my core still pulsing as I clenched his length.

"*Sihaya,*" he groaned, burying his face in the crook of my neck.

He began to thrust slowly, letting me adjust to his size, then faster and harder until he was pounding into me. He unleashed all of his anger on my body and I took it, savoring his strength as he slammed into me.

"Gods, yes. Theron."

His breathing grew ragged. "You feel how this perfect cunt takes me?" He drove his cock home, grinding against my sensitive clit and making me cry out. Every inch of him throbbed inside me and a sob escaped me—it was almost too much after his torture yesterday. All of my nerves were on fire. "I'm going to fuck you until your cunt curves to my cock. Until you can't even remember what it felt like to have another man inside you. Because you're *mine.*"

My climax built again, coursing through my veins, drawing ever closer. Theron's body shuddered as I clenched around him and he let out an animalistic growl that sent a thrill through me. A wave of pleasure crashed over me as we reached the peak together. Theron's length jerked deep inside me, hot ropes of seed filling me as I screamed his name. Pleasure so intense it was almost pain filled me and I arched off the bed, my breasts rubbing against his sweat-slicked skin.

"Theron," I moaned as he peppered kisses over my face as if apologizing for his ferocity. His cock shifted inside of me, still hard as our combined spend dripped down my thighs.

"I need you again," he growled, and I bit my lip, a shiver going through me as my nipples hardened.

He pulled out and flipped me over onto my hands and knees. I arched my back, offering myself to him. He entered me from behind, feeling even bigger in this position, and I moaned.

My moan turned into a yelp as a finger brushed my puckered flesh, rubbing our combined wetness into my asshole.

"Theron?" I wasn't sure what I thought about him taking me there. I tensed up, but his hand was gentle on my skin, slowly circling my hole before dipping inside in time with his steady strokes.

"Relax, *Sihaya*," he murmured as he gently stretched me open with his finger before sliding in two of them. "I'll always take care of you."

I groaned, the sharp ache morphing to pleasure as he stroked into me. "So full."

He thrust them in a circular motion until I relaxed completely around him.

"Good girl," he breathed, and I growled, making him laugh.

He spread his fingers inside of me and I gasped, unused to the burn as he added another finger.

I shook my head, unsure I could handle more. "It's too much."

He paused, reaching to stroke my clit, running his fingers around my opening, feeling how he stretched me, how we were connected, his cock pulsing inside of me.

"You can take it. You're mine, Kael."

He rotated his hand, pressing harder as he moved his fingers in and out of me. He continued, accustoming me to it, until my muscles no longer fought him and pleasure sparked in me, deeper and darker than before. I tightened around him, my body shaking as sweat beaded my forehead before he stopped. He kissed the back of my neck and pulled out, turning me so I laid my back again.

"Theron?"

Lifting my legs, he spread them wide and lined up his cock at my asshole.

I gasped when the head pressed against my opening, and he smiled down at me.

"I'm going to claim every inch of you," he growled before pushing slowly inside. I shuddered as he stretched me, the ring of muscle burning as he invaded me.

"You're too big," I moaned, and he pressed his thumb against my clit, rubbing in soft circles. Slowly, inch by inch, he slid deeper inside me until I gasped for breath. The sensation of invasion, of *surrender*, shook me and my eyes locked on his, unable to look away as he seated himself fully, claiming me in a way no one else ever had.

"You're so fucking tight, *Sihaya*," he groaned,

His thrusts were slow and deep, allowing the pleasure to build. He murmured soft words, praising me as he thrust harder, until it was too much for me to take and stars began exploding behind my eyes with every movement of his hips. He lifted my leg onto his shoulder and I thrashed, nearly wild with the riot of sensation. Every touch was magnified, erotic in a way I'd never experienced. He dragged his teeth over the arch of my foot and I shuddered.

"Theron, *please*." I didn't care that I was begging. It was too much. My body tightened, all of my muscles straining for release. Theron's breath was ragged as thrust faster, his cock swelling impossibly inside of me until I thought I'd burst. He slammed into me with a shout and I broke, waves of bliss radiating from my core as I keened his name. My vision went white, and he groaned as he came, filling my ass with hot spurts of his seed. I floated in a sea of pleasure, unaware that I'd lost my hearing until it returned, Theron murmuring praises as he trailed kisses over me. His cock was still deep inside me, and it pulsed in time with my heart.

He finally pulled out, and I felt a strange emptiness as he stood. He stared down at me, his eyes dark with emotion as he unhooked the chain from the bed frame, but not my wrist. "Come."

I looked up at him questioningly as he held my chain.

"Theron?"

But he merely raised an eyebrow before scooping me into his arms and carrying me to the tub. I groaned when he laid me into the water; the heat soothing the ache from our lovemaking.

"Gods, I missed this tub," I said as he slipped into the water behind me, drawing me into his arms.

"Only the tub?" He breathed into my ear, letting his lips ghost over the sensitive tip.

"Of course not." I waited for a beat before adding. "I missed the food, too."

He laughed, the sound echoing in his chest as he pulled me closer. "I'll have to work harder then."

He poured soap into his hands and massaged it into my hair, his clever fingers gentle as he worked it into a lather. He bathed me like he was worshiping my body; moving over my skin, exploring every curve of my body.

When I was clean, he dried me off, wrapping the towel around me, before washing himself.

"Come here," he sat on the couch, pulling me onto his lap. He grabbed a piece of melon from the tray, lifting it to my mouth and waiting for me to take a bite.

I chewed slowly, savoring the sweet taste as he fed me.

"If you unchained me, then I'd be able to feed myself."

He shook his head. "I can't let you move freely around the castle."

"But why did you capture me if you don't trust me?"

"The same reason they kept me in chains when I was in that cave." He held my gaze. "It doesn't matter how we may feel about each other to those around us." I sucked in a breath. Was he going to tell me he loved me again? I didn't know how I'd react if he did. I'd never said that to anyone but family... "They don't trust you. And to be honest, I don't know what you'll do."

"This is different than when you were captured," I tried to reason with him. "I had to answer to Teodosija and Haemir." I moved to my knees, placing my hands on his bare chest, ignoring how his towel was slung low. "You're in charge here now. Not your brother. You can make different choices."

"What choices?" He grumbled, biting into a pastry. "All I've been doing since you killed Rhazien is reacting."

"You could join with rebellion," I said slowly, gauging his reaction. His body tensed beneath my hands. "You hate your mother, and you don't want to be the next emperor. We could be on the same side together—standing shoulder to shoulder—"

"Kael. Stop." He ran his hand through his hair. "The rebellion will never win. There's a reason we've conquered half of Maeoris, and it's not just because we're stronger, faster." He leaned forward, capturing my gaze. "We're trained and well-equipped, with secure supply lines. Say the rebellion manages to retake

Adraedor. You may have a chance of holding the city. It has sturdy walls, difficult terrain to traverse with an army, no resources for an army to utilize. But that's just one city. There's no way you can beat the Niothe."

He was echoing Haemir's worries about what would happen to the rebellion once Teodosija had Adraedor. Too many supplies were shipped in for us to support the entire population on what we gathered... I shook my head. "That's why we need your help. You could train us. Teach us how to defeat your mother, so you never have to be under her thumb again." I paused before. "Please. We need you. *I* need you."

"*Sihaya*..." His brows drew together, and he buried his fingers in my hair, his thumb brushing my cheek. "I—"

The door opened, cutting him off as Raenisa came in, closely followed by the other Harvestmen and Roza, who wore chains similar to mine.

"Enough fucking. We need to talk about the mission." Raenisa stomped into the room as if she owned it. I'd once thought it a sign that maybe Theron wasn't a monster given his easy friendship with the woman, but now I found the lack of privacy irritating.

"For Atar's sake, Rae." He growled, wrapping my towel more securely around me. "You need to start knocking."

"Or you could fuck in the bedroom like normal people," she countered, and Zerek chuckled. "Some of us couldn't enjoy breakfast because of all the screaming."

I let my hands fall from his chest, my cheeks burning. Roza was staring daggers at me. To her, I'd betrayed our people by being with Theron. There was no more hiding behind my mission, or pretending. The truth was written all over my body.

"I'm going to get dressed," I muttered, standing carefully to keep my towel from falling.

"Why bother?" Roza sneered. "You're his whore. You might as well look the part."

I stilled, my hands balling into fists, but before I could say anything, Theron beat me to it.

"She's not anyone's whore," He growled, stepping closer to me.

"Yeah, right," Roza spat. "The entire castle could hear you two." She narrowed her eyes at me. "I fucking knew that you were helping him in the caves. You let him go and then sold us out so you could get back to riding his prick."

"Fuck you, Roza," I snarled, making towards her. I didn't care that both our hands were bound. I'd still kick her ass. "You don't know shit."

"Ah ah ah." Raenisa stepped between us, holding her hand out to prevent me from advancing. "As much as I'd love to see you two wrestling—preferably with oil all over you—we have more important things to deal with right now."

"Like killing my dad?" I threw at her and she shrugged.

"If he's part of the rebellion..."

I turned to Theron. "You can't seriously be thinking about hurting Haemir. He's a good man who is doing the right thing."

"Kael—" He began before Roza cut him off with a derisive laugh.

"You dumb bitch. Do you think that'll stop them? You're nothing to them."

"Careful," Theron growled, glaring at Roza.

"I'm not afraid of you." She spat back, but there was a quaver in her voice that gave her away.

"You should be."

Zerek stepped between them. "Sorry, Theron. I didn't want to leave her in my suite. She'd be liable to kill the servants."

"As if I'd hurt slaves." Roza sniffed, turning up her nose. "I won't stoop to Kael's level."

"I swear to Cetena that I'm going to stick my foot so far up your ass th—"

Raenisa interrupted me. "Again. Something I'd love to see, but not the right time."

I glared at them before stalking away into the bedroom to dress.

There was no way I'd let Theron go through with this.

Chapter 25
Kael

I dressed, deftly tying on one of the skimpy garments left in the closet. It was little more than strings and black beads, but I could put it on even with my hands bound, so I didn't care. All the dresses with more coverage were gone, still in the bag that Theron had brought when he fled with me that night. A flicker of guilt went through me when I realized I hadn't even unpacked it, leaving it with my family's things. I checked myself in the mirror, dragging a brush through my damp hair. The strings clung to my body in a series of loops, strategically covering my breasts and lower half, while leaving my stomach and back on display. It wasn't what I'd chosen for myself, but I'd work with what I had.

I stepped out of the room and into the living area, where Theron was sprawled in front of the fire in only his breeches, a low growl rumbling from his throat at my entrance. My cheeks heated, but I kept my eyes straight ahead, determined to ignore his reaction. Otherwise, we were liable to fall back into bed all day. Roza's gaze zeroed in on me.

She sneered, her voice dripping with disdain. "You say you're not a whore, but you sure look like one."

Fire raced through me, and I clenched my fists as I glared back at her. No. I shouldn't fight her. I had to convince them of my side and I couldn't do that if I started shouting again. "Keep it up and you'll be in one of my dresses by lunch, Roza."

She glowered at me, and Zerek snickered from the corner where he had been watching us. He checked Roza out appreciatively as if liking the idea of seeing her in such an outfit.

Theron stood, towering over me as he ran a hand down my bare back. I shivered at the sensation, unable to deny the sparks of pleasure that surged through me.

"I'll get you more clothes soon," he murmured, his breath warm against my ear.

I nodded, stepping away from him before I did something foolish, like kiss him. Instead, I cleared my throat before speaking. "What about negotiations? We can talk to Haemir. Find a solution."

He sighed and ran a hand through his dark hair. "Yes, but that doesn't mean I'll be successful or that it'll stop the fighting. They'll want concessions I can't give."

"Then I'll come with you. Broker a peace—"

He shook his head and took a step closer to me so that our bodies were almost touching again. "It's too dangerous," he insisted softly. "I need you to stay here, where it's safe."

I growled. "I'm not some maiden in need of defending, Theron. Keeping me locked up here is about your weakness, not mine."

His gaze bored into mine, his jaw clenching. "I don't care if you think I'm weak." He stepped closer, crowding me. "Do you know how many times I've had to stand over your broken body, unsure if I could mend you? Staring down the tunnel of eternity as the world closed in on me and your heartbeat stuttered?" The rest of the group faded away until it was just him and I. "I've seen my future without you, Kael, and it's bleak. I refuse to do it again. If that means I keep you chained and angry, I'd do it a hundred times over." I opened my mouth to interrupt, but he spoke first. "I asked you to run away with me, *Sihaya*. Twice. You refused to leave the rebellion. Now I have to find a solution we both can live with."

My heart sank at his words. "Can you live with it, though? Remember what you said about Caurium? This would be more of the same." I put my hands on his chest, uncaring anymore of Roza's presence. "They're starving, with no water. This isn't honorable. Please, Theron. You've already taken one father from me. Don't take another."

His eyes burned with pain, the column of his throat moving as he stared down at me.

An explosion rocked the palace walls, shaking the ground beneath our feet.

"What the fuck?" Raenisa shouted, jumping to her feet. I rushed to the patio, looking out over the city as smoke rose from the direction of the second gate. I could make out a crowd of rebel soldiers in the streets sprinting toward the palace gates.

Theron cursed and turned to Herrath. "Take Kael and Roza inside and guard them," he ordered. He grabbed his armor from where it hung on a nearby stand and put it on quickly, not bothering with a shirt.

"Theron." I hurried over to him. His eyes blazed as he strapped on his swords. His armor gleamed, his features carved from stone as if was Atar himself.

"Stay here," he growled before gripping the back of my head, his lips descending to mine. I kissed him fiercely, tasting blood when he pulled away.

"I'm not going to wish you luck."

He smirked. "Good, because I don't need it." He stepped back and motioned to Raenisa and Zerek. "You two come with me," he said as he stalked out of the room.

I watched him go, dread heavy in my gut. There was no winning for me here.

I turned around to find Roza watching me with confusion. She shook her head and turned back to the patio to watch the rebel incursion. I followed her, looking for Haemir in the melee.

Small groups of rebel soldiers peeled off from their primary force and ran into the city ahead of them, disappearing down alleyways. What were they doing? I watched anxiously as Theron's soldiers formed up into a phalanx, locking their heavy metal shields. Their commander shouted orders as they pushed forward, trying to retake the gate of the city from the rebels.

Roza stood by my side, silent as she stared at the soldiers below us with barely contained rage in her eyes. Theron sprinted into the fray, his twin bone swords unmistakable. My heart dropped as he threw himself into the fight, cutting down the rebels that attempted to escape into the city. I watched until I could no longer see Theron in the throng of fighting men below us, swallowed up by a sea of steel and sweat and violence.

"Look," Roza murmured, canting her head to the left. Far from the initial attack, a group of rebels were on top of the wall. But they weren't coming over en masse, they were tossing bags of grain and barrels of water over to the other side, no doubt to waiting soldiers.

"It's a diversion to gather supplies," I breathed, turning my attention back to the rebels. They weren't pressing the soldiers as hard as they could, just enough to keep them busy.

Herrath swore, no doubt seeing what we did as he shouted for a servant. A man I didn't recognize jogged in and Herrath directed him to take a message to Theron and the men on the wall immediately. He took off at a run and Herrath scowled, watching as another group of rebels carried off more supplies over the wall on the right side. Smoke curled above us like a blanket of death slowly descending.

"They're drawing back," Roza muttered, and I nodded. The rebels were retreating in the face of the phalanx.

"They have to be in awful shape if they're not pressing this. That force wasn't even a quarter of the men they should have."

Roza hummed in agreement, turning away from the scene to look at me as the last of the men drew back into the second line.

"Gods." My breath caught as Theron leaped off Zerek's shield, his armor flashing as he twisted through the air. He was incredible.

Roza frowned at me. "You and the Marshal have some weird shit going on."

"Shut up, Roza. What do you know?"

"I know that he's obsessed with you," she began. "And that you two have some weird pull toward each other." Her brows drew together. "Do Elves have mates like Inferi or Zerkir?"

"Uhhh. I don't know."

"No," Herrath spoke up from behind us. "Not since the Lightcurse."

I turned to face him, anger simmering inside me. He watched me, his lips drawn into a thin line. He stepped closer and my muscles tensed.

"Do you remember what I told you the first night you came to the palace?"

"That you'd kill me if I ever hurt Theron?" I said, not backing down from his gaze. My voice was steady despite how my blood pounded through my veins. I may have grudgingly liked Zerek and Raenisa, but I'd never liked Herrath. "You know that rebel you tortured? That was my little brother. Maybe I should be the one threatening you."

He narrowed his eyes on me. "I never trusted you. And I was right. The first chance you got, you captured him."

"Technically, she passed out. Gavril and I captured him." Roza put in, smirking as she leaned against the railing. She'd been there the night Gavril was tortured. No doubt she hated Herrath too.

I glanced at Roza, but she didn't meet my eye, even if she'd seemingly allied herself with me. "What do you want, Herrath? You want me to congratulate you for figuring out I was lying?"

"I want you to stop stringing Theron along," he growled.

"He kidnapped me." I pointed out, raising my shackled hands.

He shook his head, ready to keep arguing when the door opened, Mirijana breezing inside.

"Kael!" She squealed, running forward and squeezing me tightly even with my shackles digging into our stomachs. "Kearis' wings. It's good to see you up and about. How're you feeling?"

"I'm good. How're you? Were you safe after I left?"

She blushed, glancing at Herrath before meeting my gaze once more. "Is it terrible if I say I've been great? I know everything is falling apart, but..." She waved it away. "Never mind about me. You look thin. Let me call Aella and have her bring you some of her cakes. She has a knack for it, just wait."

I smiled, happy to hear the Sirin Remnant was doing well. "It would be good to see her."

"She's excited that you're home. I'll be right back." She placed a delicate hand on Herrath's arm as she passed. He looked down at her, an intense emotion flashing across his face before it cleared again.

A few minutes later, Aella entered with a tray of tiny cakes and drinks. She smiled brightly as she placed it on the table, but her gaze hardened when she saw me in shackles.

"Kael? Are you alright?"

I nodded. "I'm fine. Don't worry."

Roza sucked in a breath, her gaze fixed on Aella as though seeing a ghost from the past. I glanced at Roza before turning back to Aella, not wanting to embarrass her by asking if something was wrong in front of Herrath and Mirijana.

Aella had no such compunction. "Is something wrong?"

Roza's expression softened slightly and then hardened again as she shook her head. "You just remind me of someone." She cleared her throat. I knew who she was thinking about; I'd thought the same. Orya.

"What about you, Aella? Were you alright after I..."

"Killed Rhazien and fled into the night?" She raised a brow, and I scowled.

"Yeah."

"I'm glad they're dead," she growled. Her expression was dark. "They deserved all that and more."

"Absolutely," Mirijana agreed, her normally cheerful disposition souring. "After what they did to you, Kael..." She crumpled the napkin in her hand. "Poisoning was too good for them."

I ducked my chin, strangely embarrassed, even though I knew I shouldn't be. I blinked hard, willing the memories of that night to pass. "Thank you for helping me."

Mirijana smiled. "It was the Lord Marshal who healed you. I just helped."

The room quieted. All I could think of was Theron; his bronze eyes filled with an emotion I couldn't name as he'd carried me—half-dead and unconscious—to his vanira. I'd never seen him like that before; all he'd cared about was getting me to safety. And I'd repaid him by capturing him.

I looked up to find Mirijana giving me a reproving look as if she could read my thoughts. "I didn't plan to capture him, Mirijana. And I tried to help him when he was imprisoned."

She lifted a brow before relenting. "I know you didn't. You weren't even conscious when he ran with you." She elbowed Herrath. "And you should know that, too."

He huffed a laugh, and a dimple appeared on his cheek, shocking me. "Miri..." He murmured, and she gave him a small smile before turning back to me, her cheeks pink.

"Things will get better now, yeah?"

My expression faltered. How could I tell her that, no, none of this would get better? Not for all of us. Either the rebels would die, or they'd storm the castle and she might.

No one would win here.

A new sound drew my attention, and I hurried to the patio to find the gates opening once again.

Only this time, Theron was marching through them with a company of mounted soldiers.

Chapter 26
Theron

I mounted Vaernix and rode out of the inner keep, surging through the smoke-filled streets of Adraedor. The battle cries of our enemies echoed in the distance, mingling with the chittering of the vaniras as we advanced. They thought they could steal our supplies and attack once they were fresh. No. Tonight, we'd strike, seizing the opportunity to surprise our foes when they were distracted by their ill-gotten spoils and weak.

Gazing back at the determined faces of the men trailing behind me, I steeled myself for the conflict to come.

"Zerek," I called, and he rode up beside me. "Return to the district and hunt down any rebels lurking within our territory. They probably left assassins."

"Yes, Lord Marshal." Zerek nodded, his eyes burning with determination. He had to be upset to be using my title, normally only doing so in formal situations. He veered off, disappearing into the night.

With Vaernix's powerful strides, I pressed onward, alert to every subtle shift in the shadows. The air crackled with anticipation, the scent of impending battle hanging heavily around us. A voice sounded up ahead, and I motioned them forward with hand signals, the only sound of our approach the clicks of the vaniras' chitinous exoskeletons. We came upon a group of rebels, caught unawares as they drank water from a barrel with their bare hands.

"Attack!" The clash of steel resounded as swords clashed and sparks flew in a symphony of violence. I drew my blade, its familiar weight comforting in my grip. Every strike was calculated, each parry swift and precise. Raenisa cackled as she fought, laughing with the mad joy that sometimes took her in battle. It was uncanny; her golden armor gave her enough strength to send men flying with one blow.

As the moon bathed the streets-turned-battlefields in ethereal light, I searched for the faces of Haemir and Gavril amongst the rebels. Relief surged through me when I didn't see either man. At least I could tell Kael that I hadn't hurt her family.

But would that be enough?

"Forward!" I commanded, our movements fluid and coordinated as we broke their line. The desert breeze carried the scent of blood and sweat, mingling with the dust kicked up by our relentless pursuit. We were a tempest like one of the sand wyrms that had once ruled the dunes.

"Retreat!" Called one rebel, and they ran in a rout, their line collapsing.

"We got them now!" Raenisa shouted beside me, a streak of blood marring her cheek.

"Pick them off!" I yelled, pursuing the fleeing rebels.

I watched them run, shame at my commands coursing through me. Kael would never stand for this, her moral code demanding that her enemies be given a fair chance at victory. And yet here I was, hunting down the helpless and desperate with ruthless efficiency.

A place I never wanted to be again.

"Hold," I shouted, pulling up on Vaernix's reins as we entered a large water forum, my men panting behind me on their mounts, letting the rebels get away. I didn't want to be this man anymore, murdering the defenseless for a cause I didn't believe in. There had to be more than this. Raenisa sent me a questioning glance, and I held up my arm for my soldiers to hold their place. A sense of unease prickled at the back of my neck.

Something wasn't right.

I scanned the surroundings, my eyes trained for any sign of danger.

"What is it?" Raenisa asked beside me, hefting a large war hammer over her shoulder.

"I don't know." My magic tickled at the edges of my senses as if to tell me something was wrong. But I didn't know what.

It reminded me of years ago when Calyx died...

The rebels had set a trap, and we had walked right into it.

"Run!" I shouted, my voice slicing through the night. But before the word had fully left my lips, the world erupted in a blinding explosion. The force of the blast sent me hurtling through the air, screams of pain and terror filling the night around me.

When I came to, I was lying in a pile of debris on the ground, Vaernix nowhere in sight. Half of my men lay motionless, their lives taken in an instant. The others screamed in pain or coughed, their lungs rejecting the clouds of stone. Grief and rage rolled within me like molten metal, threatening to consume me as my ears rang.

The rebels had anticipated our movements and set a trap for us, intending to exact revenge upon us after retreating.

An icy wave of realization overcame me as I comprehended their cunning; any other commander would have fortified his base, knowing the defensible position was preferred, rather than pursue them into their territory. This was an attack specifically for me.

Haemir knew I had Kael.

"Rae?" I shouted, looking for her in the chaos. *Gods, no, not again.* "RAE!"

"I'm over here, dumbass," she groaned, shifting under a pile of stone.

"Rae, thank Atar you're alive." I pulled a slab off of her and she winced.

"Careful, my arm is broken."

"You're lucky it's just your arm and not your skull."

She huffed a weak laugh. "My head is harder than that."

"You got that right," I said, my voice shaking with relief. I'd thought I'd lost another friend. I pulled out my healing plate, running it over her arm as I pushed my magic into it. She gritted her teeth as the bone popped back into place before heaving a sigh. I helped more warriors out of the debris, expecting an attack while we were wounded and vulnerable.

But it never came. They left us alone in the wreckage; devastated but alive.

Haemir was mistaken if he thought this would deter me. Kael was mine and there was *nothing* I wouldn't sacrifice to have her. There was still a battle to be fought, a war to be won, and I was going to win it.

But as I took a step forward, my gaze fell upon Vaernix, motionless on the ground. Anguish tore through my chest, threatening to shatter the iron resolve I had fought so hard to maintain.

"No," I whispered, my voice choked. Vaernix, my loyal companion, my partner in battle, had fallen. The loss cut deeper than any blade ever could. I knelt beside her, tracing a trembling hand over her crumpled legs. We had shared so many battles and faced countless adversaries together. And now she is gone.

I bowed my head and whispered a last goodbye to my fallen friend. Some elves didn't bother naming their vanira, hardly recognizing them in a group. But I'd raised Vaernix since she was an egg. She'd been my companion, listening as I spoke to myself on long treks... The need to charge into the rebel stronghold by myself, to kill all of them and damn the consequences, filled me, but I took a shuddering breath, letting it pass over me and through me. I had to remain strong if I was going to survive the surrounding chaos. We were at war, and I would make them pay for what they had done.

They weren't a weak and helpless adversary, and it was time I fought them with the respect they deserved.

I strode through the palace, my body aching from the explosion and grief. I could feel the ones I'd lost under my skin, scratching at the surface as if trying to break through. The war room was empty as I entered and I sighed, my shoulders loosening. It was impenetrable; with layers of false walls and hidden passageways in the thick stone, allowing for escape when cornered. There were no windows or natural light sources, but several torches illuminated its depths in an eerie dimness that cast long shadows across maps and charts scattered on the tables. Shelves filled with books lined one wall while weapons hung from hooks on another. A large hearth stood at the other end of the room, providing both heat and light for those gathered within its confines.

The air here was heavy with tension as Herrath strode in behind me and closed the door with an echoing thud.

"What happened?" He asked, taking in my disheveled appearance.

I shook my head and swallowed hard. "They ambushed us. I lost half my contingent. And Vaernix."

Herrath's face softened as he crossed the room towards me. He placed a hand on my shoulder. "I am so sorry," he whispered, his voice heavy with compassion. "I can arrange for her body to be brought back if you wish."

"Thank you."

"Does it ever get easier?" he asked, his straight brows drawn together in a line. "To lead men into battle, knowing you won't bring them all home?"

I let out a sigh, the weight of responsibility settling within me. "No. It never gets easier. And if it ever does, then I wouldn't be fit for leadership." The lives I'd spent, the sacrifices my men made—they were forever etched on my heart. And what had I bought with their lives today?

Nothing.

"That sets you apart from your family," he said. "They revel in power without consequence, while you carry the weight of your decisions with dignity. You would be an excellent emperor."

I shook my head, dismissing any notions of ambition or conquest. "I have no desire to ascend the throne, Herrath. Power doesn't motivate me, nor do I want to extend our reach beyond Athain." I sighed, tracing my finger over the mountainous peaks of our homeland on the map. "We were once kings, and that was enough."

Herrath hesitated, his gaze unsure as he spoke. "You could change things, Theron. You hold the reins now."

His words echoed Kael's, adding to my irritation. As if things were that easy.

"What about your parents?" I challenged.

Herrath shrugged, a glimmer of rebellion in his eyes. "Now that Raura is dead, there's no reason to continue bending to their will." He paused, his eyes distant. "I-I think it's time for me to swim in strange waters on my own." He lifted a shoulder. "There are fates worse than poverty. My parents will have to find their own way. I refuse to be a pawn in their schemes any longer."

I raised an eyebrow, a grin tugging at my lips. "So, you're not going to wed an heiress anymore?"

Herrath shook his head, a wry smile gracing his features. "No, I've found someone else... if she'll have me." His smile widened, and he continued. "And I wouldn't have done it if it weren't for you. Seeing the way you went after Kael—then standing against Rhazien and Nyana." He leaned back, eyeing me with respect. "I figured that if you could stand up to them, then I could tell my parents that I'd be living my own life from now on."

I clasped him on the shoulder. "Good for you, friend." I don't think I'd ever referred to him as such before. But it was true. When I'd first heard that Herrath was holding Adraedor, I hadn't feared for the city, knowing that I could trust him. He was one of my Harvestmen in truth now.

Herrath ducked his chin to hide his pleased expression. "What will you do now? With the rebels?"

I sighed and shook my head. "I don't know. Whatever I do, someone loses in the end."

"You mean Kael won't forgive you?"

I nodded slowly, weariness settling within me. "Yeah," I whispered. The truth was that she might never forgive me—no matter what I did or how hard I tried to make it right. "I want to slaughter them for killing Vaernix and our soldiers. But I can already hear her argument. That all the men I killed today had people who loved them..." I let out a long exhale. "Could you reach out to our rebel contact? I have an idea."

"Of course." Herrath pursed his lips. "I won't pretend to understand your relationship, but she obviously cares for you." He leaned against the table. "She watched you the entire time in the fight, grumbling strategy under her breath—as if she wished to join you to show you how it was done."

My mouth curled into a small smile at his insight. "She may well be able to."

Herrath patted my arm. "Take heart," he murmured. "You'll find your way through this."

I nodded but didn't answer. There wasn't any way to come out of this situation clean for me. If I didn't kill the rebels, my mother would send the Niothe to slaughter everyone in the city and start over.

If I did, then I'd lose Kael...

Chapter 27
Kael

I paced the living room, dragging my chain behind me as I waited for Theron to return. He should have been back hours ago. Unless he'd been hurt in that explosion... I tried to keep my worry at bay as I moved from one end of the room to the other, counting every step along the way. The thought of Theron being hurt or worse was too hard to bear; it seemed like all my fears were coming true. I was going to lose someone I cared about—loved—no matter what. My breath caught in my chest. I loved h—

The door opened, and my heart leapt, but Raenisa stepped inside.

"Where's Theron?" She asked, her voice cold.

"He hasn't returned yet." My stomach twisted, guilt filling me as she turned to leave. I'd liked Raenisa when I was in the palace. Thought of her as a... friend. Or potentially one. That I'd hurt her with my subterfuge didn't sit right. "Raenisa," I called out. "Can we talk for a minute?"

"Fine." She crossed the room with her head held high, eyes fixed on me as if itching for a fight. "What do you want? I'm not unchaining you."

I swallowed hard, knowing that I'd hurt her. It was time to own up to my actions. "I'm sorry," I whispered. "For lying to you."

Raenisa sighed and glanced away. "It's alright," she said after a moment, though it was clear she didn't mean it. "You did what you had to do."

"No," I said, shaking my head. "My need for revenge blinded me. It wasn't just a mission for me." I took a deep breath. "I wanted to hurt you all, even after I realized you were as trapped as I was, and for that, I'm sorry."

Raenisa nodded, her expression unreadable. She studied me for a moment before asking, "Why did you want revenge?"

My heart squeezed as memories of that day flooded me—the flames and screams and chaos that had changed everything. I took a shuddering breath before speaking, feeling as though each word was being ripped from me against my will.

"I was at Caurium when the Niothe razed it," I said, trying to keep my voice steady and Raenisa sucked in a breath. "They—you—destroyed everything in their path. My father included." The tears welled in my eyes, but I fought them back down with gritted teeth. As much as it hurt to talk about what had happened, it felt right to tell Raenisa the truth at last. "When the Niothe sent me here, I was ten..." I began and the rest of the story tumbled out of me, being held captive, Haemir's rescue, being assaulted in the mines, and finally Orya's death. I fought off a sob, trying to relay the information in as factual a way as possible. If I let the memories truly touch me, I'd be weeping for hours.

"Atar's anvil," Raenisa breathed, shaking her head. "No wonder you hate us."

I let out a heavy breath, exhausted. "I don't hate you, Rae," I said softly.

Raenisa chewed her lip. "I don't hate you either," she murmured. "Caurium was brutal and I've always regretted it." She met my eyes, her gaze apologetic. "I'm sorry for threatening to kill Haemir. That was wrong of me."

"Yeah."

"I don't know how you can even stand to be in the same room as us. After all that," She said slowly, turning back to meet my eyes once more, "How do you have feelings for Theron? I'd want to kill him."

"I did. Before." I lifted a shoulder. "Now. I don't know. Maybe—"

"Let me stop you right there," she said, holding up a hand. "I don't want to hear anything about how he tongue-punches your cunt."

"Gods, Rae," I laughed. "I was just going to say we understand each other."

"Good, because I hear enough of you two as it is. I need to move into a new suite, preferably at least three floors away."

I rolled my eyes, settling on the couch. "Have you heard from Caelia?"

Raenisa's expression changed, her face becoming carefully blank. "No. When the court left, she followed shortly after and hasn't reached out since."

"I'm sorry."

"I heard some things," she said, her voice strangely neutral. "About Caelia. Rumors say that she's gone back to her family estate and is mustering allies—no doubt preparing for a bid to challenge Nyana." She swallowed hard. "And probably getting married to Zerek's brother to solidify the alliance..."

I reached out and took Raenisa's hand in mine, squeezing it. "Nothing is certain yet," I told her. "If it makes you feel better, Xadrian didn't mention anything about her wedding anyone."

She blew out a breath. "I can't believe that idiot joined the rebellion, no offense."

"None taken," I said with a wry smile.

Raenisa looked away, her gaze on the horizon outside the window. "Though I won't say it isn't tempting. One day there won't be any more land and people to conquer outside Athain and Nyana will turn her eye inward toward us..." Raenisa trailed off, shaking her head. "Empires only work when they're expanding."

I opened my mouth to respond when the door swung open and Theron stepped inside. He was covered in dust, a trickle of blood dried on his forehead. His gaze immediately found mine, and he froze, taking in the scene before him. Raenisa's expression changed to one of surprise as she looked at us.

"Well," she said slowly, standing up. "Our conversation can wait till later." She gave me a wink before leaving, the door clicking shut behind her. I rose to my feet, feeling unsure under Theron's gaze. He didn't reach for me, and I thought the worse.

"Are you alright?" I asked, my voice barely above a whisper. I moved closer and ran my hands over his hard body, looking for injuries. He caught my wrists, stopping me.

"I'm fine," he growled, meeting my gaze. "It was just a minor explosion."

I let out a relieved breath and stepped back. My anger returned as I remembered why he had been chasing after the rebels in the first place. "What the hell were you thinking?" I demanded, crossing my arms over my chest. "They were just stealing supplies! You didn't have to pursue them into their territory."

"This entire city is my territory." Theron narrowed his eyes on me. "I can defend it, however I see fit."

"Not if it means that you're going to get yourself killed," I shouted.

Theron stalked forward, his gaze searching mine. "As if you'd care."

I scoffed and stepped away from him. "Don't be ridiculous," I said sharply. "I protected you in the caves. You know I don't want you dead."

"You also captured me," he threw back. "Twice."

"And you've chained me. Twice." I shook my manacles in his face.

Energy crackled between us as we stood locked in a silent battle of wills. Theron's eyes softened just a fraction before he yanked me to him, crushing my lips with his own.

"Stubborn woman," he snarled against my neck as he tore off my dress, beads scattering on the ground.

"Arrogant prick."

I moaned as his hand found my breast, pinching my nipple in rebuke.

"It's not arrogance when you're the best."

"Shut up." I pulled his shirt open, yanking until he let it fall to the floor. I ran my hands over him, his muscles tense beneath my touch. His lips moved down my neck, sending shivers through me as his tongue found my sensitive spots. He licked and sucked until I trembled with pleasure, my breath coming out in soft pants.

I reached into his breeches, grasping his hard length and stroking it. Theron groaned as I freed his cock. It sprang forward, the slit already shining with pre-cum. I sank to my knees and took him into my mouth, tasting his salty sweetness.

"*Sihaya*," he growled, threading his hand into my hair and gripping it tight, guiding my movements as he pushed deeper into my throat.

I pulled back and looked up at him from beneath my lashes. "This is what you want, isn't it? Me on my knees before you...submitting. Chained to your bed for eternity."

He thrust back into my mouth before answering, his voice strained with pleasure. "No. I want you by my side."

I hummed in pleasure, and he groaned. He pulled me to my feet and crushed my body against his, burying his face in my neck. "Come here."

He picked me up and carried me over to the couch, falling back onto it with me in his lap. Heat radiating off him, soaking into my core. He ran his hands down my sides until he reached my hips. I lined up his cock with my entrance and sunk onto him.

I gasped as he filled me, pleasure flooding through me. Theron's eyes were locked on mine as we moved together, sparks of desire shining from them like stars in the night sky.

"I love watching you ride me like this," he growled. "Let's me play with these gorgeous tits."

I ground against him, pleasure sparking between my breasts and my clit. "Free me," I whispered, my manacled hands resting on his chest as I rode him.

"Never." His grip on my waist tightened as he thrust into me, pushing deeper with each stroke. I moaned against his lips as pleasure rushed through me in waves, the sensation of our connection sending sparks through every nerve ending in my body. He looked at me with such intensity that it felt like he could see straight into my soul. "I'll never let you go."

I moaned as I whipped my hips forward, causing us both to cry out. I reached up to grasp the back of the couch; the chain connecting my manacles pressing against his throat. He didn't break my gaze as he lifted his chin, thrusting into me again.

My breathing was ragged as we moved together, connected and lost in each other. His heart pounded against my chest, our breaths syncing up with the rhythm of our movements. His grip on me tightened as if he was trying to get closer even though there was no room left between us.

I reached a fever pitch, pleasure washing over me in waves. Theron held my gaze as I rode him faster, letting me press the chain harder against his throat as if he knew I wouldn't hurt him. He trusted me and it sent a surge of desire through me that pushed me over the edge. My core clenched tightly around him as I came, sending shivers down my spine. My orgasm exploded through my body like liquid fire and I choked on a guttural growl, clinging to Theron as he climaxed with a shout.

We stayed there for what felt like an eternity; skin slick with sweat, holding each other in an embrace so tight I knew we were both thinking the same thing.

That this couldn't last.

Chapter 28
Theron

I watched Kael sleep, her expression serene and her silver hair spilled across the pillows like a wild tundra. She was completely relaxed, her breath coming in little puffs as she slept, no longer waking at the slightest provocation. I rubbed my chest, a now familiar ache hitting me in the sternum. The overwhelming emotion seemed to consume me from head to heel. I'd thought I'd been in love with her before, ready to run away with her when I'd told her that night. I remembered the moment so vividly, the way she'd looked away from me and then drawn in a deep breath and told me what a fool I'd been. She'd been right. The way I felt for her now couldn't compare to then. Because now I *knew* her. Her inner pain, the aspects of herself she thought made her a bad person, and all the parts of her that showed me how wrong she was about that.

I knew her, and I loved her.

I ran my fingers through her hair, savoring the softness, before tearing myself away. It was time for me to find a solution we could all live with, otherwise, I was going to lose her.

I stood, heading into the living room. I pulled on my metal armor, loading up on gold, silver, copper, and bronze. It wouldn't be enough to protect me if they caught me in enemy territory, but it would give me a chance. A chance to come back to her. I could still feel the silk of Kael's hair as it slipped through my fingers and the softness of her skin as I'd run my hand over it. I was determined to do so every morning from now on.

Making my way through the palace corridors, my armor clanked against every step. It was time to talk to one of my Harvestmen and get more information about the undercover agent embedded in the rebel camp.

When I stepped into Zerek's chambers, an argument was already in full swing between him and Roza. They clashed like fire and ice, sparks flying between them.

"You don't know what it's like to live in the desert," Roza snapped, her aqua eyes flashing. "I've been living here for years. I know how to make camp without getting caught."

"Oh yeah? Well, I've been searching the desert for years," Zerek shot back, his voice tight with frustration. "I can stay hidden and survive out there."

"That's not enough! You need someone who knows the desert and its people," Roza argued, her hands balling into fists at her side. "Someone who can anticipate their movements and hide us from detection!"

"And that's exactly what I'd do!" Zerek said, throwing up his hands in exasperation. "If you would just listen to me, you'd see why my plan would work."

I cleared my throat, and they broke their stare down, neither of them hearing my approach, despite the clanking. "Everything alright here?"

"It's great. I love being held prisoner by a fool," Roza sneered. She looked different—fuller cheeks, clean clothes, healthier than before. Zerek had been looking after her, regardless of their constant bickering.

"We're fine," Zerek assured me. "Just a hypothetical argument."

"One that he lost," she muttered, sitting down on the couch. She wore men's clothing, Zerek's... I glanced between them but didn't think they'd slept together. She'd probably just refused to wear a gown.

I ignored her comment, turning to Zerek before he could respond and start it over again. "Did Herrath get in contact with our rebel contact?" When I walked past his room, the noises coming from within made me reluctant to interrupt.

Roza scoffed. "Contact? More like a spy."

"I spoke to her," Zerek confirmed, glancing at Roza. "But she's demanding a hefty price, Theron. Passage out of Adraedor, a fresh start, and a ton of fucking money."

"I don't care. We'll pay it." That was nothing compared to what I'd pay to have Kael. This was the path I had to take, regardless of the challenges and uncertainties it presented. "Where's the meet-up supposed to happen?"

"Andreja said she'll meet you at the Slave Quarter water forum."

"Andreja?" Roza questioned Zerek, her brows drawing together. "You're wrong. She would never do that."

Zerek smirked. "I assure you she would. She's been our informant for years, though she didn't give us any actionable intel until recently."

I lifted a brow, remembering the Inferi Remnant from the caves. I didn't relish the idea of having her as a guide, but I'd do whatever was necessary to keep Kael by my side.

Roza stared at him, her eyes wide. "She told you about our camp in the Red Wilds?"

Zerek nodded. "She used to work for Rhazien before approaching me." Roza's lip wobbled before she pressed them together, her gaze going distant.

"Sea whip?" Zerek murmured. He reached out to comfort her, but she shook her head before standing up from the couch abruptly. "Roza?"

"I need to be alone." She brushed past him and walked into the other room, slamming the door shut behind her.

Zerek sighed, dropping his hand back down by his side and watching the door with a pained expression. "What was that about?"

"Andreja is her closest friend. She just found out that she sold her out." I explained, and he growled.

"Don't give her a cent." He looked at the door once more, sighing. "I liked it better when she was yelling."

"Just give her a little space for now. She'll come out when she's ready."

He shook his head. "It doesn't feel right leaving her alone. I'll go talk to her. Unless you need backup?"

"No. I have to do this alone."

He was already walking toward the door when he turned back to me. "If you're not back in three hours, I'll come and drag your ass out of there."

"Same goes for you." I grinned, and he rolled his eyes before turning the knob.

I stalked through the Slave Quarter, watching for any sign that Andreja had betrayed me. The streets were quiet and deserted, so different from when I'd been here last. When Rhazien had forced me to kill those slaves... I blew out a breath. Never again would I have to bow to his will. Kael had made sure of that.

I reached the water forum and my eyes narrowed when I saw Andreja there waiting for me; her smirk made my blood boil.

"You're late," she said, her voice dripping with arrogance. I ignored her, and she stepped closer, swaying her hips as she walked over to me. "I'll forgive you though, if you earn it."

As if this woman could compare to Kael. "Where are Haemir and Peregrine?"

Her face fell, but she recovered quickly. "They're in the tavern on the other side of town. I'll show you, but first I want payment."

I crossed my arms. "No money until after we get back to the palace," I told her firmly. "You'll need a guide and a vanira to leave Adraedor. And to carry the chest of gold you demanded."

"Fine." She scowled but nodded grudgingly before turning on her heel and marching down the street.

"And Andreja?" She stopped, looking back at me. "If you sell me out, I'll kill you. "

She swallowed, her eyes widening. "I won't."

I didn't speak, instead jerking my chin for her to continue. We passed through winding alleys and cobbled streets until we arrived at an old tavern. The windows were blackened with paint from the inside, but I could just see light coming through the thinner strokes.

"We have to go around back," she whispered, gesturing for me to follow her to an alley. It was strangely clear, as if ready for a quick retreat. She pushed open the door and gestured for me to enter.

"I'll wait out here." Of course, she would. Didn't want everyone to know who'd sold them out.

"Fine."

My hand itched for my sword, every instinct telling me that coming here was a mistake. The scent of stale ale and wood smoke filled my nostrils, mingling with the murmur of a few voices and the clinking of glasses.

A sinking feeling entered my stomach as I stepped forward. *Atar, let this work.*

Peregrine stopped talking when she saw me approach and Haemir stood up, his eyes dark with anger.

"What are you doing here?" He growled as he hefted a war hammer from the ground. "Where's my daughter?"

I held up my hands as Gavril picked up the maps and battle plans spread across the table. "She's safe. I'm just here to talk."

"I don't want to hear a godsdamn thing you have to say until Kael is here."

"Dad..." Gavril glanced between us, his expression less hostile than his father's. "Just listen to him."

"I'd never hurt her, Haemir."

"You already did."

His accusation stung, and I rubbed the back of my neck, feeling like a chastened youth.

"Why are you here, Marshal? And what's stopping us from killing you right now?" Peregrine fixed her birdlike gaze on me.

"Other than the thirty men I have surrounding the tavern?" I bluffed. "And I'm here to negotiate."

"Your surrender? We accept." She smiled, and I matched it.

"No, yours."

Peregrine scoffed. "You want us to submit? To the people that oppressed us for centuries?" Her lips pressed into a thin line.

"Yes," I said firmly, ignoring the simmering tension in the room. "But I'm offering you more than just submission." I leaned forward, my voice low and intense. "I'm offering you freedom; citizenship in Adraedor with fair wages and protection under my rule. No more slavery. No more public killings or beatings." I waited for a beat. "And no more water restrictions."

Peregrine snorted. "That's a nice sentiment, Marshal, but it doesn't change the fact that Adraedor is already ours. This entire country is. Your people came and stole Kearis and our immortality, and you think to offer me a pittance?"

I frowned. This wasn't what I hoped for, but she hadn't stabbed me yet, either. "What do you want?"

She looked up at me with icy determination flashing in her eyes. "I want the city that was my people's birthright. I want the elves out and to never step on our sand again." She lifted her chin. "And if you grant it to us... then we will pay a yearly tithe of metal to the empire, as payment for never journeying into our country again."

Haemir turned to her, his fiery eyes blazing. "You can't be serious." He growled. "The rebellion works together towards freedom for all the Remnants—not just the Kyrie. Or did you forget you have a cohort of many races, not just your own?"

Peregrine didn't flinch at his outburst and kept her gaze trained on me. "That's what I want, Marshal—what do you say?"

My thoughts flew to Kael, standing tall and proud in that dim cave, refusing to run away with me because she couldn't abandon the rebellion. I knew she would have agreed with Haemir, and never accept a deal like that.

"No deal." Peregrine narrowed her eyes as I continued. "The moment I leave this city, the Empress would send the Niothe to retake it. This is a chance for peace, for a better life for your people."

Haemir glared at me. "Let me guess. All you want is to keep Kael."

I held his gaze. "She's worth more than a kingdom to me. I'd trade the entire empire for her and consider myself getting the better deal."

Peregrine interrupted our stare. "You may have to choose sooner than you think, War Marshal." Her yellow eyes were cruel as she continued. "An army is already on the move to reclaim Adraedor. From you."

Fucking Theodas.

"All the more reason for you to take my deal, otherwise you'll be pinned between two armies. Only one of which offers something other than death."

She smirked. "We'll see."

Gavril caught my eye and glanced nervously at the door.

I spun around to see men pouring in—weapons drawn.

"Attack!" Peregrine shouted.

I roared as I sprinted across the room, my swords outstretched. I funneled magic into my armor, giving me the speed and strength I needed. I twisted and turned, parrying blows and counter-attacking with precision. I connected with their swords, sending broken metal flying as my blades cut through theirs.

A shout came from behind me and I whirled around to find Gavril there, his back pressed to mine as he blocked a rebel's strike.

He looked at me over his shoulder. "Go!" I didn't have time to heed him, though.

Haemir swung his war hammer, the weapon whistling past my head as I dodged at the last second.

"You steal my daughter? Try to make her your whore?" He charged me, striking his hammer and I blocked, leaping backward.

I shook my head as I circled him. "It's not like that. I love her."

He sneered. "You don't know the meaning of love." He rushed me and I dodged again.

"I don't want to hurt you."

"You won't," Haemir growled, charging at me again.

"Dad, stop!" Gavril shouted and Haemir glanced at him, giving me the opening I needed.

I turned and sprinted for the exit, unwilling to risk hurting Kael's father. I fled into the alley, Andreja nowhere to be seen as I ran back for the palace. Had she sold me out? Or had someone seen us approaching? It didn't matter now. None of it did.

My plan to keep Kael had failed.

Chapter 29
Kael

I woke with a start, reaching for Theron, only to find his side of the bed empty, the soft light of the fireplace casting a warm glow upon the room. I shifted and my chains rattled, a constant reminder of my captivity. Theron hadn't freed me as I had hoped. It seemed his trust didn't extend far enough to grant me my freedom. Disappointment settled heavily in my chest, mingling with a flicker of worry for his whereabouts. Was he out attacking more rebels? Or had he been caught in another ambush? Haemir wouldn't wait forever for him to return me.

Mirijana stepped into the doorway, hesitating before entering. "Kael? Are you up?"

I offered her a weary smile as I pulled my blankets up to cover my breasts. "Yeah, I'm awake. Where's Theron?"

"He left word that he had an early meeting and to wait for you to wake," she explained, eyeing me with a mix of happiness and concern. "I've brought you some more clothes and breakfast."

"You're a lifesaver. I need to bathe first. Give me a minute."

"Of course."

She bustled out of the room as I reached for my robe, only to realize I couldn't put it on with my bound hands. Grumbling under my breath, I settled on wrapping myself in a towel before joining Mirijana at the tub. She'd already run it, pouring in a scented oil that reminded me of a flower from my childhood in Caurium.

I set down the towel and sank into the hot water, sighing as the heat relaxed my sore muscles.

I grabbed the bar of soap and began to wash myself. "What happened in the palace after I killed Rhazien?"

A shadow passed over her face, and she winced briefly before offering me a cloth. "It was difficult at first. There was suspicion that a servant might have killed him, but Herrath protected me and Aella."

Shit. "I'm sorry, Miri. I didn't mean for you to get in trouble."

Mirijana waved off my concerns. "Don't worry, Kael. It's alright. Herrath has been great." Pink stained her cheeks as she pretended to busy herself gathering more bathing supplies.

My mouth dropped open. "Herrath? I thought you were afraid of him, or at least didn't like him."

Her smile was soft as she stared off at the horizon. "I used to be. He seemed so stern and distant. But as I got to know him better, I realized he's just... formal, especially when he's upset. And he has every reason to be, considering his family."

The thought of Herrath opening up to Mirijana seemed impossible. "You've become close?"

Mirijana nodded, her smile tinged with a hint of bashfulness. "Yeah. I really like him. He's kind and brave, despite his past. And it turns out, he's easy to talk to. Funny."

Fascinated, I forgot to rinse my hair and a trickle of soap went into my eye, making me wince. "What do the others think of your relationship? With you being a Remnant and him being an elf?"

Mirijana lifted a shoulder. "I don't care what anyone else thinks. I learned that from you and Theron." Her smile was serene. "It's our happiness that matters, not their opinions."

My face heated as I sank further into the tub. I hadn't openly claimed Theron as mine, only hinted at it to my brother and father. Mirijana might be inspired by me, but she was the courageous one.

Not me.

I forced a smile. "I'm happy for you."

"Nothing is official yet. It's all really new." She blushed again, and I smiled in truth.

"Don't worry, if he tries to string you along, I'll kick his ass."

A laugh escaped her. "I'm the one making us go slow, Kael." She winked at me. "Well. Not that slow."

"Oh. Uh, good." I finished awkwardly as she chuckled.

"Can I ask you a question?"

I rinsed, stepping from the bath into the towel she held up for me. "Sure."

"Why did you capture Theron after he'd saved you?"

I sucked in a breath, not expecting the question. But Mirijana was my friend. I'd been sincere with Raenisa... A plan had been brewing in the back of my mind and if I wanted it to work, then I'd have to be honest with everyone. Including myself.

"I didn't want to," I admitted. "I was so out of it I didn't realize what was happening at first. Then there were so many of them, and he was hampered because he wouldn't let me go." My mind went back to that day, the pain so deep in my bones that hadn't receded despite him healing me, the feeling of disconnection from the world around me. The only things that had been solid were Theron's arms. "He rode right in there, demanding help, not realizing that they would kill him no matter what he said. I had to take him as my prisoner to prevent them from killing him where he stood."

She nodded, a relieved grin lighting up her face. "I *knew* it. I told Herrath that you cared for him, that it wasn't all an act."

I ducked my chin. "Yeah, well. You were right."

Her smile turned smug. "Of course I was."

I rolled my eyes. "That elven arrogance is rubbing off on you."

"It's not the only thing," she winked, and I laughed.

"Will you help me dress? It's hard with these." I held up my manacled hands, and she pursed her lips.

"Sure. And I'll give the Lord Marshal a piece of my mind when he returns. Putting you in chains is ridiculous. Come here." She rifled through the pile of clothing she'd brought, muttering as she looked for something that would fit around my manacles before settling on a floor-length black skirt with slits up to my waist. The top wasn't a shirt, but a skeletal black breastplate that clipped around my neck, hanging to cover my breasts and part of my rib cage.

"Let's put your hair up, and show off your back."

I nodded, watching as she tied it up, securing it with braids and obsidian hair clips shaped like talons with matching arm and ankle cuffs. Tilting my chin up, she smudged kohl around my eyes, smiling when she finished.

"Perfect."

I sighed as I looked at my reflection. "All dressed up with nowhere to go."

"It won't be long until the Lord Marshal sets the city right."

I frowned. "Killing slaves isn't right."

Mirijana's eyes met mine, her expression unreadable. "No offense, Kael, but the rebels can't be trusted."

I crossed my arms, leaning against the couch. "Why not?"

Mirijana looked out the window, her gaze lingered upon the sprawling desert. She reached up to touch the scar on her face, her fingertips tracing it absentmindedly.

"I used to work in the mines," she began, her eyes distant. "When I heard whispers of the rebellion, I thought I'd found a way out. I saved up all my water tokens to pay someone to smuggle me to their base, to a life away from the Elves' clutches."

My brows drew together. The rebellion never took payment to get people out. "What happened?"

"They betrayed me," she said, her voice laced with bitterness. "They sold me into a brothel, drugging me with areca, thinking it would stop me from fighting back. When the first man came in to rape me, I bit him. I could barely stand, but I managed to take a chunk out of him. He hit me, knocking me into the fire..."

She swallowed hard before continuing. "Theron heard my screams, and he burst in with Herrath behind him. They were terrifying... I feared Herrath for years after that. Well, until recently." She sent me a small smile.

I let out a breath. "I'm so sorry, Mirijana. That's horrible."

She nodded. "I was one of the lucky ones. I got out." She held my hands in hers. "The Lord Marshal is a good man. You can trust him."

"I know," I murmured. "Mirijana. The rebellion doesn't take tokens to get people out. They help those that they think can survive in the wilds on their own or want to fight." I shook my head. "Those were grifters."

She scowled. "I know you think—"

"No." I interrupted her. "I've lived with the rebels for five years. I know that they'd never do such a thing."

Mirijana pursed her lips, considering, and I held my breath, hoping I had made some headway.

A knock sounded as the door opened and Herrath stepped in. His eyes softened when he saw Mirijana. "Well, don't you look beautiful?" He murmured, leaning against the doorframe.

She blushed. "What are you doing here? I thought I wouldn't see you until later."

Herrath brushed a strand of hair away from Mirijana's face, his thumb brushing over her scar. "Just wanted to see you and I figured Kael would still be—"

"Right here?" I called out, grinning from the couch as his shoulders straightened, his rigid bearing coming back.

"Yeah," Mirijana chuckled. "Don't worry, I already told her."

"And?" He looked at me warily, as if unsure of my reaction.

"I'm happy for you two. And if you hurt her, I'll castrate you."

He smiled, his face lighting up, and it was like he was a different person. I could see now how Mirijana could fall for him. A fluttery hope filled my chest; if these two could find love together, then perhaps my plan would work.

"If I screw this up, I'll let you," he chuckled, and I stared at him in shock. I don't think I'd ever heard him laugh before. He turned back to Mirijana.

"Can I talk to you for a moment?"

"Of course," Mirijana said, stepping out into the hall after I waved her off.

A scrape sounded on the patio and I whipped around. I froze, waiting to see if it came again. Unease settled in my stomach and I walked out to investigate.

I glanced behind the billowing fabric. Nothing.

"Get it together, Kael," I muttered to myself.

I turned to go back inside, and a hand clamped over my mouth from behind. I threw my elbow back, smashing into my assailant's ribs.

"Ow, Kael. Stop," he grunted, and I stopped, recognizing his voice. I whipped around.

"Xadrian?"

He grinned, his dark eyes twinkling. "In the flesh." He gestured around him. "I'm here to rescue you."

My mouth dropped open, and I closed it with a snap. "What about the others at the base?"

Xadrian's face softened. "They're safe," he assured me. "I made sure they were alright before I came for you." He stepped closer and placed a gentle hand on my shoulder, giving it a comforting squeeze.

"Come on," he said with a small smile. "We should get going before they come back in."

I shook my head, my heart thudding in my chest. "No. I can't leave."

Xadrian's brows drew together. "What do you mean?"

"I have a plan, and I need to stay here to make it happen."

Xadrian sighed heavily and ran a hand through his hair, the moonlight glinting off of the silver highlights in his dark locks. He stared at me, searching for something in my eyes.

"Kael," he said softly, "you can't convert them to the rebellion. I grew up with people like them. Trust me, it's a lost cause. They like their comfortable lives. It's easier for them to ignore what's happening."

"No." I set my jaw. "I'm going to make this work."

"You couldn't even convince the servant," he pointed out. "What hope do you have of changing their minds? Theron treats you like his property." He grabbed one of my hands, holding the manacle up to my face. "Is this what you want? To be chained? To be kept like a pet?"

"I'm not a pet," I growled, but he didn't stop.

"You're no better than that servant if you stay. Come with me," he pleaded. "We can win this war. Together."

My heart beat hard in my chest. He wasn't just asking me to leave. He wanted me to be with him, to choose him. But I couldn't.

Theron had already stolen my heart.

"Xadrian..." I looked up into his face, trying to find the right words.

His expression hardened as if he knew what I was trying to say. "We don't have time for this. The Vennorin brothers are on their way to Adraedor right now with the Niothe. We need your help to take the keep before they arrive."

"What?"

"Caelia told me with our speaking stones," he explained. "Theodas sent Trevyr and Tikas in his stead. They're supposed to secure the city and take it from Theron."

"How much longer until they get here?" I grabbed his forearm and the door to the suite opened.

"Kael?"

Theron walked in, his expression darkening when he saw me in the arms of another man.

Chapter 30
Kael

"Xadrian," Theron growled, his face twisting in rage as he realized who had come to steal me away.

Like a predator baring its fangs, he lunged forward, his swords materializing in his hands. Xadrian dodged, slipping past his blades without a second to spare.

"Theron, wait!" I shouted, as he pressed Xadrian harder, his movements so fast he was a blur. Shit, he was going to kill him.

"You think you can take her away from me?" Theron roared, his voice echoing over the city. "Steal her in the night?" His eyes had flooded fully black, layers of midnight in his gaze as he struck.

"What? Don't want to lose your pet?" Xadrian taunted as he blocked, his dark eyes darting to me. "At least I don't have to chain a woman to keep her."

"Fuck you."

Xadrian pulled magic, tossing a chunk of the palace at him. Theron's rage gave him an edge as he reacted, pulling so much power that his swords passed through stone like butter. Xadrian's smile faltered and Theron pressed his advantage, forcing Xadrian to the edge of the patio.

"Run, Xadrian!" I shouted, and he shot one more glance my way before throwing himself over the side and out of Theron's reach.

Theron pulsed with an intensity that defied comprehension, his magic surging forth in torrents that I could feel pressing against me, calling my own power. Xadrian was a skilled warrior, but he couldn't stand against the force of nature in front of me.

"Theron?"

He turned his wrathful gaze on me, his features twisted with unspent rage. "No one takes you from me."

"You can't blame him for thinking I need help," I growled, unafraid of the anger blazing from him. "I'm not a beast to be chained."

"You're dangerous."

I stepped into his space, my face inches from his. "You wouldn't want me if I wasn't."

He closed his eyes and took a deep breath as if trying to regain control. Finally, he looked at me with a mix of wariness and admiration. "I can't lose you."

"Then trust me."

"I do."

"So prove it." I breathed, my gaze never wavering from his. "Release me."

He shook his head slowly. "You'll leave me," he whispered brokenly, his eyes tortured. My heart ached for him, for the man who feared nothing but facing eternity alone.

"That's a risk you have to take," I murmured, my mouth inches from his. "To see if what we have is real."

Theron let out a shuddering breath, his gaze searching mine. He leaned forward and brushed his lips against mine in a gentle kiss before pulling away and reaching into his pocket. With trembling hands, he pulled out a key that glinted in the moonlight and knelt, releasing my manacles.

"You're free, *Sihaya*."

I stood there in disbelief, hardly believing what had just happened.

He stalked across the room, the sound of metal clinking against stone echoing in the night air as he removed his armor piece by piece until he stood in only his breeches.

"Theron?" He didn't turn, instead pouring himself a large glass of wine before sitting down on the couch, he stared at me with such an intense sadness that I knew was waiting for me to walk out the door. He drank deeply, the column of his throat moving. His eyes were still entirely black despite his feigned nonchalance. I took one step, then another, and his eyes tracked me. Not with the same fire as before, but a resignation that hollowed my chest.

I grabbed my sword from the rack, running my fingers over the engraving I'd done so many years ago, promising to kill the man before me. I unsheathed it and moved to stand before him. He looked up at me, his gaze guarded, but I could see the hurt there and my heart ached. I slipped into his lap, pressing the tip of the blade to his throat.

"Is that what you want, Kael? To finally take your revenge?" His bronze eyes searched mine.

"No." I shook my head, my eyes never leaving his.

"Then what do you want?" His voice was low and intimate in the dark.

I stood, carefully removing my sword. Pain flashed in his eyes and I could tell he didn't understand, that he thought I was leaving him. But I knew what I had to do now. He was mine, and I'd have to fight for him. For the life I wanted for us. "You'll see."

I strode into the martial gallery, my heart racing as I went over the plan again. The glass case holding the celestial tiara glimmered before me, its power calling to me. I shattered the glass, the tinkling sound echoing like fallen stardust, and reached in, claiming the crown as my own.

The metal flowers and leaves pulsed within my mind. Not just one celestial metal, but all of them. I placed the tiara on my brow, embracing the power, its pulsating energy promising endless possibilities. Xadrian was right. I had to claim my power, trust it. This crown was my birthright. And I was ready to reclaim it.

I stepped out into the night, feeling Theron's eyes on me. He was letting me go... not knowing that I did this for us. I whispered a promise to him as I approached the first gate that whatever happened, we would find our way back to each other one day soon.

"Stop," a guard commanded, his sentries falling in behind him, and I sent a wave of power through the earth, knocking him to the ground. Reaching for my magic came without thought and I mentally clasped the gate in my grip, ripping it open.

"Don't try to follow me."

As they scrambled to their feet—shock and fear painted on their faces—I walked towards the second gate before they could recover. My newly discovered power sang within my blood with every step I took, the pulsing energy in my veins urging me forward.

I called upon my magic again and it swirled around me like an invisible cloak. I urged the sand to join it, creating a maelstrom. The air rippled and shifted as it sought those who tried to enter, preventing anyone from getting too close to me.

With a shout, I ripped open the gate where the rebels were amassing.

Their voices rose and a battle cry echoed in the night air as they moved forward, shouting my name. I let the sand fall, holding up my sword.

"Hold," I commanded, my voice rising above the din.

I waited until the murmurs quieted before continuing.

"There will be no more bloodshed today. The Marshal and I have come to an understanding." He may not have agreed to it yet, but he would. I'd do anything to be with Theron, and I knew he'd do the same.

Even if it meant taking down the empire itself.

The sudden silence was like a vacuum, sucking away all sound. The soldiers behind me were shocked, but they didn't move as I lifted my hands, using my magic to rip their weapons away from them.

"We will no longer be divided," I shouted over the mass. "The Marshal and his people have joined our cause. We will stand together against the empire."

Disbelief rippled through the rebels, whispers and shouts going up as they tried to figure out what was happening. Teodosija pushed her way to the front of the group, her yellow eyes flashing.

"How can we trust him?" She spat, her stunted wings flaring. "We should kill them all and be done with it."

"If anyone touches Theron, I will tear this city apart." I glared at her, my expression hard as I shook the ground beneath them with a wave of my hand, the buildings around us swaying. Whoever had the power to destroy the city controlled it. I wouldn't let Teodosija stand in the way of what I wanted anymore. No one would.

My voice was low and full of power as I spoke. "The Marshal is the key to winning the war. He's mine."

I felt his eyes on me, and I looked over my shoulder, sending him a wink.

"And I'm his."

Chapter 31
Theron

I stood on the patio, my heart thundering in my chest. Kael was a tempest incarnate, effortlessly tossing soldiers aside as she conjured a swirling sandstorm that enveloped her. She exuded power; a force of nature in her own right. At that moment, I realized what a fool I had been to think I could ever contain her. Kael was never meant to be chained; she was meant to soar, to conquer the world with her ferocity.

I'd fooled myself once more, believing she'd stay. That she loved me as much as I did her.

As she ripped the gates open, I braced myself for the onslaught, expecting chaos and destruction to follow in the wake of Kael's rebellion.

But it didn't happen.

She approached the rebels, telling them something I couldn't hear because of the distance. The rebels, who had been poised for battle a moment before, lowered their weapons, their body language relaxing. What had she done?

I funneled magic into my aluminum, strengthening my senses until I could see her clearly, picking out the sound of her breath amongst the crowd.

As if she could sense my bewilderment, Kael cast a glance over her shoulder, her gaze finding mine with a sly glimmer. The night breeze whispered secrets, lifting her hair in the air as we stared at one another.

"He's mine." She winked, before turning back to the army before her. "And I'm his."

A grin spread across my face as she continued speaking, telling the rebels how I'd teach them how to defeat the Niothe. I'd said that Kael was worth an empire.

Now it was time to prove it.

Acknowledgements

In the whirlwind of finishing this book, I couldn't have made it without some amazing people in my life. Foremost, my rockstar of a best friend, Ginger Kane. From the early beta reads to the meticulous proofreading, you are simply incredible. Your sharp eye and unwavering support have been instrumental in shaping this book into its final form. I freaking love you. To my understanding husband, whose patience knows no bounds, thank you for putting up with my writing-induced madness and allowing me the time and space to bring this book to life. I promise to actually cook soon. A special shout out to Tears of the Kingdom for distracting my children during crucial editing moments. (Now it's my time to play fuckers bwahahaha) My sweet kitties, you're my writing muses. Your purrs and snuggles brought comfort and inspiration when I needed it most. Also, you kept me in my seat writing since I didn't want to move you, so a double bonus. Shout out to the Arctic Monkeys and their song "I Wanna be Yours" for inspiring the chemistry between Kael and Theron in this book. And to my incredible writing groups, your support and advice have been priceless. You've shaped this book more than words can express.

I have a lot more projects in the works! I'll update my website and social media soon so you know what's coming! Until then, happy reading and I hope you loved my desert.

About the Author

Atley Wykes is a lifelong reader and writer of fantasy romance. She adores writing love stories (the steamier the better), always with a HEA guaranteed... eventually. She lives in the Great Lakes region with her family, where her children outnumber her and her husband. When she isn't writing, you can find her daydreaming about her characters, accidentally swearing during a PTO meeting, baking a cake at one in the morning, and trying to coax her two cats into taking adorable pictures.

Sign up for her newsletter to receive free bonus content and announcements for new releases: atleywykes.com

You can also find her hanging out here:
- Facebook
- Instagram
- Twitter
- TikTok
- Reddit

Newsletter Signup

Join the Newsletter
If you'd like to stay up to date with new releases, click the link below to join my free, bi-monthly newsletter.

Subscribe
and receive a FREE copy of To Etch a Promise in Bone, The Frozen Prince, The Frost Lord and other great reads!

Made in United States
Troutdale, OR
12/27/2023